THE
CANASTA PLAYERS

WAYNE TEFS

TURNSTONE PRESS

Turnstone Press
607-100 Arthur Street
Winnipeg, Manitoba
Canada   R3B 1H3

Turnstone Press gratefully acknowledges the assistance of the Canada Council and the Manitoba Arts Council.

Cover illustration and design: Scott Barham

This book was printed and bound in Canada by Kromar Printing Limited for Turnstone Press.

The author would like to thank Mark Duncan, Birk Sproxton, David Johnston, and Pat Sanders.

"Better Be a Financial Tortoise," page 120, is from David Christianson's *The Financial Planning Report*, September/October 1987; the quotation on page 121 is from "Our Allotted Lifetimes" in Stephen Jay Gould's *The Panda's Thumb*.

Canadian Cataloguing in Publication Data

Tefs, Wayne A.

    The Canasta Players

    ISBN 0-88801-149-0

I. Title.

PS8589.E37C35 1990   C813'.54   C90-097123-1
PR9199.3.T4C35 1990

Canasta, in its many forms, is the most popular game in the branch of the Rummy family where the main object is to score points by melding as opposed to scoring by "going out." From 1950 to about 1952 it was the biggest fad in the history of card games.

—*Jacoby on Cards*

I came to Carthage, where a cauldron of illicit loves leapt and boiled about me. I was not yet in love, but I was in love with love, and from the very depth of my need hated myself for not more keenly feeling the need. I sought some object of love with loving; and I hated security and a life with no snares for my feet. For within I was hungry, all for the want of that spiritual food which is Thyself, my God; yet I did not hunger for it: I had desire for incorruptible food, not because I had it in abundance but the emptier I was, the more I hated the thought of it. Because of all this my soul was sick, and broke out in sores, whose itch I agonized to scratch with the rub of carnal things—carnal, yet if there were no soul in them, they would not be objects of love. My longing then was to love and be loved, but most when I obtained the enjoyment of the body of the person who loved me.

—*The Confessions of St. Augustine*

Every epoch not only dreams the next, but while dreaming impels it toward wakefulness. It bears its end with itself, and reveals it by a ruse. With the upheaval of the market economy, we begin to recognize the monuments of the bourgeoisie as ruins even before they have crumbled.

—Walter Benjamin

In play there is something "at play" which transcends the immediate needs of life and imparts meaning to the action. All play means something.

—Johan Huizinga

once again, to A.G.

—and to the canasta players

One

Michael is driving home from Alley's Piano Bar. A light rain is falling on the city—mist really. It's past midnight and the streets are nearly deserted. Eerie blue light from sodium vapor streetlamps reflects off the hood of his Tercel, distorting the glimpses of street he catches between strokes of the windshield wipers. Michael peers out the glass, compensating for his weakening eyesight by squinting. On the seat beside him the flower he bought in the afternoon for Mary, a red rose, shriveled now from the heat, still gives off faint whiffs of perfume. Textbooks, magazines, and student essays litter the backseat. He is on his way home from the bar where he stops Thursday nights for drinks with his students. Michael drives slowly, eyes riveted to the wet asphalt, both hands steadying the car down the street's center lane. He is a careful driver at all times—but when drunk, he becomes cautious and plodding. He's driving north on Pembina, a divided street which originates in the city center and cuts through the strip villages it creates to the fields marking the city's southern limit. Past the Rib Shack a vehicle pulls up alongside in the curb lane. Michael glances over. It's a big Harley. The biker is wearing black leather—boots, pants, and jacket. His helmet is black with a tinted visor. Michael has seen it before. Where? He cannot recall, though it makes him uneasy the way greasy hair does. There is almost no traffic on Pembina, but the motorcycle stays tight to the Tercel's front wheels. They pass Mother's Pizza, the Holiday Inn, and the Keg, the motorcycle holding position just off the car's wheels. Michael doesn't like this. He squints through the windshield, trying to still the shaking of his hands on the wheel. At the side of his vision he notices a second motorcycle on his left. Black Harley, black jacket, helmet with tinted visor. Darth Vadar. Sweat starts from Michael's armpits. Who are these guys? What's going on? He lives in the suburbs where crime is having the sideview mirror of your car smashed, where drug abuse means too much scotch, where more people die from exposure than murder. He thinks of turning down a side street to escape but is trapped in the middle lane. His heart has speeded up. His mind jumps to lurid news items involving bikers—stabbings, sawed-off shotguns. Does somebody want to kill him? Michael glances in the rearview mirror. Headlights flickering through the rain, flashing advertisements on storefronts, a taxi's lit dome light, but no sign of a friendly police cruiser. A drugstore's neon sign reads KNIFE SETS 12.99. Michael's neighborhood. At Windermere Street he brakes sharply, gears down, and wheels to the right, watching the motorcycles glide through the inter-section. Michael sighs with relief—but suddenly his hands clench the wheel. A gray-haired man with glasses is stepping right into his path! Michael didn't see where he came from and his mouth drops open in a silent scream as the Tercel leaps forward. He swerves. He sees the man's hand flail out and graze the side mirror as the Tercel fishtails past, striking the curb. Gravel scatters in the gutter, rubber thumps on concrete, a metal part from the undercarriage drops to the asphalt with a clank. Michael is sweating hard now. His heart is a clenched fist in his chest. He looks back in the rearview mirror, expecting to see a heap of bloody clothes on the asphalt, expecting to see disaster, a crowd gathering to indict him for murder, but the man stands on the curb staring after the car, one hand over his heart. Michael slows. Should he go back? The smell of burning rubber rises from the front of the car, mixing with the fug of Michael's fear. What was he doing? What was he thinking? The Tercel coasts through another block while Michael studies the man's receding image behind him. Everything seems okay. He shifts into second, then third.

* * *

Minutes later Michael stands in his yard listening to night sounds and smelling the air. His hands still tremble. In one he holds the rose for Mary, in the other the sneakers he left in the grass after his morning run. He was lucky not to have killed someone tonight—or been killed. Dumb luck. Once a cousin of Michael's was killed in a car accident on the way home from a dance, a bloodbath at a railroad crossing Michael had been spared only because he was passed out drunk in the bushes. Not virtue or even cunning saved him, just dumb luck. Michael looks at the sky. The stars shine bright as they have throughout this spring of stifling heat. Greenhouse effect, they say on the radio, the old planet running down. The Big Dipper hovers over the Yims', his neighbors, whose terrier yaps at his own dog through the caragana hedge between their houses.

This neighborhood is called Woodydell. Isolated by the river on one side and perimeter dikes on the others, Woodydell is not the most pricey neighborhood in the city, but it appeals to ecologists and New Left holdovers from the sixties, including, Michael has come to accept over the past decade, himself. It's a planned community. Diagonal sidewalks converge on a central park where children swing from wooden gymnasiums and then scoot down walkways to homes renovated according to *Architectural Digest*. Mary gushes over Woodydell. No cars, no crowds. *Gorgeous*, she calls it, one of her favorite words. Woodydell boasts ten acres of parks, a community club on the river, and forty species of trees. Volvos, Saabs, Subarus. Strangely, Michael feels at home here among civil servants, architects, and stockbrokers—types he once snubbed, suspecting their trimmed beards and button-down morality. Now he chats them up at the health-foods counter and shares tubes of Primo Caulk in the fall. Happy. Fat. He likes the trim wives who ferry their kids from Highland dance to ringette in Suburbans. His neighbors come over on warm summer nights and they play canasta and listen to old records. They bask in the glow of good scotch, the glow of middle age, the glow of success. Michael signs petitions protecting Woodydell from freeways, he referees little league soccer, he sprays his trees for bark beetles. With his neighbors Michael agrees that if it weren't for Dutch elm disease Woodydell would be perfect. Like them he votes Liberal and wears toe rubbers over his loafers during spring thaw.

And jogs. It's supposed to keep his weight down, but it isn't working. So far all he's got from running is pain. Cramps, stitches, a twinge he hasn't felt in his knee since the days when he played high-school basketball in Belvu. Was it really thirty years ago? Lately there've been spasms in the back. Still, they're nothing compared to the gut-aches he gets brooding about Angela.

He feels sweat on his brow. He wonders if it's the heat, or the terror of seeing the bikers, or nearly killing the man on Pembina. Or Angela. Coal-black hair, black nails, the scent of

4

mint on her breath, the scent of sexual excitement and danger in every twitch of her young body. Angela. Some things are better not thought about. Michael closes his eyes and listens to the rattling leaves. It feels hot even though it's been raining. But this heat is good for him. It burns fat. Which he's got a lot of, now that he's living the soft life—teaching graduate courses, pecking out his newspaper column. Life's treated him good, better than he deserves, and he's thickened to 230 pounds, as heavy as when he left his first wife. In those days he guzzled Johnny Walker like he owned an interest in the company. He smiles. The idea appeals to him, owning shares in a big conglomerate. Seagrams gained two bucks last week after the CEO announced a move into coolers. You could do worse than put your money into booze.

Michael pats his stomach, calculating pounds to lose. When you near fifty you think about how much weight you're carting around and what the old ticker can take. Not like when he was forty. His mind flattens back through time and he remembers scampering through parks to meet Mary. She wore a turquoise dress the summer of their affair, and she hiked it up over her hips when she straddled him under the trees in Barrier Park. He recalls the way the material scratched his bare legs as it worked up their thighs. He recalls, too, hurried meetings in coffee shops and restaurants. Was it only ten years ago? Though he was crazy in love with Mary, that was an awful time. He was wracked by guilt and fear. His nerves were shot. He doused them with nicotine and alcohol, waiting for Mary's phone calls, terrified that Patricia would discover them. His pulse raced as if he were high on speed. How did he escape without one seizure? Lord. The only ailment he had in those days was headache, and it came from too much scotch.

A willow branch teased by the wind beats on the Yims' roof. *Thuck, thuck.* A sound like feet on asphalt, which reminds him of the run he makes most mornings around Woodydell. His buddy,

Stephen, jokes they're killing themselves with exertion, but Michael likes to think he's toughening his body. *Granite thighs,* Angela said, her long fingers working his zipper, her hair tickling his legs. There are things about women he'll never understand, things having to do with fingers and mouths, the way a woman smells stepping out of the shower, or the pursing of lips chewing over a crisis late at night. And he likes it that way—a little mystery. Angela. He spits into the grass before he turns to the house. Places the Avias on the deck so they'll be dry in the morning for his run with Stephen.

* * *

As they near the war memorial Michael signals with one limp wrist that he can just make it to the halfway point if they go easy. He needs to stop and catch his breath, he wants to linger there and talk about Angela, unburden himself—Christ, what can he do, a man of fifty pursued by a woman half his age? But before he regains his breath Stephen blurts out, "I'll tell you what's killing us." He glances up to the sky, and Michael's eyes follow his, focusing on a pair of ducks flying over the river. "What's killing us is the crap they put in food these days."

Michael can smell the river curling by out of sight beyond the trees, a cool dark bouquet that reminds him of happy summers at Willow Point where he fished with his brothers and had a rowboat painted green. The peace of open spaces and no responsibilities. "Cholesterol," Stephen continues. "Eight thousand Canadians will have heart attacks this year, mostly from poor diet." Stephen subscribes to *Living Health* and *Harrowsmith.*

Michael says, "We don't buy butter any more." Mary's idea, actually—he loves it on potatoes and greens. "Though margarine is loaded with hydroxy-whatever."

"Hydrogenated oils," Stephen says, breathing hard. "And salt. Both bad for blood pressure." Stephen scratches his brow after he says this. He talks often about heart attack, claims that the men in his family die young. So he's made out his will and has bought a burial plot at Green Acres. Not Michael. Making wills is a concession to death, and that's something he won't do.

This is not a pleasant subject. Michael dabs his brow with the facecloth he tucks into the waistband of his sweatpants. He senses that Stephen wants to talk about global extinction, but *he* wants to talk about Angela. He looks around for his dog, Ruggles. Left for a moment, the golden retriever jumps in the river and smells like skunk for days after. Then Mary turns up her nose and sulks, though she was the one who brought Ruggles home as a puppy.

"Who I'm really sorry for," says Stephen, "is the kids. Meltdowns and toxic ash aren't bad enough. Now they're getting poisoned at the burger joints. At Chicken Shack, for godssake!"

Michael looks past the war memorial toward the river. Talk about kids reminds him of Jane. On the telephone last night she accused him of being cheap—him, when he coughed up two grand for that Jap car? Then they got into the shouting. The kid always needs something. She's always brought home losers for boyfriends and now she's screwing a psychopath who can't hold down a job, so Michael has to support them both. Brad the Bum. Poor Jane, nothing's ever been easy for her. Taunted by kids at school. Never fitting in. Then he and Patricia got divorced when she was in junior high. What a way to grow up. No wonder she drags Michael into shouting matches, no wonder she's a bust with men.

"They're more scared than we are," Michael says.

Stephen softens. "Shit scared." He runs his hand back through his black hair. Jogging behind him, Michael noticed a bald spot starting to form there and wanted to reach out and touch it. Something makes him feel sorry for Stephen, although he also knows he needs him as a confidant. Someone to share his life story.

Stephen asks, "Were we like that, scared shitless at twenty?"

"No," Michael says flatly. He mops his brow again. He's happy to get off the subject of Jane, he's happy to reminisce about the past. "We had the promise of hoola hoops and whiffle balls. The promise that things worked out. That anyone could make it." These are his father's words, Michael realizes, his father who owned a '52 Meteor and on Sundays drove to the city to visit Uncle Charlie and argue politics past midnight. Michael's father insisted free enterprise did wonders for the country, which in those days was wallowing in post-war euphoria and consumer demand. Michael is tempted to paint the fifties in the gold of nostalgia, though he stops himself with thoughts of race riots, the Berlin Wall, the Seaway scandal.

"Everyone was on the make—in more ways than one."

"On the make," Michael says, "but never making it." This is something they share, memories of frustrated teenage lust. Whoever was screwing in the backseats of Chevies, it wasn't Michael and Stephen. They were in the pool hall, or working on the yearbook, or shagging flies on some twilight diamond, but that was the all-male world of loud guffaws and slapping backs, far from panties and condoms and squeaky backseats. In fact most of the guys Michael knew in high school never got much beyond petting. Although there was a lot of talk. And still is. "Not like today," he says, hoping to swing the talk around to Angela, "when everyone's making it."

Stephen snorts. "What I remember is hand-jobs."

"One girl at Belvu High carried Ivory Liquid in her purse and smeared it on her hands for lubrication."

"The girl in front of me for home room came in Monday mornings with a big hickey on her neck. The back. We used to wonder where else she had them."

"Lover's nuts," Michael says. "Christ, I had such a bad case of those one night in 1959 I nearly cried. Joanne, I think was the girl's name. It was a week before I could piss right."

"We used to say, 'I touched the Little Man in the Boat' when we got to third base."

"Hooters."

"Knockers. But how to get your hands on them."

Michael sighs. "That's the curse of teenage lust. Ignorance and terror. Fear you're going to look like a klutz." He adds in a confiding tone, "Not like today."

"You say." Stephen raises his brows archly. "I feel more a klutz around women today than I did thirty years ago." He states this with finality and glances up the road, a signal to resume their run.

Michael studies the grade up to Crescent. He feels cheated, knowing he'll have to wait to talk about Angela, miffed Stephen won't take up his lead just when they're warming to the subject of sex. He touches the facecloth to his brow one last time before tucking it into his sweats and says, "Another thing to get you down."

"Right. One of the many."

Stephen moves off behind Ruggles, the issue apparently closed. Conversations conclude this way now, Michael's noticed. Everybody's hunkering down to take whatever blows are coming. The other day on TV a crowd gave Paul McCartney a standing ovation for "Let It Be." It scared him. He's never much cared for fatalism, though he recalls a time when he just let things happen to him, when it seemed enough to survive, when he was stuck between desire for Mary and duty to Patricia. Stuck, hell. Frozen is more like. Impotent. That was different, personal and temporary. This new thing goes deeper. Everyone's ready to give up, to pay the price, whatever it is. Why, no one even haggles with shopkeepers any more, they just shell out. They've given up, the bastards. They've given in. And then Michael wonders between breaths why he's using the third person. Hasn't he given in, too?

* * *

One hand braced against the house, Michael leans forward and vomits into the grass at his feet. The sharp stucco stones dig into the palm of one hand. He holds his other hand over his stomach as if coaxing the vomit up. He does this between his house and the Yims' where there are no windows spying on him. The vomit drops to the ground, speckling leaves of grass the burnt color of dried blood. Ruggles backs away whimpering. Stars dance in Michael's eyes. He smells the mixed odors of sweat and alcohol coming out of his pores, the smells of life—or is it decay? Strangely, he feels no pain once the vomiting is over. Inside the house he will gargle with Scope and feel fine. He has been to see his doctor about the vomiting. Tests. Tubes down the gullet, tubes up the anus—painful even when slathered in petroleum jelly. His doctor, an Arab with a pencil mustache, has prescribed small brown pills which Michael takes before bed. If he remembers. The pills relax him so he falls asleep faster, but they do not stop the vomiting. When he leans against the wall after his run, the spittle comes out burnt blood streaked with chalk white. At first it was just a mouthful, but lately he's coughing up enough to fill a cup.

* * *

It's the feet that go first, that's what a reflexologist on TV claimed, and looking at his soles Michael is sure she's right. He's taken off his sneakers and socks and is resting on the steps after running. He picks at a callus. What did the reflexologist say about heels—not something to do with the heart, was it? He can't remember, though he recalls clearly the young woman in a dun caftan who held up charts of feet and pointed to areas with her long red nails. But he cannot recall what she said. Dammit, now his memory's going too. First the eyes, then the lungs, now the brain. More and more he has to concentrate on simple things.

He finds himself in the basement holding a pair of pliers but unable to remember descending the stairs or what he meant to do when he got there. Soon he'll have to do what his father does—scribble notes in a little book which he keeps in the breast pocket of his shirt and checks every hour or so.

Ruggles noses Michael's leg, wanting water, and looks up from brown eyes. What a simple life the dog leads at emotional ground zero—food, sleep, sex. No consequences. Michael envies that.

Before he can get up, the screen door flaps behind Michael's back. "Hey, big guy," Mary says in her singsong voice. She stands on the top step, holding a coffee mug in one hand. In her house shirt she looks ten years younger than when she's made up for the office, a girl really, shiny cheeks, breasts swaying in her cotton shirt. Mary's legs are still hard and firm and her skin turns golden every summer like a teenager's. Michael can't remember when she's looked better. He thought women were supposed to age badly.

"Hey, sweetheart." Michael looks up. The scent of shampoo and powder hang in the air around her. Mary.

"Look at that sky," she says. He hadn't noticed but colors have flooded in from the east, purples and pinks. Two hours and the mid-May sun will be high and hot. She asks, "Have a good run?"

He hasn't told her about the vomiting and won't unless she finds out. "Yes," he says. His chest feels hollow with exhaustion, his legs tight and solid, good feelings he remembers from high-school days. He was strong and resilient then, but he wouldn't trade his life now for that one. He knows people who wish they were still twenty and on the make. Not Michael. Though he feels it all slipping away. He says, "We did the circuit around the war memorial."

"You and Stephen?"

Michael nods. "Stephen's on about weight training now. Not

power-lifting like in the Olympics. Aerobic stuff for the gut and back. I'm not up to that."

Mary says, "I had a call from Jane."

"Oh." Michael turns on the step toward Mary. The kid brings the pain. Shouting on the phone, abusing Mary. When she left home the last time—the last in a long series of flights—she stole two hundred dollars from a dresser and some of Mary's jewelry. Still, it's Michael and Mary who feel guilty. Mary thinks her sharp words drove Jane away, and Michael thinks he's never given the girl enough encouragement, enough unqualified love. He asks, "What does she want this time? More money?"

"A car." Mary brushes an imaginary crumb from her lip. "She's got an appointment at the clinic."

To Michael "clinic" means hospital which means something bad. Some disease? Pregnant? Though the thought of a grandchild pleases him. At his age he wants to dote on creatures with tiny hands and feet. During the Easter holidays he held a nephew's baby at the dinner table and was surprised at the strength of its grip and how little it weighed. But that's not what Jane needs right now, a squawling infant. He asks, "What's all that about?"

"Don't ask me. You know how much she tells *me*." Mary's hand trembles, so she steadies it on the deck railing. In the other hand she holds a brown mug with white lettering that reads, GUEST ON CBC'S COFFEE KLATCH. A realtor now, Mary does radio shows from time to time, hyping property. She's smooth, explaining depreciation and mortgages. Listening on the kitchen portable, Michael admires how she mixes breezy chat with slick sales pitch. Off-air the hosts say she soothes people, they tell her she could get a job in broadcasting, and one station manager has taken her out to lunch.

Michael wants to change the subject—it's too early in the day to quarrel about Jane. "Can you get off early?" he asks. They can make the cottage in an hour, open space and soft sand. Peace.

He finished the deck at the cottage last summer and likes to sit and read under the maple boughs and feel the cool breeze off the lake. That's what he needs, the feeling of being hollow and full at the same time. Spent. In the city the only way he can get there is through scotch—that and the spent exhaustion of sex.

"I want to close the Riverview thing by noon." Mary's voice, guarded while they talked about Jane, grows warm now. "But there'll be time to stop at the track, won't there?"

In the past year she's started following the ponies. She goes to the track weeknights during the summer and lately part of the weekends, too. A novice, she puts her money on ponies with fanciful names. When her horses come in she dances and throws her arms around Michael's neck. It embarrasses him, but he feels a secret thrill. So much energy, passion. It was that passion that attracted him to Mary over a decade ago. She dresses to go to the track—bright skirts, red scarves—and he notices other men looking at her as they stroll past. When she loses, Mary stamps her stubs under her feet. She bets on intuition. And it works. Michael was raised by a father who gambled away thousands each season at the two-dollar window, so he knows track lore and studies the form charts with a practised eye. He plays his money smart. But Mary wins as often as he does and it irritates him, though he laughs when she gleefully counts her winnings. "One race," he says, since it's Friday, "one bet."

"Swell." Mary taps her feet as she contemplates her schedule. "I'll be ready by three o'clock. Maybe two."

Michael massages his neck. The cottage. He spends as much of the summer there as possible, away from petty college politics and the heat of the city. He likes the solitude. He relaxes, he sleeps better. Daydreams. He spent much of last summer at the lake curled up on the sofa reading old magazines or sitting on rocks at the point drinking from a bottle of scotch while he gazed at the stars. Studied the constellations. Slept at odd times and started to feel like a hermit. When he came to the city, the traffic sounds scared him and people seemed to be pressing in. Dirt, noise.

Now he says with a conviction he doesn't feel, "I'll clear up this business with Jane." He stands, stretches his back, and toes his sneakers along the cement pad. "Give her the Tercel." Maybe that will bring the kid around. He adds, "That coffee smells great." When he takes the mug and sips, he looks into Mary's gray eyes and sees them slip past his shoulder across the lawn to the house opposite where the two gays live. Jumpy eyes.

"Swell," she says, "because I'll be on the run in Riverview, so I need the Merc all day. In fact I should be over there now telling Mrs. whatshername about mortgage assumption. You'd think selling at two hundred grand she wouldn't fret about penalties, but that's the first thing she asks. Honestly, Michael, the more they have, the squeakier they get." She touches his cheek as he mounts the steps to her and says, startled, "You're warm."

Some things constantly surprise him. The way he goes fluttery inside when Mary's skin brushes his, the effect her scent has on him in the morning. She embraces him now, quickly with her free arm, and he smells the bath salts he gave her for her birthday. Forty-five, she looks thirty-something. His wife. He puts his hand on her back and guides her through the door. "I'll call," he repeats, sounding, he hopes, both compassionate and authoritative. "Tell Jane to take the Tercel."

"Do that," she says. "And Forster, too." When Michael hesitates she adds, "About the stack?" and tips her chin toward the rear of the house. Out back it's a wreck. The small bedroom Michael uses as a study is the scene of remodeling, the walls bleeding bats of insulation and plastic vapor barrier. Renovations. Hardly in the house one year, they began to sense its inadequacies—old wiring, a dark living room, the small bathroom. So Mary hired Forster, a German with a good reputation and expensive taste. A shark, Michael thinks. Forster charges twelve bucks for a sheet of Gyproc and three for framing studs.

Bathroom fixtures two hundred. Forster's take off the top must be thirty percent, Michael figures. But Mary's paying out of her commissions, so what can Michael say? He nods, he agrees, he phones Forster about building permits and toilet stacks.

In the kitchen he selects a mug from the cupboard. IN SPACE YOU CAN'T HEAR A FART, it reads, a gag gift from Mary's partner, Fred. As he pours coffee, Michael thinks about the calories in cream and congratulates himself for giving up sugar two months ago. Mary moves between the bedroom and the bathroom, dressing. The smells of powder, soaps, and perfume compete with the aroma of coffee. Another of women's mysteries Michael happily nibbles at—their ablutions. He loves smelling Mary's hair. Angela's. Nice, he reflects, women are nice. And then, thinking of Jane, sometimes. Sometimes.

"She didn't say anything else?" he calls when Mary crosses the hall between the rooms.

"Only that Brad's truck's down and she needs a car."

When isn't Brad's truck down? Michael dislikes the boy, even though he's the first one who's stuck with Jane longer than a few weeks. Most of her men have been one-night stands. At least Brad has stayed around long enough to talk to Michael. In the backyard one night they had a beer and fifteen minutes of strained conversation before Jane rescued them. "But she didn't say anything about this clinic business?"

Mary sighs with exasperation. "She's twenty-two, honey." Whenever they talk about Jane their voices have an edge to them. They're angry at the girl but they end up shouting at each other. And though they've talked this over late into the night, they can't help themselves. "Maybe she ran out of birth-control pills," Mary adds. Her voice is muffled in the closet as she rummages through clothes. Silk blouses, cotton shirts, racks of jackets. Michael figures she blows half her commissions on clothes and cosmetics, another big chunk on the Mercedes.

He picks up Ruggles' water dish, rinses it under the tap, and fills it. As he opens the door Ruggles nudges his leg. Water slops onto the crown of the dog's scruffy angular head, which seen from above reminds Michael of a coconut and which he cannot help fondling tentatively, like he fingered his babies' skulls. Maurice, Jane. A grandchild?

* * *

Back inside, Michael switches on the radio. News. In New York, a voice says, markets are higher in large volumes. An update will follow. Elsewhere, OPEC ministers emerged from closed-door meetings, promising a joint statement on Iraq's latest moves in the crude oil market. Another three bodies have turned up at a notorious dumping ground used by El Salvador's death squads. The English poet laureate is dead at sixty from heart attack. Probably smoked, Michael thinks, they all do. And they never take any exercise. This jump in the markets excites Michael—what does that work out to for him? A couple grand, maybe. Mary's been pestering him to extend their leverage loan and he should have. Chances missed, millions missed. Sports. Football's first. Stamps 32, Argos 28, but Calgary's in financial trouble. Last year Montreal folded and Ottawa had to be bailed out by a *Save the Roughies* appeal. The CFL's doomed. He waits for news of the Blue Jays, one game up almost halfway to the All Star break. Last night Bell cracked home run number ten and Henke is on a record pace for saves. He loves the way the Jays play, the swank. On Sunday the rookie McGriff smacked two homers out of Fenway and said in the post-game interview he's not swinging good. Cheeky! Michael loves the fleet Fernandez, burly Whitt with arms like hams, and the sleek Moseby. They have to be going to the World Series, he figures.

* * *

When Mary appears in the hall he says, "I was thinking maybe it's *because* she ran out of pills."

"How's that?" Mary has come into the kitchen. In one hand she carries shoes, white pumps, in the other a leather case with realty papers spilling out. Dressed for work she seems smaller than in the house shirt, her soft lines bullied by a navy suit into functional trim. Cool, her clothes say to the world, a message she's fine-tuned in her decade of selling property. But on top of things, too. Michael can't help but reach out to her.

"Jane, I mean," he says. "Pregnant." Holding her he smells lily of the valley, a new scent for Mary, and he buries his face in her hair. Her perfume reminds him of the delicate spice of Angela's pale skin, but the curve of her back is purely her own, giving, rounded to take the shape of his need. This is what life is all about. If he could only stop time at one of these moments— holding Mary in his arms, or getting dreamy at the lake.

"Pregnant?" Mary's voice has gone brittle. "She'd announce that. Guessing we're certain to object."

Michael pulls back from their embrace. "Aren't we?" In the uneven light of the kitchen Mary's irises seem pale green.

"Not necessarily. That girl could use something to shake her out of her everlasting funk."

"Well," Michael says, suddenly defensive about his daughter, "you know things are tough for the kid."

Now Mary pulls back. "She's not a *kid* any more—though being told she is is one of the reasons she's so screwed up."

He can feel the heat of argument on her breath but he says anyway, "She's screwed up because no one wants her."

"Michael, honestly."

"You don't think?"

"That's a handy excuse. Nothing more."

"What then?"

"God. You refuse to face the facts."

"And what are the facts—in your humble opinion?"

"You're the one insisted she leave here. If you remember."

"I gave her a choice," Michael says. "Following the famous

Kirkbeck's advice. Advice for which you shelled out fifty bucks an hour, if *you* remember."

"Dr. Kirkbeck was worth the money. At least he gave us direction. Told us not to smother Jane, to let her find herself."

"Huh." Michael feels caffeine driving his heart and enlarging his anger. "So we found her a beat-up Honda. And what she found was a punk with a fried brain and no driver's licence. Filthy little creep. And what *he* found was somebody eager to take the shitbox off his hands for five hundred bucks, which the kid and the punk turned into dope and rock concerts before you could say rip-off. Five hundred bucks and I paid seventeen!"

"We. We paid seventeen."

He deserves her retort but not the headache he's getting. Too early in the day to fight. Too hot in the city. What he needs is a morning at the cottage, a long vacant walk. He glances at the clock. In a couple hours he'll be sitting with a glass of scotch and the only sound in his head the rhythmic pulse of lake water. When he doesn't answer, Mary says more gently, "Let's forget about all that. The past. And concentrate on what's in front of us." She taps one shoeless foot on the hardwood floor and adds, "Let's not worry about who did what to who but about what we *can* do. Now."

Michael agrees but all he can think to do is pour more coffee. This is when he misses his Winstons, abandoned in the pursuit of pink lungs and virtue two years ago. He asks, "You think this clinic business is serious, then?"

Mary sits at the table, fussing at smudge marks on her pumps with a tissue. When they lived on Furby Street she wore black Chinese flats around the apartment. That's when he started buying her roses. He glances around the room. She's put the one he brought last night—surprisingly, recovered, its petals opening again—in a slim crystal vase on the dining-room table. Mary says, "With Jane anything is an overture to disaster."

"So you *don't* think it's serious, then?"

"I didn't say that either. In fact things might be worse than you guess."

Worse, what could be worse? Cancer? A disease that turns people into vegetables? "Worse?" he asks.

"Abortion." Mary says it so coolly Michael's uncertain the word actually came out of her mouth. She might have said *acne* or *headache*. He almost laughs aloud but he sees Mary is serious.

"Why do you say that?"

"That's what they do at Mountain View. Abortions. It's the one clinic where a woman, a young woman, can get a fair shake." For a moment Michael pictures Angela sitting in the waiting room of a doctor's office, hands folded in her lap. The image startles him, though he doesn't know where it came from. Mary has wiggled into her shoes and straightened the papers in her case. "The one place where they hire women doctors for women patients and treat girls like something less than sluts when they come in carrying some jerk's baby. Some jerk like Brad."

Abortion, Michael thinks. A little baby, a grandchild with tiny paws for hands? Michael smiles at the idea of babies and Mary says, "Makes you feel old, eh?" She glances at her Rolex. "Anyway, Michael, look at the time. If I don't get over to Riverview, Mrs. Johnston's going to get cold feet and then where will I be with the payments due this month?" She dangles the Mercedes' keys in Michael's face to remind him of the sixty thousand still owing on the car and brushes his cheek with her lips as she squeezes past.

"I'll call Jane," he tells her as she goes out the back door and down the half-finished deck toward the cars. Her silver Mercedes gleams in the sunlight filtering through the Yims' maples. "Say she can take the Tercel."

"And Forster," she throws over her shoulder, firm, the tone she uses when she talks to lawyers on the phone. Then she stops on the sidewalk and looks back. "And don't get all worked up about it, Michael. Be cool."

* * *

Cool, he repeats under his breath. Easy for Mary to say as she sails off to scalp Mrs. whatshername of seven percent off the top. How does she do it, take people's savings like that with a flash of her gold-filled pen? He calls out after her, "Should I ask about the abortion—right out, like?" But Mary's either beyond range or pretends not to hear.

The car starts and he shrugs before he puts down the coffee mug. "C'mon," he says to Ruggles, jumping off the deck. Ruggles bounds around looking for the tennis ball they use to play fetching games. Animal joy, animal dumb. It's cool in the shade of the trees, and Michael feels the heat of argument subsiding. Piss on Jane. Overhead the sky is bright blue through the interlace of power lines and TV cables and elm branches. Above the rooftops of his neighbors' houses, a jet to the south spreads a fluffy track. He listens and hears his own heart thumping—a good sound, a very good sound. When the dog comes up with the slobbery ball he flips it under the honeysuckle bush. "Go!" Dank stuff under there, discarded peony stalks from spring cleanup never quite completed, matted rotting leaves, heaps of cedar needles. In a few seconds Ruggles is back. So little room back here now. The addition to the house cuts the yard in half.

It's the same everywhere. The big yards where people grew vegetable gardens years ago have been slashed to postage stamps by extensions, and pools, and double garages. Everybody's hacking up their yards, shrinking the green space, really. Soon there won't be any left. They'll have run that down, too.

For some reason he thinks of Angela again. It's got so he can't help think of her whenever his mind isn't occupied by something specific like a grocery list or the news on the radio. She's become an obsession. And like a high-school kid in love, Michael's alternately ecstatic about her and tortured by her. He runs his hands through his hair. He sighs. When Ruggles brings back the ball, Michael kneels and puts his arms around the dog, feeling hot and musky breath on his cheek. Ruggles' heart is knocking in his chest. So is Michael's. He thought he was all done with this, the giddiness of infatuation and desire. Why is he like this? Michael knows what he should do. He should forget about Angela. He should appreciate what he's got with Mary and work at making it even better. Christ, ten years ago he went through all this shit to get *her*. And he doesn't need all the distraction, all the pain. *Grow up*. Other men seem to go about their daily lives without falling in love, without punishing themselves with desire and guilt. He sees them shopping at the Safeway with their wives, helping them apply Tanglefoot to the elms in fall, strolling through the park hand-in-hand. What's wrong with him? Is he the only one wracked by lust and despair?

* * *

Hot water pouring down his back, shampoo streaming over his skull and through his beard, Michael is showering. He closes his eyes. The taste of Scope in his mouth, minty, reminds him of Angela, though residues of vomit taint his palate, too. Spray falls directly on his face. Fatty taste of soap. In the movies starlets have suds up to their nipples. It must take hours to arrange, he thinks, shaping the foam, hurried shots before it dissolves and exposes naked breasts. Wonderful wobbly things, they're all so different. Mary's have pink tips the size of dixie cones. Patricia's were flat and baggy, like Colleen Dewhurst in those O'Neill plays showing up as reruns on the late show now. Angela's? She's still a girl, really. Water runs down the hollow of Michael's chest and over his gut, and streams into the drain. Steam clouds his sight. He spent an afternoon naked in a pool with some college girls years ago. Nineteen-sixty-something. Before he married Patricia. A friend invited him to his ranch in the country where one weekend they held kite-flying contests and the next enacted *commedia del arte*. The one Michael's thinking of was "karma weekend," complete with hash and white wine. And skinny dipping. They held hands and circled the pool, playing ring-around-the-rosy while the Grateful Dead boomed out of the stereo. The water was warm, the girls giggly. It should have been a hippie togetherness experience, communal ritual, but the skin under Michael's beard itched from chlorine, and he felt out of place, naked in front of strangers whose voices rose as the THC worked its way through their veins. When they started playing pinch-the-penis, he feigned a turned ankle and retreated to a deck chair. He was never invited back.

Michael towels down. He clips his mustache. When he's snipping the hairs in his nose the phone rings. He expects to hear Jane's high voice and is surprised by his mother's. She asks, "Were you working?" He tells her he was jogging, leaving out the part about vomiting. Like his father, she is convinced Michael spends too much time at a desk. An account of his running, he thinks, will make her feel better about that, though he can't remember either of his parents taking exercise or playing games. They lived without leisure. When he's done she says, "Your father tells me you're writing for the newspapers." He pictures her saying this to the aluminum cake pans and copper utensils hanging on the wall opposite the telephone table in his parents' kitchen.

He explains that he's writing the first columns on a trial basis and that the paper may kill the project if the editor doesn't like it. "I see," his mother says. But he can tell she doesn't like the idea of two jobs. His visits are already too infrequent to suit her, but she would never say so. Michael rearranges the towel around his waist and sets the scissors between two family photos on the telephone table. On the right, Mary outside the ROM in Toronto, on the left, his parents seated on a bench in their backyard. His mother peers out tortoiseshell glasses too big for her face and tinted like Hollywood stars'. Her arms are solid with fat where they stick out below the short sleeves of a summer blouse. In the past decade she has grown stockier while his father has lost weight. He asks, "How's Dad's back?"

"A whole week without pain. Or pills." She lowers her voice. "He missed you Sunday."

She could never say she did. And his father's the same. Only Uncle Charlie came right out and said it: *love*. He explains, "I was meeting with this editor."

He hears her breathing against the mouthpiece, then a long silence in which he imagines her fussing with her glasses. Finally, she asks, "You're not working too much?"

"I'm fine," he says, knowing what she really wants to say. So many moves in a game. "We're both fine." And he sighs. Maybe she'll take the hint from his voice and move on to another subject.

Instead she says, "Your father finds it very hard. He spends a lot of time staring out the window." Michael doubts this. Since retiring his father seems busier than ever. Over the winter months he refinishes furniture in the basement and fusses with a vegetable garden from April to October. Michael's never seen him staring out a window. His mother either. But that's not what she's getting at. "And we miss the kids," she adds. She means Michael's children, about whose lives she has opinions he'd rather not hear. "How is Jane?" she asks, trying to sound casual. And, before he can respond, "If you want my opinion, this Brad is one big mistake."

Opinions are precisely what he doesn't want. Silence he would love, the silence of his parents' meticulously groomed backyard where he sits with a large gin and tonic, listening to the birds in the trees, watching his father water the tomatoes. Laughs with his mother over the antics of a forgotten cousin. "Jane is no treasure herself," he says. This is something Michael's mother could never understand. She is intent on spoiling her grandchildren and turns a blind eye to their faults. If she had money she would have ruined them without realizing it. "And Brad seems good-hearted," he lies.

"Fuh. You can't trust a city boy who drives a truck."

"I believe he uses it for his work," Michael says, and then winces at his tone.

"Exactly," his mother responds with belligerence. "Delivery boy. Is that what you want for Jane? Our grandchild?"

When he was young, Michael's mother could crush him with one word. "Michael," she'd say, "not *those* shoes." He hates her for that and answers with a sharpness he regrets instantly, "Dad drove a coal truck at one time. Was that so special?"

"In the thirties, yes. But your father made the most of what came his way. He rose in the world."

"Some people might not think shipper at Liquid Chem a big deal."

"Plant foreman. And it was good enough to put you through college. You and your brother."

"Did that make him think any better of us—college?"

"No. But—"

Moves on a chessboard, Michael thinks after he's hung up. I say this, you counter with that. You protest that, I insist on this. Do fifty years with parents come down to this, a series of maneuvers ending in hurt feelings? His own kids feel this estranged from him, sometimes. Hurt, angry, and guilty about that, Michael has a sudden impulse to pick up the receiver and call his mother back. But he leaves the phone on the hook, her voice echoing in his head. He has no idea why she called. Surely not to make him guilty. To make sure he came on Sunday? Over the years his parents' demands have shrunk with their bodies, but that has not kept his guilt from growing. He picks up the photo and studies their eyes. His father's look right into the camera, still sharp blue. His mother's don't meet the camera's eye. That's the way he averts his gaze when his picture is taken, her son in that, too. Mary is different. Whenever she snaps his photo, she says, "Look into the lens, you're always gawking into the distance." When she poses, she stares right at the camera, but she won't meet his eyes when he wants to talk. He revolves the photo in his hands. He wants to smash it against the wall. He imagines the Kodak-tinted faces startled by the blow, glass spraying down the hall. Elation. Release. Instead he brushes lint from the frame. He takes the scissors back into the bathroom and finishes snipping his nose hairs.

* * *

Michael's Tercel, copper metallic, is economical but cramped. At six foot two, he hunches over the steering wheel, his big face filling the side window as he peers out. He's crossing the steel bridge separating the south end of the city from the north, where Jane lives. Below, trains scree and scraw in the railyards spanned by the bridge. Smells of oil, machinery, and diesel fumes. The city was built on the railroad, the "Hub of the West" they used to call it, though now the railways have fallen on hard times and with them this part of the city. There's little movement in the yard below this Friday morning, and the men waving arms along the tracks seem to be drowning in space, signaling distant watchers before they go down for the last time. Once thousands of cars choked this yard, but in the last year the railroad has cut eight hundred jobs, and rumors of more layoffs circulate monthly around city hall. Railways are dying.

At the foot of the bridge Michael gears down and the Tercel bucks, *whunkawhunk*, a sound Michael knows he shouldn't ignore. Forty thousand kilometers and these Jap cars start to fly apart. His father had a '67 Parisienne he drove two hundred thousand miles without changing plugs. *Miles*. When the car bucks this way Ruggles slides around on the backseat, whimpering as he struggles to right himself at the open window. Michael eases the Tercel into the curb lane and strains to read street signs. Last year he bought reading glasses, but he's vain about his eyes, so he's without them again today. Squinting, he makes out some names: Sutherland, Jarvis, Dufferin.

Jane's place is a dreary apartment in a rundown building at the end of a short side street, Lizzie.

At Selkirk he turns east. This is the main drag in the city's north end. On this colorful thoroughfare Polish barbers once stood elbow to elbow with Jewish bakers and German butchers. A welter of tongues and skins. But in the past decade Selkirk Avenue's once-vibrant heart has slowed. The immigrants who came to the north end in the twenties and thirties were indifferent to the swank of department stores, but their children and grandchildren have embraced the vulgar sprawling malls of the eighties with their acres of parking, their arcades, their video shops, lottery kiosks, Green Machines, tanning parlors, astrologers, lawyers, dentists, walk-in clinics, instant film booths, cinemas.

On the corner where Michael turns east a defunct drugstore's windows and doors have been boarded over to protect the plate glass. A dead neon sign on the roof announces RX. Everything here seems pinched and defeated. Across the street stands a decaying branch of the Toronto Dominion Bank. Bankers, druggists, they're going down together. On the sidewalk two old women in black dresses as big as parachutes gesticulate, unaware of everything except the soiled shopping bag between their feet which first one and then the other prods with a black brogue as they talk. Their words float into Michael's open window as he glides past, a foreign babble. Ukrainian? *Baba*, he whispers to himself.

A horn honks and Michael realizes he's slowed to a crawl. In the rearview mirror he sees he's being tailgated by a Trans Am. The driver wears a black watchcap and dark glasses, and for a moment Michael thinks he's seen him before. Where? His heart skips. His fingers tighten on the wheel. Then Michael thinks of Brad swilling beer while Jane frets about carrying his baby, and he tastes coffee backing up his gullet. Whenever he thinks about Jane he feels sick.

He passes an empty lot between two collapsing storefronts and glimpses the glitter of the city's commercial center a mile to the south. Rose-tinted skyscrapers reflect each other's glass and steel. When he stops at a red light the Trans Am pulls up alongside, blaring heavy-metal music. Now that the car's beside him, Michael feels the menace in its two occupants. Maybe they have guns. Maybe there's a gang after him, a gang in leather jackets. When the light changes the Trans Am squeals away and Michael thinks, that's it, wrap yourselves around a light standard, you punks.

He pulls into an ESSO for gas. Here it's a cent a liter cheaper than at the Woodydell self-serve, and when he hops out of the Tercel a man in overalls emerges from beneath a hoist to fill the tank. Old-style service, Michael remembers it from his boyhood in Belvu. On the crowded lot there are Buicks and Chevies, great rusting tubs, but no Volvos or Saabs. Across the street goods are displayed in wooden bins in front of stores, prices marked on white construction paper: ATHLETIC SOCKS $1. Michael is tempted to walk over—he pays ten bucks for three pairs at MGM. Oretski's Warehouse. Gunn's Bakery, where a bell over the door tinkles when an old man emerges with a pretzel in a napkin. Here garbage is tossed in plastic bags on the curb and, dog-torn, spills into the street. Windows of stores are opaque with grit, filmed with grime. A FOR SALE sign is tacked to the facade of one. Dying, dying.

When he hands the pump man ten dollars Michael sees he's dirtied his top-siders, and, glancing about, spots a pool of oil, iridescent on the sun-speckled asphalt, reminding him of the bellies of fish pulled out of Willow Creek. Once when he was hunting he turned over a dead doe and was stunned by this hue, blue shimmering into green and green into gold. Beautiful. And he remembers, too, his uncle Charlie laid out in the morgue after he killed himself, skin unbeautiful, not at all iridescent—flesh a washed-out green as if Uncle Charlie'd had one too many and felt sick. How old had he been? Only fifty-two? At the time it seemed ancient to Michael.

Back in the Tercel he adjusts the radio dial to CBC, hoping for comforting voices. He pokes along Selkirk, straining his eyes for Lizzie. He's been here before but he can't recall the sequence of streets on the way to Jane's. His mind *is* going. Names tick by, McGregor, Andrews. Past the next intersection Selkirk brightens a little. A brick fire station stands back from the street, and firemen in blue shirts loll on lawn chairs beside white vans marked EMERGENCY. Next to the station is a post office built of cinder blocks and smoked glass, a squat cubicle painted institutional gray with surprising crimson trim—Post Canada aping postmodern chic? Then a clutter of boutiques, Legs Alive, The Second Cup, House of Wicker, Next Trend, and a deli bring him to Frances Street, and now Michael recalls the sequence of once-fashionable names ending with the one he's looking for—Lizzie.

At the light he swings the Tercel right, expecting to see Jane's shabby walk-up, but he's remembered this poorly, too. He discovers a yellow brick high rise blooming before him, a retirement home for old folks, he'd forgotten this strange sunflower rearing its twenty-story head above the crumbling neighborhood and deserted railyards behind. A very fat woman stands at the edge of the lawn pointing at something Michael strains to see but can't because of the Tercel's fore-shortened roof.

Two blocks down he's at Jane's, at Brad's, really. The kid moved in with him last Easter when she and her girlfriend gave up their apartment in the Core. It wasn't much either, but compared with this, quite comfortable. He pulls the Tercel to the curb, parking in front of a battered Cadillac slumped over on bum shocks. No sign of Brad's truck. Michael's heart throbs in his temples. These sessions with Jane kill him. He takes several deep breaths, a technique he uses to relax, and closes his eyes.

The smell of burning leaves is in the air. On the radio the music stops and the news comes on. A voice says: "Markets continue sharply higher on Wall and Bay Streets." Michael licks his lips. He'll extend that line of credit Monday. If things continue this way he'll be able to buy a new car. Maybe a BMW. The voice rushes into the weather forecast. Sunny, warm. It will be a good weekend at Willow Point.

He locks the car doors but leaves one window down for Ruggles, who thumps his tail on the backseat. The door to the apartment is right at the curb. Beside mailbox 6 he reads DUNCAN/SAMUELS, and he smiles to see his daughter's name linked this way with Brad's. Part of him wants to like the boy, but part is wary. Like the others, he'll probably dump Jane because of her tantrums. Michael steps over trash on the concrete steps. He mounts the green carpeted stairs inside, the smell of cat piss richer at each landing. Number 6, he remembers, is to the right, but he doesn't recall the stack of tires he has to dodge, oversized, with raised white letters, he's seen them on muscle cars and the 4X4s which plague drivers on the dirt roads near Belvu. Is his daughter part of that crowd now? A tough like her leather-jacketed boyfriends?

* * *

After the climb up the stairs, Michael's chest is heaving, and he hesitates before the door to catch his breath. Middle age surges blood in his ears. But that's not all. Tension. Ten years ago when Michael left Patricia for Mary, his kids suffered the brunt of the pain. Maurice, his son, has forgiven him, Michael thinks. But Jane is different. An overweight teen in junior high, she's never recovered from the upset of his departure—or forgiven him. A look in her eyes turns everything from his gut to his heart into one knot.

When he knocks she calls out, "Come in Pa." He hears the thump of feet across the floor, and the rock music pulsing from beyond the door stops suddenly. Pa? Tentative, he pushes the door which swings open on squeaky hinges and releases a warm gust of air scented with soap powder. Chemical lemon. Jane's been cleaning. "Out in a sec," she shouts from in back.

Michael stands in the living room. The tattered couch he gave Jane, which materialized here after Easter along with the kid's clothes and record collection, has a broken leg now, propped up by a stack of magazines. Above it hangs a calendar. Otherwise the beige walls are bare. A stereo sits on the floor, a TV set on an orange crate under the window. The shag carpet, sickly green, is new but already stained with two big circles of grease. He expects to see carburetor parts lying about, but there's nothing on the floor except a stack of old *Rolling Stones*.

"I was polishing my boots," says Jane, coming into the room through a curtain beyond which he glimpses a futon. She lifts one boot to show him. Oxblood. She's wearing a miniskirt, black leather belted with a huge silver buckle. Michael thought mini-skirts were out of style. Or are they just back in?

"How'd I do?" Jane asks of her job on the boots. Her legs are short but shapely, like Patricia's. He nods and she says, "They were this off-white and I hated them when they got wet." She blows into a tissue. On the bridge of her nose a forked vein she's had since a baby turns vivid red when she's sickly.

Though he's touched that she still needs his approval, he can't meet her gaze. "I parked out front," he mumbles, searching for words that will show her he cares. Why is it he has lots of sympathy for students, strangers, but none for his own daughter? All he can think of is the seediness of the apartment. It's the orange crate which has thrown him off, taking him back to the time when he and Patricia lived in a dingy basement apartment. Graduate school. Babies, wicker-basket chairs, and pizza in cardboard boxes. Michael built a bookcase out of orange crates. He clears his throat. His conversations with Jane follow a pattern—strained silence leading to outbursts of rage. Once he'd like to avoid that.

"It's a dump, right?" She follows his eyes around the room and makes a little gesture with one hand, palm flipped up. Around her neck a locket flashes gold. "Right?"

"It could use a little . . ."

"A lot," Jane says with finality. "You wanna split?"

"What time—"

"Those dickheads will take *me* anytime."

"You don't have an appointment?"

"Of course. But you know doctors. Keep you waiting while they're fondling the nurses—or whatever." Jane sticks out her jaw and adds, indicating the stereo, "I'll kill this." Michael looks from one shabby object to another and drops his eyes to the floor. Too aware of his top-siders, designer jeans, and cashmere sweater.

Jane stoops to press a button on the stereo. Her shoulder-length hair is stringy and she rakes it off her face. "This place, you know, I need to buy some new stuff. Chairs, maybe. Pictures."

She hasn't come out and said it but she's angling at money. Which they agreed not to talk about after the Honda fiasco. Still, if he thought that would be the end of it, Michael would press a fistful of twenties into her hand or buy whatever she needed. Instead he says, "When we began, me and your mother—"

"Yuck," Jane says, "don't mention the Bitch."

"She's not so bad, you know."

"Gimme a break. Sure she sends a lousy check every now and then, like conscience money I guess, but there's always a note in her secretary's scribble telling me what to do—and what not to do. Like move in with Brad. Jesus, Pa, she's always on about Brad. Just because she can't get it on with anyone." Jane tilts her face to Michael as if he'd be specially interested. "Brad says that's her main problem, she's sexually uptight."

"She does her best," Michael says, angry at the image of Jane and Brad laughing at Patricia—probably at him.

"Oh right." Jane stands, hands on hips, a defiant posture she learned from rock videos. "When she isn't screwing me over. Or shutting me out of her life."

"I suppose Brad put that idea in your head."

"No, he didn't. I am actually capable of thoughts of my own. But neither you or Mom ever noticed." This is so obviously unfair Michael looks out the window. The curtains in the apartment opposite are drawn, but he can see a hanging plant behind the glass and cheery ceramic plates lined up on the sill. Jane continues, "But while we're on the subject, he said it was shitty of you not to give me money just because of the Honda."

"Two thousand dollars, peanut."

"Brad says you could've got most of it back. *If* you'd known the right people to sell to."

"He has opinions on our family affairs, does he?"

"Only when you get taken—like you always do."

"Opinions he'd like passed on when he isn't here in person?" Michael hears the irritation in his voice. He should be trying a different tone altogether, sympathy of the sort he got from his uncle Charlie, who always knew what to say. But Michael can't help himself. They're on the downslide into fury. "When he's out swilling beer at ten in the morning? While I drive you to the hospital?"

"The only thing you drive me," Jane says as she flounces to the closet to get a coat, "is fucking crazy."

"Jane," Michael says, "come on. Calm down."

"You're so damn unforgiving."

"And you're so damn demanding."

When she yanks a jacket off a hook, two anoraks fall from their hangers. She kicks at them and says, "You won't give me love, you won't give me money. Now you won't give me a lousy ride."

"That's unfair."

"I'll walk to the goddamn clinic."

"Jane," he says, "come on already."

"Fuck off. Just go fuck yourself, will you?" Blind with rage, she wrestles with the leather jacket she's pulled out of the closet. Michael stands with his hands in his pockets. He could use a drink, and he glances around the room. From the apartment above he hears feet scuffing the floor. Someone walking between rooms. Jane says, "And Brad's not swilling beer, he's out hauling Dwayne's motorcycle."

"Dwayne?"

"Who races dirt bikes."

"Great." The oversized tires in the hall must belong to Dwayne. "I suppose he lives here, too, this lunatic on wheels?"

Jane laughs. Her lower teeth are stained and chipped. Years ago he and Patricia quarreled over these teeth, Michael wanting to get a dental plan for the kids but Patricia arguing it was too expensive. Or was it Patricia who said the new car was too costly? The years blur everything. There are times when he can no longer summon up Patricia's face, though he does recall the way her eyes darkened in anger. Jane is that way, too. "Get a life, Pa," she says now, dabbing her nose with a tissue. "He's shacked up with his own girl."

"Convenient," Michael says. "Find a girl who pays the rent."

"Convenient enough. That way we can fuck in private."

Again Michael hears the thump of feet overhead. His own shoes seem rooted to the carpet. He feels heat in his cheeks, he feels the futility of the conversation. And a sudden weight on the back of his neck that makes him shrug his shoulders in an effort to shake it off. "Yes," he says, finally, "and make babies. Something you apparently *do* know about."

"Damn right." Jane's slipping into the jacket now, an old one with frayed cuffs and cracked leather. Clumsy, she catches an arm in the torn lining. Michael reaches over to help and he smells musty leather, a smell that takes him back thirty years to when he wore a jacket like this and had a sweetheart Jane's age. Their hands touch. She's trembling, poor kid. What a hard-hearted bastard he is.

"Look," he says, softening, "do you know for sure?"

She pretends to be occupied in straightening the arms of the jacket. "About being knocked up? I've missed a couple periods is all. But what else could it be, with my shitty luck?"

"Don't say that."

"At school I was always the dumbest kid, and then I had to stomach those cheerleader types in junior high. Everything's always been the pits for me."

Michael swallows. "You're too hard on yourself."

"The world just dumps shit on me. Look at this apartment."

"It's not so bad."

"Look at it."

"Jane."

"Face it, Pa. I'm a loser."

"No," he lies. "There are no winners and losers."

"Wrong. You have this stupid Woodydell idea that things always work out. Well, they don't. This isn't one of those dumb stories where the handsome prince rescues the princess and they live in the castle happy as larks. This is 1990 or whatever. The world is going to shit and it's taking people like me down with it—fast."

He puts his hand on her arm, but she wrenches away, her green eyes narrowed in a way which scares him. She snatches up a big leather bag and bangs the door of the apartment shut. In the hallway Michael stands aside to let her negotiate the tires, and he smells over the cat piss and stale rubber her delicate scent as her neck brushes past his face. Baby powder. She *is* his baby, bounced in his lap, and a surge of emotion floods through him as he follows the flash of her tanned legs down the stairs and into the street. Is it wrong to want to hold her?

* * *

When he pulls away from the curb Michael says, "Look, we're off to Belvu for the weekend, so take the Tercel." He can't wait to escape Jane's whining, his whole day is being pinched shut by the kid, he can't wait to get out of the overheated city and relax near the water. There's a place at the point where he watches pelicans wheeling over the rocks. Maybe if he can get Stephen out there, he'll tell him about Angela. At the intersection Michael studies the roof of the old folks' home, but whatever the fat woman saw escapes him. Not a cloud in the sky now. He turns back onto Selkirk, past the jazzy post office. The traffic has thinned and the lights are with him as he guns the Tercel west toward the bridge. He drives hard, wishing he hadn't given up smoking. He needs a cigarette before he plunges back into talk.

"How do you feel?" he asks.

"Like hell," Jane says. "Last night I kept waking up, so I took some of Brad's mineral water, but it didn't help much."

"Mineral water? I thought Brad was a beer man."

"Not always. When you get to know him."

He avoids the barb and runs a yellow light past the ESSO where he swings south at the defunct drugstore and speeds up for the bridge. So much for the north end. Dying. Dying.

"I didn't mean your health, exactly. I meant more your state of mind."

"Okay, I guess." She leaves a silence filled by the rumble of the car's radials over the iron bridge. Michael can see her in the side of his vision, foreground to the bleak railyards spreading west over her shoulder. He could turn in that direction and be at the cottage in fifty minutes.

"Scared?"

"Not really."

"But a little?"

"Just enough to make me wish I was dead."

"You don't mean that."

"Don't I?"

"You know," Michael says, searching for the tone he hears in fathers' voices on the TV, "you're not the first one to go through this thing. Girls in my time got married 'cause they were knocked up, too. Most of them." He gears down for a streetlight and hears the transmission clunking again. Jane's silence at his elbow is hostile but he rushes on, trying to find the words which will bring her close to him. "We didn't have the pill, you see." Michael doubts this line is going very well. The story he wants to tell her is one of triumph and success. His heart is filled with compassion for the kid. But whenever he's with her they end up arguing about their failed family. Still, he presses on. "Things were kind of dicey for your mother and me, too. I don't know if she ever said anything." What Jane most likely recalls are shouting matches, Patricia flush with rum and threatening to kill Jane, Michael intervening. Once Jane had a black arm for weeks. "So it runs in the family," he continues. He thinks she coughs and, when he looks over, he sees she's rubbing her eyes with the back of her hand. "You want me to pull over? There's a stop up ahead."

She says sharply, "I'm all right."

"Has Brad done something?"

"It's not Brad." She's angry and suddenly he understands the meaning of her pointed silences. She wants something and is working herself up to it. She asks, "Why are you guys always on about Brad?"

"He's not our idea of the ideal son-in-law."

"You're not his idea of ideal parents." Jane says this through clenched teeth. "In his family everyone isn't running off to get divorced because they got hot pants for one of their students."

"But he takes off when you need him most."

Jane turns her face to the window and blows hard into a tissue. "Just get off my back," she says. "You should hear what you all sound like, Brad this, abortion that. Mom screams over the phone and Mary gives me the silent treatment. Boy, talk about sisterhood. That's one big load of bullshit."

Michael passes her a tissue from the dashboard.

"You all bug me," Jane adds. "Like you're the ones scared."

"What nonsense," he says. But he knows she's put her finger on a truth. When grandchildren start coming, the grave can't be far away. That's how nature's got it worked out. This isn't what the kid needs to hear, so he says in a level voice, "We just don't want you going through the stuff we did. Being poor. Tied down." Michael glances sideways to see if Jane is listening. She crumples the tissue in her fingers as Michael passes the trendy shops on Osborne and turns onto Pembina Highway. "The way I see it," he says, "you're scared. You never wanted it to happen—Christ, we don't actually know if it has happened—but you're not sure that you can hack it. Right? Maybe Brad won't stick around, eh? And you don't want to be tied down. Who does at your age? At any age?"

"Don't put words in my mouth. Grandma tells me one thing, you something else. Mom. Everybody's pushing and pulling, so I don't know what I think any more. Me."

She's right, they have been at her. Michael taps the wheel with his palm as he drives. Why is it the abstract compassion he feels for Jane before he sees her evaporates so fast in her presence? At the next intersection he sees the flashing neon sign of the Garlite Grill where ten years ago he told Patricia over dinner that he was leaving her for Mary. Its newly stuccoed walls seem garish to him, uninviting, though the owners must have remodeled with the idea of attracting more people. He likes red-checked tablecloths but doesn't go there any more. Jane is staring out the window. The way she crosses her ankles reminds him of Angela, waiting in her apartment for him to phone. Or is she out for lunch with some football type on a Friday while he ferries his kid to a clinic? He fights down the resentment tightening his chest.

Jane asks suddenly, "What if I went ahead whatever happens?"

"You mean have the baby on your own?"

"Yeah. Do what I want—for a change."

"Jesus, kid, it's a big undertaking even when there's two people raising the little buggers. Alone, I don't know."

"You won't let me try. You don't trust me."

"Then there are these small items like clothes and diapers and food and rent—and the little buggers need medicines for this, that, and God knows what all else."

"Money, right?"

"Jane. We're talking necessities here. Things you can't decide not to have—like pizza on Saturday night."

"Pizza," Jane says. "Fuck that." Michael keeps his eyes on the road. He gears down to let a teenager scoot across Pembina—he wears high-topped red and black sneakers, like the old basketball shoes. Michael wants a pair just like them. Jane clears her throat.

He asks, "Have you thought about that?"

"Yes. Rent, for one. I can move in with Sally again if it doesn't work with Brad. Or Mom."

"Patricia? I can just see it. You two can't agree on the timing of an egg." At the underpass Michael slows. Water's collected at the bottom and workmen wearing blaze-orange vests are doing something in the manholes. "How in hell can you and Patricia live under the same roof with a squawling kid?"

"Why do you keep coming back to this squawling kid stuff?"

"Because babies are not a picnic."

"Because you're scared. What is it, Pa, do kids remind you you're getting old or something?" She senses that he's cornered and she sticks her chin out defiantly. "That's it, right?"

That headache is coming back—at first just a flutter in the corners of his eyes. "You have no idea, Jane—the sleepless nights, the constant feeding and washing." Should he tell her that she had colic for two months and stopped crying only when he walked the floor singing to her? "I can't see you being ready to go that alone."

"No. All you can see is me screwing up."

"Having trouble. What we want—"

"What *you* want?"

"What I want is—" Is peace, Michael thinks, the sound of waves slapping sand, the cry of gulls in the distance. "I want to go to the beach," he says, finally, defeat in his voice, but anger, too. "To sit on the sand with a cold drink and a good book and the waves at my feet. I want *not* to think of all this—all this crap." The light is red at Windermere and Michael brakes for it, too sharply in his agitated state, and he and Jane pitch forward. His heart skips a beat. This is right at the spot where he just about killed the man in glasses, not a good sign.

"Well, don't think of it, then."

Michael turns down Wildwood and swings onto the gravel shoulder. He shifts into neutral and yanks at the parking brake. "I won't."

"Good," Jane says stonily.

He jumps out of the car, calling the dog with him. His feet meet the ground unexpectedly and he feels one ankle give way. "Just don't fucking bother," Jane shouts. She guns the Tercel's motor. As she pulls away she scatters gravel over his top-siders.

* * *

At the track, Continental Divine holds off a late charge by a filly named Star and wins by two heads, netting Mary sixty dollars on the ten she bet. She's buoyant afterward, tugging Michael's elbow as they cross the heat-baked parking lot to the Mercedes. His horse, Joe Deuce, faded to third after leading down the backstretch. Is this a surprise? No more than Forster telling him over the phone that the cedar deck is going to cost closer to three thousand than the sixteen hundred he originally quoted. What would he have bet on that? And the argument with Jane has knocked the wind out of his day. But balanced against these there was good news, too. He talked to his banker, who told him to come in Monday about the line of credit, like Mary, insisting that this bull market will continue. He can be rich if he plays his cards right.

On the drive to the cottage Mary's preoccupied with numbers, her nails tapping the InstaCalc as he drives. She tells him that at one hundred and eighty grand Mrs. Johnston's place brings the agency $13,500 commission. When you subtract the government's employment tax, the agency's profit is down to $11,700, of which, Mary tells Michael, two percent goes to advertising and the Multiple Listing Service, that's $3600, two percent for office overhead—pension, unemployment, and disability—so they're down to what? Mary is lost in numbers but looks up when Michael points into a farmer's field at rusting machinery, sitting immobile since last fall. A red tractor whose engine parts have been pilfered over the winter looks like its heart's ripped out. A bad year for grains, the farmers say. He knows two near Belvu who went bankrupt. Mary nods. Anyway, she says, answering her own question, that brings the net down to $8100, plus the percent she and Fred put into the company's reserves, so now they're at $6100, and that's the actual commission she makes on the Johnston sale—it works out to about three and a half percent without taking into account her car and clothing expenses. He knows, he knows, he *knows*.

From the way she cuts her eyes at him, Michael can tell Mary's put out with his silence. Since they left the track he's tried to grin and be jolly, but thoughts of Jane and Angela have left him brooding. Michael considers himself a sunny, sociable type, but lately he's staring into space a lot, blank in the way of old men he's seen in geriatric hospitals. Recently he's been brooding about Angela, whom he pictures now in a red shirt with a button-down collar. She's athletic yet delicate, a girl who should be dating the football captain instead of throwing herself at him. He'd like to tell her simply to go away, but she holds some fascination for him. It's not merely lust, though he can't put his finger on what else it is. The answer which comes to his mind— *she lisps*—doesn't make sense, so he dismisses it. He thinks instead of her blue eyes and the way she smiles at him, almost mocking, hinting there's something she knows that he doesn't, and which she won't tell him.

At the junction of the city bypass and the Belvu highway his stomach starts to gurgle and he peeks at Mary to see if she notices. She's busy with calculations, unconsciously fingering the pendant he gave her for her fortieth birthday, a bone amulet he brought back from a conference in Australia. Mary hasn't taken it off since he fastened it around her neck. When she's post-sale fidgety like today she fiddles with it, she gives off the scent of nervous excitement, she gets horny when they go to bed. The thought of her desire deepens his guilt.

They make the cottage by 4:15 with tension hanging in the air between them. Michael feels it as the gray of the low sky they've been driving into since the city. The haze settles over the shore and obscures the lake. They unpack mechanically, Michael struggling to shake his distraction, Mary muttering about tonic water, hinting she'll have to drive to Belvu, both working hard to keep the tension from flaring into anger. They bump together passing in the door of the cottage and laugh, but strain is what Michael hears in their voices. When Mary announces she's going to town for gin and something for dinner, it's a relief to both of them, though Michael politely offers to go with her, and she as politely says she'll be fine on her own. From the deck he waves as she wheels the Mercedes onto the gravel road. The car disappears in dust. Michael yanks on a Greek fisherman's cap and considers pouring himself a scotch. Instead he hops into the old pickup they keep at the cottage and heads down the road three miles to Stephen's place.

* * *

If it were just a question of lust, he tells himself. Sure, he wants Angela. In idle moments he thinks of breasts, he thinks of the way her bottom pouts out of her jeans, his mind conjures scenes in beds, on car seats, under open skies. Even when he is occupied with other things—students, reading investment reports—his mind comes back to her. Mostly he thinks of Angela's face, her toothpaste-commercial smile, the dark knowing in her blue eyes. What is it she won't tell him? When she's with him, Michael is unnerved. She wants him and isn't afraid to let him see it. She's the aggressor. So Michael puts it to himself, seeing himself as the object of Angela's desire. Does he want her? This may not even be the question. Will he submit to her—to that look in Angela's eyes which attracts and repels him with equal force? No, it isn't a case of simple lust, Michael tells himself, knowing that it is, denying it—as he must.

* * *

"Hey, buddy," Stephen calls when Michael pulls up. He's on his deck in blue terry-cloth shorts, about to go for a dip. He offers Michael a pair of trunks, but Michael argues for returning to Willow Point where the beach is sandy and private. Stephen beetles his brow, but he trudges out to the pickup behind Michael after locking the door to his cottage.

They are silent going past the tennis courts, but when they turn onto the highway Michael blurts out, "I'm brooding on a dilemma." He tugs the peak of his cap, knowing he sounds pompous, and when Stephen clears his throat Michael guesses he's rushed into things. But he's been holding back for days, and one thing Michael is not good at is holding back. He tries again. "Yesterday a woman came into my office. She made me an offer." This sounds worse, so Michael laughs what he hopes is a disarming laugh. He should have waited until they'd had a drink and were relaxing on deck chairs. But he can't help himself. "She kissed me," he says. "At one point we're standing in my office and she kisses me on the neck and says she can't keep her mind off me." Michael sighs. Why can't he be the strong silent type who avoids disclosure and goes to the grave with secrets? Stephen's like that. Michael fingers his beard. "Christ," he says, "her breath on my neck." He feels again the way the tiny hairs above his collar tingled, the scent of mint from her mouth.

Stephen has found a flyer on the seat and is twisting it into a funnel in his hands. "You know," he says, "when you're excited your eyes bug out like a toad's." He taps the flyer on his knee. "Anyone ever tell you that?" This is a signal that Stephen is not interested in the subject of Michael's passions, a signal Michael chooses to ignore. He slows for the rise where the railroad tracks cross the highway. In the trees birds are whistling, *whueet whueet*, a mating call he once knew but now cannot identify.

When he gears up he says, "I used to know the birds around here. But with shifting weather patterns the past few years the species have moved and I need to learn all over."

"I'm not good at that," Stephen says. "Birds in the bush never look like the ones in the books. But I saw a bald eagle once."

Michael's never heard of anyone spotting one in this area, but he says, "Really?"

"Sitting on a fencepost. Of course it wasn't actually bald. White-headed as an old man." Stephen purses his lips in reflection. "I was hunting with a bow and came through this stand of trees and there he was, not fifty feet away. Another thing I was never much good at—hunting. Never had the eyes for it." Stephen touches his glasses with his free hand. "You still get out, don't you?"

"The old man likes shooting geese," Michael says, uneasy suddenly at the talk of hunting. The feeling puzzles him.

"That's nice," Stephen says. "That's real nice you're getting out together like that."

They rattle over the plank bridge across the shallow creek leading to Willow Point. The water below is algae thick and scum-flecked, though bullrushes nod in the afternoon breeze and blackbirds call to each other sharply. Far out over the lake a single-engine plane dips its wings to bank. From its angle over the water it appears to be going down like a falling arrow—and suddenly Michael knows why he's feeling queasy. When he was a kid he used to hunt with a bow in the wooded lots north of Belvu. He shot a grouse in a spruce once and was sure he'd hit it. He saw it flutter into the undergrowth. It made a mewling, choking cry as he thrashed through branches and leaves to close in for the kill. He saw movement behind a spruce. He took out his hunting knife to finish it off. What he saw when he came around the tree made him sick to his stomach—a little Indian girl on the ground with her head resting on her knees and a spilled pail of blueberries near her feet. Her white dress was spotted with sprayed blood. Michael's arrow was sticking through her throat. Luckily, it had caught a fold of skin below her ear. A doctor in Belvu removed it in five minutes and sent the girl on her way with a small bandage and a chocolate bar.

Michael watches the plane hover in the gray sky. "My dilemma," he says, starting again, "is this beautiful student."

"Umm." Stephen taps the flyer on the seat between them.

"So once again I'm confused about a woman. . . ." Michael trails off, thinking of Angela's lips, her black nails. "And she's a real beauty. Tall and dark. Skin that could be called alabaster."

"That's good, alabaster breasts. Can I quote that?"

Michael wheels the pickup onto the spit and slows where the asphalt drops to gravel. Unlike the Mercedes, this tub jolts the spine. "Angela," Michael whispers. "Angela."

"I knew an Angela once," Stephen shouts over the rumble of washboard and the pickup's rattling valves. "Bitch ran off with my Elvis collection. 1965."

Michael's stomach is gurgling again, but he continues. "I

44

thought I was done with all that nonsense. Running after women. At that conference in Australia I spent the better part of one night explaining to a woman from England that I couldn't sleep with her—ended up paying for the drinks, too. But I came home feeling sweet and good. Pure. But this one—I don't know."

"If—"

"If I should *go for it*, as the kids say."

"Maybe it's just that she's come on to you."

"That's part of it," Michael says, wanting to tell Stephen about what he feels around Angela, but sure it's futile to say, *she lisps*. So he says nothing. The silence suits Stephen. He looks out the window. Red-winged blackbirds in the gravel along the ditch twitter to each other. The clouds have lifted and the point is visible now, a smudge of greens and grays in the distance. The plane has flattened over the lake and is winging back toward Belvu.

"So what happened?" Stephen asks.

"After she kisses me she says she wants us to do it, you know? Have me. That's how she put it, *have me*." Michael glances at Stephen before continuing. "For a minute I thought she was going to pull down my pants and throw me over the desk."

They laugh but this image frightens both men. They shift on the seat nervously. In the silence, Michael hears the pickup's engine wheezing—an old heart chugging on past its time. He says, "This whole business, Stephen. It scares me."

"We're all scared of a lot of things. Pollution. Old age."

"I'm not very good at explanations. I never know how to start the story." Michael takes a deep breath and then lets it out slowly. "You think I'm making a mistake?"

"I thought you were making a mistake with Mary."

"With Mary?"

"These past ten have been the best years of your life? Right?"

"Definitely."

"There you go, then. Ten years ago I would've said you were

heading for nothing but disaster and heartache—if you'd asked me then what you're asking me now. So you see what my opinion's worth."

"You don't think I'm making a mistake?"

"I think you're risking a lot—with Mary." Stephen had sat over many scotches with Michael during the divorce and his eyes hint at the pain they both remember from those days.

"Consequences."

"Right."

Michael brakes sharply for some washboard, and when he and Stephen lurch forward, the fisherman's cap slips down his brow. He says, "It drives me crazy thinking of that. Losing Mary, I mean."

"She's a great gal."

"Being lonely. Christ, those days in that awful apartment on Pembina. I remember them and shudder. I really do."

"We're getting old for all that."

"Exactly." Michael shifts gears and slows for a dip in the road.

"Look." Stephen points across the bay where pelicans skim the marsh, the black tips of their wings feathering the tops of bullrushes. Michael's eyes follow them. Ponderous on land, they're elegant over water. He likes the way they swoop along the shore, marking their territory. But each season there are fewer and fewer pelicans at Willow Point. They leave the bay now and move farther uplake, away from the power boats and regattas, from the Sunday anglers cutting into their feeding grounds, from marauding teenage boys in skiffs with air rifles and slingshots. Like so much at the end of the century, the great birds are on the run.

"Lovely," Michael says.

Stephen nods. "But doomed."

Doomed. Maybe, Michael thinks, hearing weariness in Stephen's voice, he should never have started this conversation. It hasn't helped, and he's cheapened himself. He falls silent. The only sounds in the pickup are the splash of gravel on the under-carriage and the rattle of a yellow-handled screwdriver rolling on the molded dashboard. When Michael brakes for dips in the road, it spins on its hexagonal sides and strikes the windshield with a ping; when he accelerates it skitters over paperclips, gum wrappers, and wood screws. Michael kept a condom stashed there at one time, but it dried out and he's never replaced it. They're all on the pill now anyway. "You keep thinking," he says, "you're in the grave a long time. You know? That chances missed today are gone forever. My uncle Charlie used to say there's only so many stray pieces of tail come your way in one life. Your body knows this—like it knows it's running out of time."

Stephen arches his eyebrows. "Sometimes, buddy, you think like an old pagan." He adds, "St. Augustine maybe."

"The old lecher knew this—the prick has no conscience." Michael laughs after he says this and pushes up the peak of his cap. Then he clears his throat and adds, "And the cunt no memory."

He expects Stephen to be disgusted, but he laughs, too. "Your eyes are bugging out again," he says. He forms two circles with thumbs and forefingers over his eyes. "They really are."

When Michael laughs this time, he catches his reflection in the rearview mirror. His eyes look wide and innocent, the eyes of the eager young man in the family photo albums. His cheeks are flushed, and the bruises on his upper gums the dentist made putting crowns on his front teeth seem bluer today. Michael dates the click in his jaw from those afternoons in the horizontal chair with muzak in his ears and the smell of soap on the backs of Dr. Lee's hairy hands. He can't bite into an apple without a click reminding him of those vise-like thumbs prying open his jaws. And oral sex! "I feel stupid," he says, "about this. But I don't know what to do."

Stephen studies the lake, then asks, "What if Mary found out?"

"She'd leave," Michael says firmly. "She's told me so. *Gonzo Alonso* is how she put it." And rightly so, he believes.

"Sounds final."

"Yup. And she'd find some jerk in a business suit wearing Aramis. Some meatball at a real-estate convention with a Buick."

Stephen goes quiet and they stare out the windshield at the cottages. In just ten years, development has gobbled up all the land at Willow Point, too. Once hundreds of empty acres dotted by a handful of summer places, it's now a full-scale resort, complete with three-car parking lots and shiny aluminum boathouses. Shuttered fronts face the lake, the backyards are a tangle of motorboat parts, piles of trash, and lumber oddments. Everyone's renovating.

As they crunch up the drive Michael says, "If it was just a matter of lust. But this Angela. I don't know."

"But you want me to tell you what to do?" Stephen pushes his glasses up the bridge of his nose. "I will say this, though: try to think with your head and not with your groin."

"Something about her makes me want to take the chance." Michael takes off his cap and looks into it. "I'm not making it clear."

"No," says Stephen. "It's real clear. You need to prove to yourself you're not getting old." He opens the door of the pickup and adds, "If we could just come to terms with that."

Michael turns the key and the motor backfires once before shuddering to a stop. "Exactly." He says it simply but he knows there's nothing simple about it.

* * *

Every year the beach at Willow Point looks different. If the fall's dry the water table is low and the shoreline recedes from the cottages. Sometimes bars of gravel are deposited between cottage and beach, and barefoot swimmers have to mince across patches of sharp stones to reach the lake. Once a boulder huge as a boxcar was dredged up by the winter ice and left in front of Michael's place. Bone white, mythical. That summer everybody came to pose beside it for snapshots. Michael has one curling in a drawer, too, he and Stephen leaning on the great stone, glasses of beer in hand. The following winter it disappeared back into the lake as miraculously as it had arisen. In wet years, like the last, the water line is high and close to the cottages. Inside it seems the water will wash into the room, and on nights when the wind whips the lake, waves fling spray against the walls.

When they emerge after swimming Stephen asks, "Are you happy?" His breathing is labored. In the water he dived straight down and then surfaced doing a smooth crawl, leaving Michael behind.

"What does that mean—happy?"

"Whatever it means to you. Just answer the question."

"Well, then, very," Michael answers. "I have money in the bank, a great job, wonderful wife, fine friends. Sometimes I have to pinch myself. I feel like such a fat cat." And he does. Compared to most, he is wealthy, he's loved, he has good work. Soon the house renovations will be complete and he'll have a spacious office filled with light. He can afford a BMW.

"I haven't had a nightmare for ten years," Stephen says as he rubs sand off the bottom of one foot with the toes of the other. "That has to be a sign of something."

Michael knows what he's driving at. Why jeopardize the good life? Why risk what he's got with Mary? He wonders that himself. But he can't quite make himself say it. He wants Stephen to say it for him—or tell him to go for Angela and consequences be damned.

They stroll along the beach toward the point, still a misty blur of trees and rock on the horizon. Prehuman. Ruggles joins them and dashes ahead every few yards, expecting them to break into a jog. Michael tosses a stick for him to fetch. Stephen slows to slip on the sneakers he's brought along. His body gathers shadows to itself as he stoops. In his swimming suit he looks thick through the middle, thicker, Michael thinks, than him, though he takes little comfort from this—he could lose twenty pounds and still have a roll of fat at the waist. Stephen's skinny legs are topped by a pear-shaped gut and a torso as flabby as Michael's. They've become middle-aged farts with skinny arms and fat asses. Michael used to laugh when guys like this paraded about the tennis courts. And now he's one of them.

They are silent. Walking on the beach has this effect. The rhythms of waves aren't those of speech, Michael's learned. They're song and silence, but not the hard-edged voices of street corners and parking lots. Silence and reflection. He's noticed it in others, too—people who live by the sea. The British stare at the ocean for hours, parked in their squat cars at viewpoints on the coast or sitting in deck chairs along the beach. At first he thought they were looking for something, eyes fixed on the water, but now he knows they're listening to the rise and fall of waves—to blood pumped by a gigantic heart. Slowing their old tickers to the pace of the deep.

For this reason people raised by the sea must live longer, he's decided—an idea confirmed by a TV show he saw recently. In lab experiments rabbits placed in noisy spaces died earlier than those left alone. The rabbits' hearts sped up with the level of sound they were forced to live with. Those exposed to the highest levels died early because they ran their allotment of heartbeats out faster than the others. Michael touches his chest, thinking of his own heart, going seventy beats a minute. That's forty-two hundred an hour, he figures, a hundred thousand a day, thirty-five million a year, and about two and a half billion in a lifetime. No wonder they explode suddenly like pumps with blown diaphragms. Two and a half billion! But didn't the scientists say that mammals' hearts lasted eight hundred million beats? The figure sticks in his mind, but according to his calculations that puts the human heart three times over. He should have died—what—thirteen years ago?

Near the point the shore gets rocky. This area was the last developed, the cottages here—cedar and pine prefabs with sharp pointed roofs of black asphalt shingles and tiny windows on their second floors—loom over the beach from a prospect of land some contractor envisioned as majestic, but which is actually affected. Stagey.

Michael walked here with Mary on a summer day years ago when they were coming to the cottage secretly. He remembers the turquoise dress Mary wore and the way her shoes filled with sand when they walked along the shore. There were no buildings here then, and they sat on a log looking at the lake. A regatta was underway. Bright colors.

Since he asked about happiness Stephen has been silent, though Michael knows he's waiting for an answer. Michael would like to tell him exactly what he thinks, though he doesn't have the words for it yet, and if he did, he would probably only offend Stephen and embarrass himself. They are men of the fifties and used to thinking morally. But Michael behaves as if sleeping with a woman other than Mary doesn't matter. Like most men of his time, he cannot understand how a one-night stand can in any way affect what he and Mary have going for them. Which he calls love. He feels a little guilty about it, as he feels a little guilty about fudging items on his income tax forms, but that is not the kind of guilt that stops people from doing what they do. Michael behaves immorally and thinks of it as okay. As long as he doesn't fall in love with another woman. As long as Mary doesn't find out. That would mean consequences, and it is consequences, not morality, that frighten Michael. Memories of the pain he went through when he fell in love with Mary while still married to Patricia. Fears of the consequences of divorce. Loneliness. He waits until they've crossed to a sandbar and then turns to Stephen and surprises himself by saying, "Think of junk-bond traders on Wall Street."

"Parasites," Stephen says. "No—criminals."

"Exactly. But they're making a killing out there, young men of thirty making millions from shady dealings—and do you know why?"

"It's a sick society. A society that's crumbling."

"Sure. Because it's the lesson Ronald Reagan taught them. That the government's your enemy, that it doesn't matter what you do as long as you don't get caught." Michael jumps from one rock to the next, matching Stephen's progress over the uneven terrain. "See, Reagan himself had no morality. He was a man without values, so the most important lesson he taught people was that morals were unnecessary. Amazing, eh, the President of the most powerful country in history?" Michael pauses. It's warm and his mouth is dry. "And it's a short step from seeing the government as your enemy to concluding that you should cheat the government, cheat everyone. In other words, do whatever you want." Michael wets his lips. Stephen is flinging bits of branches for Ruggles to fetch. Gesturing wildly, Michael says, "So we're all in this moral quagmire where anything and everything is possible and all you have to do is go for it." When he stops talking Michael runs the back of his hand across his damp brow. The heat this year. A meteorologist on the radio predicted the Great Lakes would dry up soon. By 2020 Manhattan would be under water, Manitoba turned into a savannah.

Stephen has stopped to scratch Ruggles' skull. "You mean you blame Ronald Reagan because you want to sleep with Angela?"

"I mean it seems foolish after what we see daily on Wall Street and in the White House to have moral quibbles. You feel like a wimp. You feel like you're missing out on what's going by because you're too weak to just step up and take it."

"And there's no better side to man?"

"To counterbalance greed and lust? No." Michael stops and looks back along the shore. He can't quite pick out his cottage among the dozen huddled together in the little bay.

"I don't buy it," Stephen says. "How do you get to be good, then? How do you choose?"

"You don't choose. You *are*."

"Okay," says Stephen. He stoops for stones on the beach, then skips them over the water. "*Be* good, then."

They approach the point through a rocky marsh. The bullrushes on the far side sway, even though there's no wind. Coming closer, Michael sees the bullrushes are dotted with a flock of yellow-headed blackbirds, and he slows to admire them. Their satin heads are gorgeous, but before he can point it out to Stephen, Ruggles dashes down the beach and scatters the flock to the bush inland.

They angle that way to skirt the rugged shoreline. Near the point, development stops. No profits in rock and bramble for the real-estate crowd here. Rubble gathers, though, trees toppled in winds and deposited by high waves along with tangled rope, plastic buoys, and marine detritus. The junk of life. This is the one place at Willow Point where Michael feels he's escaped the city. The wind whistles through the trees, and sometimes a rabbit starts from the underbrush. The two men stand and look across the lake. There's nothing to see but it's what they came for—the emptiness. The feeling of absence that overwhelms them and fills them with peace. When Ruggles barks and races down the beach they start back, slipping on wet rocks as they retrace their steps through the marsh.

"How about Angela? Isn't that what we're talking about here?"

"Angela," Michael says, "I want to screw till we both weep. No question. When a woman like that throws herself at you, buddy, it's crazy not to." Saying it makes him feel better. He's been fantasizing about it so long it's become bigger than life—and more important. Talking at least has done this—bring it home to Michael what a dream he's been living.

"But—"

"I can't."

"You mean you won't."

"I can't."

"It's all so much talk."

"She's beautiful. She wants it. I'm a man. Is that it?"

"Why the agony? The soul-searching?"

"Going through all the shit is why. Secret meetings. Calls. A knot in the gut. Your whole life coming apart."

"So there it is, then."

"I'm too old for that shit. Can't hack it."

"Don't, then."

"Alright."

"Alright."

Now that he's said it, he realizes it's not so awful, after all, staying faithful. It doesn't bother Stephen, who has doted on his wife for more than two decades. Michael loves being part of the smug company of suburbanites who go for Dim Sum in couples on Saturdays and snuggle in for cozy sex on Sunday mornings before *café au lait* and the weekend papers. That's what Angela threatens. And he loves Mary. He needs her. "You're right," he says with determination. "I won't." Though he kicks the sand in silent rage.

Ahead a dead sunfish rots on the shore. Smells. Michael turns his face away and abruptly stops. "Look," he whispers, nodding toward the scrub oaks further up. His eyes narrow to slits. At first Stephen has trouble focusing, so Michael points. Leaning against a tree thirty yards inland is a man wearing a black watchcap and a camouflage jacket. He's totally out of place here. From a distance Michael can see he's big. With one hand jammed in the waist of his jeans, he looks casual as a beachcomber, but he's wearing black boots. Michael tells Stephen, "He's got binoculars." He feels a hot flush run up his spine. Stephen waves and calls out, but the man is silent, standing rigid under the tree. Stephen glances at Michael and they continue along the beach, parallel to the line of trees. When Michael looks back he sees the man's head following them, mechanical. Michael shudders. When they pass out of hearing he asks, "What was all that about?" He wishes Stephen had keener eyesight. And even before Stephen turns to him, Michael knows he'll shrug, but he won't have noticed the man's sinister posture, nor the fact that his other hand was resting on something standing upright beside him—on what looked to Michael like the barrel of a rifle.

* * *

At Willow Point in the morning Michael wakes with blocked sinuses and a raw throat. He snorts and hawks phlegm—and Mary rolls her eyes theatrically and turns her back to him in bed. *See the doctor about it*, she mutters, but he knows that just leads to lectures about emphysema and another expensive prescription, which he will forget to take. He coughs surreptitiously into one hand. When the sun is bright on the walls he steals out of bed, tucking the quilt around Mary's exposed feet, and makes coffee at the stove in the cottage kitchen. It's cramped with pots and pans, inadequate really for anything more than heating soup, though they manage sit-down dinners with guests twice a season. Through the screens Michael smells the lake, oxygen, sand, and the fecund ripeness of dank marsh plants growing to the south of the cottage. It's a magic time of stillness and slanting light.

This Saturday morning has a languorous midweek feel about it. On the beach two tots are chasing a cat, their towheads ruffled by the early breeze as they lurch along the sand. The water is choppy, with whitecaps out beyond the sandbars. Michael listens to the kettle boil and when the coffee's ready he takes a cup and sits out on a deck chair with *Playboy*—an issue on growing up male in America. He stops for a moment over "How I Spent the Sexual Revolution." The author, it turns out, hung around Berkeley during the heyday of free love, *not* getting laid. "Wet Dreams," another piece is entitled. Michael skims through it, reading breathy inside information on the Playboy bunnies and Hef. One of the bunnies smiles like Angela, deep brackets around perfect white teeth.

Michael's reading is interrupted by a small airplane buzzing around Willow Point, wings tilting first one way, then the other. It's the same single-engine job he saw yesterday, the pilot drunk or too stupid to know he should fly like that only over water—so if he crashes he doesn't kill anyone else. Kids are everywhere on the island on weekends. Michael watches until the plane buzzes the treetops and heads across the lake, then he hawks and spits, the arc of saliva barely clearing the toe of his sneakers. He's wearing the black and red high-tops for the first time. MGM had them in stock for fifty-two bucks. Sporty. They go with the black jeans he wears at the cottage and the blue striped beach shirt he chose this morning, thinking of Angela.

Too bad he didn't get to tell Stephen the whole story yesterday. Her visit the other day was not her first. Other times she'd sat drinking coffee and hinting she liked him. Once she'd given him poems to read. But on Thursday she was a determined woman. When she walked into his office she closed his door with a sharp smack and immediately dropped to her knees and pulled down his zipper. Her fingers were long and cool. Other than that he has few distinct impressions. The scent of perfume enveloped them, rising from Angela's black hair, parted, he remembers, as precisely as a schoolgirl's. Michael's knees went weak. He didn't know what to do with his hands—he must have spent ten minutes staring at them. The cursor on his monitor blinked regularly, drawing his eye. That, and the perfect line in the center of Angela's bobbing head. She wears her dark hair short, and tiny diamond rings flash from her pierced ears. Toward the end, her thin fingers helped her mouth release him. Then she wrapped her arms around his legs and pressed her face into his crotch. She wept. Her voice was husky. After, they sat facing each other on the floor of Michael's office. Above loomed his library. Over one of Angela's ears the works of Hardy, past the other, a stack of student essays. Angela smiled a lot. Spent and still glowing with perspiration, her face seemed ringed with an aura of serenity. "I had to," she said. They sat silent while she studied his face and he looked into his hands. His body stunk with fear, and he worried Angela could smell it. She seemed content to smile at him and stay quiet while the sound of feet padding down the corridor rose and fell and phones rang in adjacent offices. After some time Michael looked at his watch. He had a class. He stood. So did she. "You have to sleep with me," she said, "don't your senses tell you that now? Your body?" He shook his head. Staring into his, her eyes changed from blue to indigo to black. She was used to getting her way, and he was suddenly afraid of her. "Meet me," she said. "At Belvu, this weekend," she insisted, and when he told her no, she said, "If you won't meet me there, I'll come to your cottage." Her eyes swept around his office, implying that she was prepared to take the cottage by storm, too.

So he was caught.

So he's meeting her in Belvu Park.

He reads a piece called "The Phantom Sex," a rehash of clichés about the new woman, what it takes to get one—and to keep one. Understanding, apparently. According to this writer, women want to feel a man's concern for their needs. Compassion, Michael reads, sensitivity. Women want men to be vulnerable but strong. Kelly Connor said something about that when they were playing canasta the other night, and Mary, sipping liqueur, agreed.

Behind him in the cottage she's busy with real-estate stuff.

Last night she left the table covered with papers—charts, spreadsheets, her calculator. A developer's offering condominiums and she and Fred are pre-selling them. It's the only way to go, she says. Selling hundreds of units instead of scampering all over the city pursuing one crummy sale at a time. Anyway, she says, the tax write-offs for buyers are a great incentive and she and Fred get ten percent commission on condos. At the lake she wears designer sweatshirts and white pants. On her feet, Birkenstock sandals—her painted toenails peek out of them.

She looks up and smiles when he comes in for a second cup. Her blonde hair catches light from the window. She pushes a strand of it back over one ear and twists it between her fingers. When he passes, she takes his hand in hers, red nails brushing his skin. "Hey, sweetheart," she says. In bed last night she dug those nails into his back and called out to him urgently. He wanted to roll in the sweaty sheets all night, the way they had years ago when they were having their affair, nights when they made love five and six times and rubbed soap on each other's bodies in the shower after, but his back started to hurt and they had to finish side by side. In the dead of night he woke with a cramp in one shoulder, and this morning his neck's stiff. He's not forty any longer.

He swills the coffee in his mug. "Think I'll drive into town," he says. He's turned away from her, not trusting his face to cover for him. This second wife reads him better than the first.

"Good," she says. She likes having the space to herself, a chance to play Mahler and make grilled cheese sandwiches. "Get some bread. And fish." She's all business. "And some of that crunchy junk food the kids like."

"Cheezies. Are we expecting kids?"

"No." She laughs. "I'm addicted now, too."

She's such a good sport about things, even her foibles. Beautiful, vulnerable, and straight, she's surprisingly carnal in bed, his lover, his wife. To betray her would be unconscionably cruel, Michael thinks, feeling guilty now that he's on his way to Angela, now that he's assuming the role of cad again. He stoops and brushes her cheek with his lips. Soft, the skin of women. He smells Mary's hair. That scent again. "Prospectus," he reads over her shoulder, "general partner." Columns of numbers, legal jargon. "Lily of the valley," he says. "That's new, isn't it?"

"Is it?" she asks and waggles her fingers goodbye, letting him know she has secrets—that she can still be as mysterious as when he discovered she'd once blackened the eye of her former husband and had to take him to the hospital for stitches. He waggles his fingers in return and goes out the door.

To construct the U-shaped deck around the cottage last year, Michael had to cut down maples and mutilate an elm, lopping off the branches at head height. Whenever he passes the tree, though, he cringes and ducks, a tic he's had passing under tree branches for forty years. He was in grade school when his brother Moe, later a star athlete at Belvu High and a gold medalist at Queen's University, but on that day just his pesky kid brother, chased after him to get ice cream and caught his forehead on a low tree branch. Moe's scream comes back to Michael in dreams. One half-inch lower and he'd have lost an eye, Doc Hansen said. Twelve stitches. What Michael remembers most from that day is that Moe didn't cry. He stood silently as the Doc took the stitches, and it was Michael who whimpered in the car, it was Michael whose shirt was soaked with sweat when they got home. He's never been good at taking pain. He's spent his life dodging it. Find a way out, he tells himself now in the truck—badger, plead, weasel, but come back to Mary pure and good.

He drives the gravel road carefully. On weekends the kids play games in these bushes. One might dart into the path of his car. Like the man in glasses on the Windermere corner. At the wooden bridge a shadow falls over the pickup and Michael's ears fill suddenly with the roar of an engine overhead. The airplane is skimming the marshes. It's off course, and its vibrations shake the windows of the truck. As it passes above, Michael pictures the pickup plunging off the road, sending him flying into the ditch, his body drowning in a tangle of bullrushes. Someone is trying to kill him. If he could see the pilot, he's sure he'd be wearing a watchcap and camouflage clothing. Michael grips the wheel tightly, he cries out involuntarily and squints up through the windshield, expecting at any moment to be killed. But the plane veers off over the marsh, scattering birds and hammering the reeds down to the flattened water. Michael slows to a near stop, trying to make sense of things. Why is someone trying to kill him? Who?

All the way to Belvu his hands are damp on the steering wheel, and when he pulls onto a side street he wipes them on his jeans. He walks the two blocks to the park, forcing the blood in his temples to slow. It's this bloody business with Angela. It has to end.

* * *

What does he need, anyway, with clandestine sex, with betrayal, pain, confession, recrimination, rage, suspicion? The whole ugly—and once the act of copulation occurs, inevitable—scene. Why must he do it? It's not just the novelty of sex with a stranger, though there is some small truth in that. Nor even power, the ego riding on conquest, on the confirmation that despite the years, the fat, the gray hair, this body, this *me* is still desirable. More than this, Michael has to feel he's lived, that the random opportunities life offers have not passed him by. He wants to play the game of life rather than stand on the sidelines watching. Play. Risk something. Feel the thrill of danger and defeat. His life needs to be unforgettable, and for that he needs more than a snug house in the suburbs and a bank balance of five figures. When he lies on his deathbed he doesn't want to regret the chances he's missed. Because he was shit-ass scared. Or so he tells himself on Mondays, Wednesdays, and Fridays. On the other days . . .

* * *

Wrapped in thought, he's halfway across the park before he looks up. Angela is beside him, mint breath on his cheek. His insides go soft. She puts her hand on his elbow and says, "You came," but then, feeling him flinch, withdraws it. She's wearing the red shirt with black buttons, one of what must be a whole closet of shirts. They emphasize her athletic shoulders and firm breasts, a type of beauty Michael finds breathtaking. From her hand dangles a handbag in a bold abstract pattern. Around her neck a gold chain. Her nails are painted black. He realizes suddenly this girl's rich. She dresses like models in *Elle* and probably went to a private school.

He asks, "You go to Sister Mary's?"

"SJC." She lisps. Sexy. Girlish. "What gave me away?"

He lies. "The way you speak. They teach you that?"

"To be nice. And to get what you want."

"And what *do* you want?" He doesn't mean to be bitchy with her, but his resolve to have done with her has hardened his heart.

She refuses to return his anger. "Oh," she says brightly, "the usual." Where the park merges with the beachfront, the Chamber of Commerce has installed wooden benches. They sit and Angela says, "At one time it was a super house and Bonwit Teller. I was a foolish girl." She gazes off across the trimmed grass. "Now it's wines, a dog, a quiet place in the country. And food." She brings a package of peanuts out of her handbag and pops several into her mouth. She offers them to Michael and, when he shakes his head, crunches down another handful. She sighs and holds the package in both hands in her lap.

"Children?"

"I don't think so. Travel, for sure."

"London? New York?"

"Africa, actually. South America."

"What about a caring man?" Michael asks, recalling the magazine article. "One who's vulnerable but strong."

"Strong is optional." That lisp again. He wants to kiss her. He wants to slip off to a motel on the highway with Angela and make love on sweaty sheets. What's he thinking? He wants to be back at the cottage with Mary, snug in conjugal bliss. Anywhere but with this girl, this siren.

Michael touches his upper lip. Beads of perspiration, though it's cool by the lake. "Then why do you want me?"

"I don't *want* you. Not that way." When she leans forward her breasts sway beneath her red shirt. "I want an affair with you," she says. "A simple affair."

"No affair is simple. It's one of the things you learn after thirty." That, and how to lie. He feels bile rise to his mouth. Desire and anger. Wanting her so much he hates her.

"Please. No talk about age."

"But that's just the point," he says. "I'd feel ridiculous making love to a girl." Michael glances over his shoulder before correcting himself. "With a woman half my age." By which he means guilt has started to worm through his guts. What if somebody sees him here? His brother in town for groceries? His aunt Julia?

"Age," Angela says firmly, "means nothing." She stands and repeats, "Nothing." With her back to the sun he sees pouches beneath her eyes, and this waste in her complexion touches him.

As they walk toward the beach he asks, "You take the bus up?"

"I drove. Parked beside the tank thing in the town center."

"The war memorial," Michael says. His two uncles were cut down on the Normandy beaches—yellowing photographs in his mother's album show twenty-year-old boys with fat cheeks and caps at jaunty angles. Kids, really. He shudders, then thinking of Jane's fiasco with the Honda, he asks, "You have a car of your own?"

"A Porsche."

It would be. Private school. Fifty-dollar haircuts. They get it all, these rich girls, right down to the perfect skin. Michael asks, "He buy you that, your old man?"

"No, no." She laughs, straight white teeth, a bounce in her hair. "Grampa's graduation gift." She puts the peanuts back into her handbag. "Daddy's in the Army. Tanks, camouflage jackets, brush cuts. That scene." She's tall, leggy. Did he tell Stephen spectacular? When they reach the concrete dike, she jumps down prettily and waits for him to follow. Michael balances on the narrow concrete strip, conscious of his stiff movements when he vaults the three-foot drop, and the way he winces when his fiftyish bones jar on the ground below. The town is behind them now. The gravel beach that runs to the marsh is nearly empty. Michael takes a deep breath, and when he looks at the lake, feels his heart slowing.

On Saturdays the bay is filled with wind-surfers and power boats as well as the commercial fishing boats that are the mainstay of the town's economy, though the lake has been nearly fished out. He read the other day that this will be the last generation of fishermen to work it. Michael searches the shore a mile away for his cottage. Home, he thinks—and Mary. If he can only swing the conversation in the right direction, if he can only let Angela down easy.

Angela is wearing black boots over her jeans. They give her a martial air. "I want to meet you again," she says authoritatively, startling him out of his reverie. "Sleep with you." She faces the lake when she speaks. "Your body interests me. Big, yet soft." The words float back like a song. "Yours is a giving body. Has anyone told you that?"

"Not lately."

"I feel I'm safe with you, secure." She turns and smiles at

him again. "I don't want anything from you in the way of commitment or whatever. Just sex."

"You scare me sometimes. The things you say."

"But sex doesn't?"

"Excites me as well as scares me." Michael studies the sky. Gulls wheel and dive over figures on a wharf near the fishermen's gutting shed. Michael and Angela move to the edge of the water. Far down the shoreline two fishermen are throwing lines into the lake.

Angela says, "The water—there's something magical about it." When he nods she adds, "You know, for all their brain-busting about the big bang, there's not much we really know about what goes on down there." Her jaw juts out, indicating, Michael guesses, the lake bottom. "About plankton, or two-hundred-year-old turtles, why sharks never sleep. Weird, eh? But marvelous, too. They can put a man on the moon and bring back rocks, but about the stuff of life, where you and me come from—blanks." She turns, studying Michael with sea-blue eyes which would be easy to drown in. Michael feels vertigo. He walks down the beach toward the two fishermen.

Angela hooks her hand through his arm and this time he doesn't resist. Her pulse throbs through her fingertips on his bare wrist. When they reach the top of a little rise he says to her, "Look." A dead marsh bird, a merganser, lies on its side. This one's a smoky blue, though they're usually washed-out colors around Belvu, grays and dun.

"No," she says. "I won't."

Michael moves closer. "Quite lovely."

"I won't look," she says.

"Come on. The colors are—are gorgeous."

She turns away and strides up the beach, boots scattering sand, and he joins her at the water's edge. She's trembling and rests one hand on his arm. The mystery of women, Michael thinks, one minute they're begging you to screw them, the next they're weeping over a dead bird. He likes this one, though, there's a directness about her. He could be more like that—demand things and the hell with consequences. The hell with pussyfooting around. He asks, "Are you all right?"

"Yes." She looks away when she says this and scuffs her boots in the sand. Then she turns to him. "We have a place," she says, "up the lake. My parents'." She points north where the water and sky blend together. "Ten miles up. In a little cove they call the Echo."

"Where the highway passes under the hydro lines from the north."

She loops her arms around his neck. Is she going to kiss him? He half turns to look over his shoulder, afraid of what she might do out here in the open. She asks, "You know it?"

"I grew up in this area," he says, but doesn't add he was in love with a girl named Janice who lived on Echo Bay. Janice what?

"Meet me there next weekend." A sudden wind off the lake blows Angela's hair about her face. Ruffles it.

He pushes her arms away and says in a voice choked with anger, "I can't." He could strike her, he wants her so much.

"Michael," she says. "Please."

"No."

"I don't get it."

"There's nothing to get."

This time she grabs his shoulders like his coach used to in the heat of the game, the crowd going wild, his heart thumping beneath the singlet. "Just go for it," she yells in his face. Her fingers are strong, he feels the urgency on her breath.

"Christ, I'd like to. You don't know how much I'd like to." His heart wasn't ready for this. It's thrashing like a beached fish. He didn't realize that saying *no* could make him so miserable. He wants her—he doesn't want her. Why didn't this happen ten years ago? But he says into her flushed face, "You're beautiful,

Angela, any man would be flattered, young guys must drive themselves crazy thinking about you." Him, too, but he can't admit it, he has to be good, to hold on to the ten years with Mary. "I want to, but I can't." The wind blows the words away as he speaks them.

"I'm no threat to you."

"You're every threat. My job. My wife."

"Oh, give me a break."

"You want too much. Period."

"Just one weekend."

"It's never just one weekend."

"For me it'll be one."

"I told you before, when you're thirty you think—"

She blurts out, "What does thirty have to do with anything?"

They stand facing each other, words swirling about their faces like beach sand blown in gusts. Michael needs words, he needs explanations to right his flailing heart, so he says, "This. Life comes down to just three ages—twenty-two, forty, and sixty-five. You follow? I'm forty now, I think of myself as forty even though I passed that age years ago. But I'll stay forty in my mind till I hit the next stage." This sounds pompous but he continues, "Sometime about sixty or so, when I'm still forty—in my mind anyway—I'll turn sixty-five and go to the grave that age." Seeing her frown, he asks, "It doesn't make sense, does it?"

"It does." Angela drops her head and looks glumly at the sand, toeing it until she's built a little ridge. "But not for me. Because I'll never reach thirty."

First Michael feels embarrassment—spouting out his pet theory. But then he feels sick because he misunderstood her— because he sees from the look in her eyes, suddenly and with no doubt, that she means she's dying. His bowels go lax. He had this happen once before, when Patricia came at him with a knife and he lay helpless in his own blood, glass embedded in his palm, certain he was going to die. He feels weak with shame.

And with knowledge, too—of why this girl has fascinated him from the beginning. Death.

He says something unintelligible and Angela answers calmly, "A rare blood syndrome. Cancer maybe." And adds when he looks into her face, "A few months. With luck, a year. They don't know, really." Yes, he sees it now. The pockets beneath the eyes. The lisp. He should have seen it before, and yet how could he? She's so young, so full of animal vigor. Desire. He lowers his rubbery legs to the sand, his fifty years a sudden weight he can't support. Angela sits beside him, her hand in his. On one finger she wears a school ring, a big ruby-colored stone with engraved crest. A girl like this should be thinking of having babies and instead she's trying to talk a man twice her age into an affair before she dies of leukemia or something. In his big grip her fingers are thin and frail as straws, he could crush them before she cried out. He asks, "Which weekend did you say?" And feels his heart come loose in his chest.

* * *

Angela stands beside her pink Porsche. "I wanted to be brave," she says. "I swore I wouldn't tell. Anybody." She puts one hand on Michael's arm but looks past his eyes and past the war memorial to the lake. "Especially you." He knows. She wanted him on different terms. Emotional blackmail's not her style. Nor is she the type to tell Michael she's dying just to get him to sleep with her. She's gutsy. So it's only happened because he's forced her into it. Hasn't he? Though he's nervous about touching her in public, he takes her hand and squeezes it. "No," he says, "you have been brave. You *are*."

* * *

Long after Mary's asleep Michael sits in the armchair beside the fireplace with a book. The light from the lamp behind him shadows his face. He lifts one hand to his brow mechanically, a movement like brushing away a fly, though the bluebottles have settled for the night hours ago. Then he rests his hand on the arm of the chair. The clock on the stove ticks, the refrigerator snaps off abruptly and sends vibrations fluttering through the floorboards. Michael sighs. His eyes stray to an empty glass. He drained the last of the scotch from it when he started reading. He listens for Mary's breathing. Outside he hears waves beating up the beach. The breeze of the afternoon is now a steady wind blowing out of the north. There's ice in its breath, a hint of winter as it pushes in through the screens. He turns the book over in his hands. Poetry he's reading for a class. Stupid words about sex and death. He tears one page out and tosses it onto the fire. It flares, bringing heat to his face. Then he rips out each page and methodically feeds it into the flames.

* * *

He dreams of the moment when he turned the Tercel into the intersection at Pembina and Windermere. The man wearing the glasses screams and beats his arms as the car bears down on him. The steering of the car is stiff and it heads directly for the man, while a voice in the dream repeats *go for it*. He has a powerful sensation of sweating. The car bears down on the paralyzed man. His foot paws at the brake pedal but it doesn't make contact. The wheel won't turn in his hands. Everything moves in slow motion. Suddenly it is not the gray-haired man but the cheerleaders from Jane's junior high. Then Michael's high-school math teacher. Michael wakes. He has a knot in his stomach. Why does he want to run someone down?

* * *

After his divorce from Patricia and before Mary moved in with him, when he was restless and lonely, Michael started the ritual of visiting his parents on Sunday afternoons. On this summer Sunday he and Mary have driven back from Belvu after breakfast, and, since Jane has the Tercel, he takes the Mercedes for the drive across town. It glides up Wildwood Street. Michael brakes for a teenager chasing a frisbee and then slows round the blind curve at the golf course where he shifts down and waves at a Woodydell neighbor out jogging with his wife. Flushed with exertion, the couple wear virtuous grins on their glistening faces. Mary won't run—hates it, she says, because it's mindless. There should be a point to exercise, she says. She prefers racketball and is trying to persuade Michael to join a club: family membership two thousand dollars—plus annual dues, plus bar and dining tab. Still, it might be nice to have a club to take friends to for meals. The Club.

When he turns at Crescent Michael eases by a front-end loader parked in the curb lane. This area is being redeveloped. Cramped bungalows built fifty years ago are being torn down and replaced by condominiums with three-car garages. Bulldozers rip up the lawns and trees in May, and by August crews of college kids lay sod around the units Mary will sell for two hundred grand. For that they get a view of the river and a racquet club within walking distance.

At Pembina he waits for the light. On this corner Michael saw a child run over. He was waiting at the lights one summer afternoon, the first car in line, when a kid on a bicycle darted from between parked cars into the path of a delivery truck. The driver swerved into the next lane, but it didn't matter. The kid, a boy of maybe twelve wearing a blue baseball cap, flew right under the front wheel of the truck—his skinny tanned legs, tumbling after he'd left the seat of the bicycle, beat the air in the few seconds before his head was crushed under the tire. Squished like a pumpkin, Michael said to the policeman who wrote down his statement in a black book, though a pumpkin was not what he thought of as he rushed from his car to keep the driver from seeing the pulpy mass on the asphalt.

A horn toots behind him and startles Michael. He swings the

Mercedes in behind a pickup truck and heads south past Burger King, Country Kitchen, Wendy's, Marigold. Fast-food joints have elbowed out the family restaurants he haunted here as a student, Mama Trossi's—where tipsters bought bootlegged whiskey on Sundays—the Pony Corral, home of the Pony Burger and fries with gravy. All replaced by tacky signs and cardboard food. Further along there's a Rib Shack and then Alley's Piano Bar.

His route takes him down Bishop Grandin Boulevard, shopping mall to one side, Dakota High School to the other. No kids in leather and jeans daring the traffic today. At his turn north there is a high rise for seniors—everywhere you look now they're putting them up and filling them with old people. He read that forty percent of the population would be over sixty soon, the baby boom mushrooming into the twenty-first century with canes and bifocals. He'll be there, too, if he lasts that long. Seventy. On this side of the river the housing is modest. Prefab bungalows. Two blocks over there's subsidized housing, side-by-sides where pickups clog the driveways— and the saplings which the city crews plant every spring are ripped out by gangs of kids overflowing the sidewalks onto the street as they make their way to the 7-Eleven for cigarettes and Cokes. He feels uneasy bringing the Mercedes in here, those kids with greasy hair gouge the paint with keys. The middling poor live here, waitresses, truckers. On the corner of Worth, his parents' street, sits the junior high. Fortressed behind an eight-foot-high hurricane fence, this squat cement building resembles a bunker with its flat roof and vertical slits for windows. Not one tree in its block-square playground. What a place to learn about osmosis and read *Robinson Crusoe*. Something about poor kids, they hate schools, they smash windows and anything not bolted down: desks, toilet-paper dispensers. It's no wonder the doctors and middle managers are lining up to get their kids into private schools. A block and a half down is his parents' place, a bungalow squeezed between two others. All three have manicured green lawns and flowerbeds out front. Michael pulls the Mercedes in behind his parents' ageing Ford.

* * *

He goes down the walkway along the side of the house and into the backyard, a long narrow strip of lawn with flowerbeds on the fence side and garage on the other. Near the bottom of the yard in the vegetable garden his father stands nozzling spray over the plants. As he walks up Michael calls out, "Everything's green."

His father turns slowly to face him. He stopped moving just his head years ago after he had a cyst removed from his neck. "Dry," he says through thin lips. "Dry as bone." He turns back to his watering and Michael stands beside him. Near their feet grow tomatoes, their yellow blooms just starting to show. The rows running to the left are peas, with a knee-high chicken-wire fence for the vines to climb. They seem stunted. On the right, carrots, Michael thinks, though it's difficult to tell, and beans. In behind, hilled potatoes.

He asks, "Trouble with the peas?"

"I think," the old man says, "we got gophers." In the last years his emphysema has got so bad he wheezes on every breath. "Damn nuisance anyway, peas. If they grow at all, the blackbirds get them." He points the nozzle to the potatoes and flutters spray their way. "Still. Your mother likes them." His hands are the same size as when he was fifty, thick and sinewy, the tools of a working man.

"I do, too."

"Huh?"

"Like peas," Michael says.

"Good," the old man says. Forty years patrolling the noisy floor of Liquid Chem have left him hard of hearing, though not deaf. He turns his better ear to Michael. "I'm done here," he says. "Let's go inside. Have a drink."

Michael goes into the house first, hesitating in the archway leading to the kitchen. His mother is kneading dough on a flat board, back to the door, and has not heard him step in. She is a vigorous woman who's stood this way washing clothes and stirring stews for as long as Michael can recall. When she hears her husband enter she turns and says to him, "Take the garbage," pointing to a plastic bag at the door. Then her eyes adjust to the light coming in at the door and she says, "Michael." She puts out her dough-caked hands to him, arms still solid, and grasps him to her large frame.

"I should have called," he says.

"No," she says and points to the table. "Sit down." He pulls out a chair and sits at one of four places where years of settings have worn the arborite thin. His mother glances over her shoulder quickly. "I wanted to tell you," she says, dropping her voice, "before your father gets back. I spoke to Patricia the other day." Since their divorce Michael's mother speaks to him about Patricia in the conspiratorial tones she used in the fifties with her cronies about girls who got in trouble. "About Jane." She has returned to her work at the counter and is speaking toward the wall where the copper pans hang. "I said that Brad was bad news."

They go over the same ground again and again. Michael hoped they were done with Brad. "Not entirely," he says. Irritated.

"But you can talk to her."

"Get yelled at, you mean."

She shakes her head and says, "A father can always exert influence. *If* he wants. My father, now, he sent a boy away from our door when I was a girl. A boy who wanted to take me dancing at the Lodge." When Michael doesn't say anything she continues, "This was before I met your father. I would have been twenty, eighteen, maybe. This boy invited me to the Lodge, a nice boy one of my brothers met caddying at the golf course, but Father got wind of who it was—he knew the family were drunks—and refused to let me go. There was some scene." She stops kneading for a moment to reflect and says in a voice he recalls from childhood, full of earnestness, "Me in my party dress, the only one I owned, it was the thirties, remember, and Father standing on the front steps with a buggy whip in his hands. He meant to drive the boy away. He had some temper, grandfather."

"Well, you should be happy I didn't inherit that."

"And a strong sense of family. Which you also seem not to have inherited." She looks at Michael now over the glasses that have slipped down her nose, and involuntarily he places his hands on the table and folds them together to demonstrate good intentions. "I only met Brad the once," she continues, "but I can smell trouble a mile off. Motorcyles and trucks is all he talks about—which is okay when you're single and have nothing better to do. Now he's gone and got a girl pregnant and it's time to stop fooling with toys and settle down to the business of family life. The question is, what does he plan to do? Marry Jane?" She's kneading dough forcefully on a plywood board and Michael can see the cords in her wrists leap out as she manipulates it. He feels warm watching her, though he knows she's pummeling him as much as the dough.

Tired of wrangling, he says in a whisper, "Mother."

"Or is that too old-fashioned—marriage?"

"Let it be. It'll work itself out."

"Ach," she says. "Charlie talking. That man never tired of leaving things alone. His job—which he lost how many times. His wife. His kids." She pauses dramatically and looks at him past the corner of the refrigerator. "The only thing he couldn't leave alone was the bottle. And look where that got him."

"He was a gentle man," Michael says, remembering the

aroma of Uncle Charlie's pipe tobacco and the way he relit it as he told Michael stories about traveling the boxcars in the thirties. Trips to the poolhall in Belvu. Cokes. "I liked him."

"Everyone liked him. But no one respected him. Not even Charlie himself in the end." She hesitates. The memory of her brother's suicide hurts her more than she lets on.

"But he was right," Michael adds.

"About what?"

"Leave things alone and they have a way of working out. But interfere, offer advice and opinions and all you do is get everyone pissed off. They do what they were going to in the first place—and the only thing you've done is make them angry at you." When she doesn't answer he looks up and sees she's lifted her glasses and her cheeks are gleaming under her eyes. He stands, shocked. Is she crying about Charlie's death or Michael's hectoring voice? In the next instant Michael's father opens the screen door behind them. He turns to his father, she back to her work. End of conversation. Though he knows his mother will fret secretly into the early hours and get little sleep tonight.

"Those punks," Michael's father says. "Knocked the cans over again. I swear. One of these days. I'm getting a slingshot." He's threatened this for years, thinking that one well-aimed stone will knock the children of the poor into oblivion. After he's removed his shoes, he opens the cupboard above the sink and takes down a bottle of whiskey and two glasses. He pours in them and then motions Michael to sit. He asks, "Did you see the ball game last night?"

"We were at the cottage," Michael says.

"Man, that Bell," the old man says. "Last night the Jays are down early. Four to one. It looks like it's all over. But Bell comes up in the eighth. Three men on. Whack. Grandslam home run. You could not write a better script."

"He's something," Michael agrees. "It looks as if he could be the first guy in years to hit fifty home runs."

74

"Man oh man. You could tell that ball was gone from the moment you heard the crack of the bat."

Michael eases back in his chair, holding his drink in one hand and running the fingers of the other along the ribbed molding of the table. Forty years ago his father coached the little league ball team in Belvu and Michael was the pitcher. The memory feels as warm as the whiskey in his stomach.

"I like the little guy," his mother says, her voice recovered from weeping. "Fernandez."

"The franchise," the old man adds. "So the newspapers say."

"Speaking of which, we read your column in the paper."

Michael leans forward. "And what did you think?"

"Nice photo," his mother says. "But I don't much understand finance. Bids. Puts." She's patting the buns onto trays and arranging them for baking, and she asks, "Coffee?" Michael nods *yes*. Once the old man gets into the whiskey he turns quarrelsome or maudlin.

"She doesn't understand finance," his father says, "and I don't trust paper investments. Saw too many fellows get burned in the thirties." The old man runs his tongue around his dry lips.

"Well," Michael says. "That couldn't happen now." He shifts on the chair to face his father. "There are things to prevent it."

"Don't you believe it."

"Government policy for one. I wouldn't worry about it."

Michael's father blinks at him. "Do your job. That's what I say. And let the company take care of your retirement. That's my motto. Mind you, it has to be a good company."

They're slipping into an old argument. "People are not happy with that today," he says, holding his tone in check.

"Happy," the old man snorts. "You're right there," he says and stares at his whiskey glass, cradled in both hands on the table. He's holding back, too, looking for that neutral territory where they can talk without fighting. Michael would like to go back to baseball, the comforts of sports clichés and shared memories of sandlot triumphs, but that would be too obvious a retreat, so he sips at his whiskey, a harsh rye that tastes of prairie flowers. His mother places coffee cups before them, and this domestic gesture unites them, the family chatting at the table.

When she goes to the stove for the coffee pot, Michael catches a whiff of cinnamon, a hint of what's coming. "We were the happiest," she says, "when you boys were in grade school. Remember?"

"I do," Michael says, though what he recalls is not his mother's tidy kitchen or the parlor with the sofa wrapped in its factory plastic, but carefree days of baseball in the summer and hockey on the rink his father made with a garden hose in the backyard. They had pancakes and syrup before bed, and one winter his mother bought an old pair of skates at a rummage sale and skated with Michael and his brothers.

"That Christmas your father put on the Santa Claus suit."

"Yes," Michael says. "And there was that bowl of punch Uncle Charlie made that got you so worked up." Michael grins at his mother. "Do *you* remember that?"

"Oh. I can laugh now, but I was some angry then. Mixing vodka into the punch. That was just like your uncle Charlie." She beams, but full of warning. "Irresponsible." She touches her fingertips to her lips, remembering. "Just a clown, that Charlie."

"I hope," his father says, "you're that happy." When Michael takes a sip of whiskey, his parents look at each other across the table the way couples do, apparently unsure who is going to speak next, though there is clearly something to say. Trouble in the air. "You *and* Mary," his father adds.

"I am," he says. "We both are."

"Good," his mother says.

His father says, "Let me pour you another." He stands and fusses with the glasses at the counter, wrestling with whatever he has to say. In the oven the cinnamon buns have started to sizzle, and their aroma fills Michael's nostrils with expectations.

His father is spending too much time measuring whiskey. Maybe one of his parents has got a dreadful diagnosis from the doctor—cancer, maybe, or heart disease. Nothing but death seems equal to this strained silence. He sees his father lying in a hospital bed with a monitor blinking behind him. When the drinks are poured Michael's father holds out his glass and says, "Well, son. Come what may." Michael's mother looks into her cup and worries her bottom lip miserably.

"Go ahead," he says, resigned to whatever trouble is coming. He looks from one parent to the other. It can't be that bad. They went through his divorce together, they buried Uncle Charlie.

Apparently his father thinks the same. "Well—"

But his mother interrupts. "This is a mistake, Bill."

"What is—for heaven's sake? What's a mistake?"

"Ach. Just talk." She turns to face her husband. Clearly, this wasn't her idea. And the trouble is not cancer. Michael's hot. He stares at his whiskey. "Stupid gossip," his mother says.

God, Michael thinks, they've found out about Angela. They hated the messiness of his divorce. He looks around, wanting to hurry to the door. Afraid of having to apologize for his pathetic life.

"About Mary," his father says somberly and sets his glass down with exaggerated delicacy. He's not used to this kind of talk and looks confused, blue eyes flickering here and there.

Michael's knees twitch under the table. He sips at his drink. "I suppose," he says, "you've heard some gossip from Aunt Julia and the sisters Bloch."

"As a matter of fact, it was Julia who told us this."

"Well, you know what's it worth, then," he says. "Wasn't she the one who sent you to that quack for new teeth?"

"Yes, but—"

"You should know from that, Dad, what her word's worth."

Michael's father flexes his jaw, testing his ill-fitting dentures. "This isn't about teeth. Is it?" he asks his wife.

"What it's about," she says coolly, "is the wild fantasies of old women with too much time on their hands." Michael's mother has gone to the oven to switch off its buzzing timer. She pulls out one rack of buns. "I told your aunt Julia that," she says to Michael, her voice raised to carry to the table. "And I told *him*," she adds with certainty, meaning Michael's father.

"A man has a right to know." The old man wipes his mouth with the back of his hand after drinking. "About his wife." The heat Michael felt earlier has spread into his ears where it tingles like frostbite. He swallows the rest of his whiskey in one gulp.

"What?" Michael asks, desperate now.

"Running around."

"Ach." Michael's mother bangs the buns off the baking sheet. "Those old women don't know they're alive most mornings. And Anna Bloch wears two hearing aids."

"Some sharpie," his father grunts. "Some guy Mary meets."

"Meets?" Michael asks.

"In the mall near Julia's," his mother whispers.

"Some guy in a fancy car. Who she drives off with."

"So your father, of course, assumes—"

Michael asks, "A Cadillac?"

"We don't know what kind," his father says.

"Well I do," Michael says. He laughs aloud. "That's her partner, for godssake, her business partner. He drives a Cadillac and meets her to appraise properties. It's real estate, you know? They have to set selling prices. Christ." He sits back in his chair. He feels the urge to butt his hands together but instead he turns to his mother and laughs again.

"You see." She's put three cinnamon buns on plates and places one before each of them. "Nothing but gossip and meddling." She raises one eyebrow at Michael, then shakes her head.

"The houses *are* empty," his father says. "What better place to carry on?" But his voice trails off. He knows he's defeated and is only talking to keep from admitting it.

Michael feels the whiskey working in him. His heart is starting to speed. "Aunt Julia," he says, "is a fool."

"Your father's side of the family."

"I should choke her. Meddling old bag."

"I told them," Michael's mother is saying. "But they're not happy in that family unless they're stirring the pot."

This is directed to her husband, whose eyes are darting around the room. Again Michael sees him lying in a hospital bed, staring up at a white ceiling. "It's okay, Dad," he says. "A mistake."

"I thought you should know." His voice shakes.

If Michael could reach across the table and touch his father's hand he would. "It's all right, Dad," he repeats. "I would have done the same myself." Not a big lie, but one both his parents see through, though they say nothing to correct it. They look at their plates. In the silence bridged by the ticking of a wall clock, Michael feels the three of them slipping back into the house in Belvu, the sound of heavy breathing over food, the smells of baking fresh from the oven.

"Butter?" his mother asks, pushing the dish to him.

Michael sinks his teeth into the cinnamon bun. Warm, sweet. Butter and brown sugar mixing together. With the smells of his mother's kitchen around him and alcohol seeping into his blood, Michael glows in the narcotic of childhood. He sighs. "Boy," he says finally, "no one makes cinnamon buns like these, hey Dad?"

Two

Michael wakes with a start and looks at his bony feet sticking out from under the quilt. He has coarse toes, large-knuckled and yellowed with dirt. His mouth feels dry. He considers getting up for a drink, but doesn't want to disturb Angela, asleep beside him. He dozes and dreams of his childhood dog, Scruffy, run down by a truck but in Michael's dream still alive and barking from the head of the stairs, which Michael is trying to mount for some reason as obscure as it is compelling. When he wakes again, Michael has a pain in one leg and lies staring at the ceiling.

Angela breathes through her nostrils, steady, regular. He envies her. The last time he slept like that was in the backseat of the family car on the drive home after weekends at the beach, his parents listening to the glowing radio as he and his brothers dropped off one by one under the wool blanket his father had brought back from the army. For years now he's been awake at 5:30. Sometimes with headaches, sometimes with a bladder that makes demands—which he stifles by thinking about other things.

The roof at the cottage has not been winterized. Inside, the supporting trusses are made of fir, stained mahogany red. The roof proper is tongue-in-groove cedar oiled to match the trusses, handiwork from an earlier renovation period. One summer he and Patricia laid the asphalt shingles. It was hot that year. In the evenings they sat on the beach and drank white wine. Three years later came Mary. Together they bricked a hearth into one corner of the main room and installed a zero-clearance fireplace. They bought a waterbed which Mary thought was sexy, and was, but the water got cold during the nights, so they sold it to a young MBA with a penthouse in the city.

Michael turns his head slowly. The clock radio at the bedside reads 8:05. In five minutes he has to get up. The red letters in the display panel read 14:8. August this year has picked up where July left off: heat waves and drought. The few remaining warblers that shelter in the willows outside twitter thin songs in the mornings but go to ground somewhere cooler by midday and give the island over to buzzing insects. Ruggles hides under the deck, panting and snapping at flies.

Feeling pain in his leg again, Michael shifts in bed and curls into a fetal position. He shouldn't arch his back when they make love, it puts pressure on his discs and brings on spasms. But he can't explain this to Angela. For her he has to be athletic. When she's excited she bites her lower lip in ecstasy. After, she drops into this deep sleep. Angela. Last night after the moon was up and the night birds had ceased singing, they stole out to the lake for a swim. Her body was a slip of bronze above the water. She made no sound entering with a dive. When they surfaced, steam rose from her hair. In the moonlight it formed a silver halo around her head.

Later they sat on the sand and looked at the lake. "Do you ever think about what's after this?" she asked him. He hadn't for a long time and he felt bad having to confess it to her. At the therapy sessions which she attends Angela and the other dying patients talk about it. One man thinks his soul will merge with everyone else's and produce a sound like the music of the spheres. Another believes in hyperspace and the transmigration of human force fields. Silly, Michael and Angela agree, but comforting. He wanted to know what she believed in. The body, Angela told him. The body is no mystery: it arrives, it grows, and then it dies. No mystery, no metaphysical angst. She had brought a bag of peanuts out to the beach and she cracked them as she spoke, flicking the shells into the darkness. He asked, no afterlife? He thought she would need to believe in an afterlife, that anyone facing the inevitable would. But she told him, no, having a belief is the only important thing, not what you believe in. It can be reincarnation, transmigration, or resurrection. Having faith is what gives you courage. For her, it's knowing that when the neurons flick out for the last time, that's it, existence is over as beautifully and remarkably as it began. Like the flash of electricity between contact points. Though she knows it's contrary to what most people think, there's actually something comforting in the thought of extinction.

Long after she had ceased speaking she sat hugging her legs, chin resting on her bent knees. There *was* an aura about her, a silvery halo which Michael wanted to reach out and touch in the deepening night, a mystery he longed to share with her. Later in bed she came on top of him, face glowing with exertion, with intensity.

8:10. Michael squirms to the edge of the bed and slips out from under the quilt, landing lightly so as not to wake her. The lids of Angela's eyes flicker, but she snuffles and her breathing regains its rhythm. Is she dreaming? She tells him she dreams all the time, lengthy complicated dreams with subplots. He looks down at her. Blue-veined pulse in her ivory throat. On the pillow a few white strands mixed with black, the first signs of age.

Standing beside the bed Michael realizes he's trembling. From exhaustion? More likely anxiety about having Angela at the cottage—where his sense of betrayal is overwhelming. When Angela lifts one of Mary's tumblers to her lips, he feels hot and sick. And there's the risk he might be found out. As a rule Mary comes to the cottage in the afternoon only, but he's jumpy just the same. She might decide to surprise him by driving out early. So he only relaxes when Angela's Porsche disappears round the bend.

He tiptoes to the bathroom. It's a little cubicle next to the bedroom outfitted with a tin shower as well as a sink and toilet. A big man like Michael has difficulty turning around inside.

He opens the cabinet door where they store towels. From the back of the top shelf he removes a gauge for monitoring heart rate. Michael borrowed it from a student, a marathon runner who uses it in his training. Once he thought he'd had a mild seizure when his arms went numb. Shortly after that he talked to the marathon runner and borrowed his equipment. The gauge is attached to a harness which fits over the chest: a flexible black strap with a pulse sensor goes across the nipples. Since he's been seeing Angela, Michael uses this gauge to monitor the effects of stress on his heart. He's seen statistics on seizures brought on by sexual exertion in middle-aged men—and he's learned the warning signs.

While he secures the strap, he listens for Angela's breathing. She'd laugh aloud if she found him with this athlete's gauge strapped to his chest. Water drips in the toilet bowl. Outside he hears birds in the marsh, a pleasant sound he associates with long mornings on deserted rivers, fishing for bass. He turns to study himself in the mirror and his elbow strikes a shelf. He jerks about and strikes the tin shower with his other elbow. Why is he so jumpy? He counts to ten to calm himself, then studies the gauge. According to his student, his resting heart rate should be no higher than seventy-five. If he has sex it should jump abruptly, but then flatten back to normal within ten minutes. If it doesn't, something's wrong.

Seventy-two beats a minute, Michael thinks. That *does* make over two and a half billion, as he figured, but he was wrong about this being a threat. He's discovered that the heart of a man beats three times more over a lifetime than any other mammal's. If you're fat or eat too much salt, the rate jumps to eighty, maybe more, and you die five years sooner. Sudden effort, like lifting heavy objects, brings on cramps, constrictions, headache, and numbness in the arms. Who knows about gymnastic sex with a woman of Angela's appetites?

Michael studies the face of the gauge. It's blank. When he taps it with the end of one finger, the plastic casing pops off the back and it drops. A flash of silver hits the floor. One of those little silver batteries pings across the tiles and with it Michael's heart. The readout will be useless if the battery is soiled. He drops to his knees, scrabbling with his hand around the base of the toilet. The damn things are so small. Along the wall skirting he recovers the disk-shaped plastic backing. But not the battery. Then he hears Angela stirring in the bedroom. Any minute she'll be coming to the door with her toothbrush in hand.

He thrusts his head along the baseboard, peering into the cramped space behind the toilet. Things always lodge where you can't see them. Condensed water is pooling on the floor. Michael smells decaying wood. It's hard to get your head between the wall and the back of the toilet seat. But that's where it must be. Propping one foot against the far wall and cocking his knee, he levers himself forward, bangs his head on a pipe leading out of the water closet. Angela calls, "Honey?" Her voice is muffled, but he pictures her crossing the floor to find out why he isn't answering. Then he spots the shiny battery caught between the baseboard and a loose tile. It winks at him. "Ummphh," he calls back. Snakes his hand around the toilet and pinches the mercury sliver in his trembling fingers.

Michael relaxes. Before his eyes stars weave in a green matrix, like the tint of his computer screen. He's recovered the battery, but now he can't move. His big head is wedged between cold surfaces, one cheek pressed to porcelain, the other to the damp wall paneling. Pain flares behind one ear. Michael blinks. He got his head in, it has to come out—it's simple geometry. He wills himself back into the center of the room. When this doesn't work he shuts his eyes and breathes to slow the thumping of his heart.

In the bedroom the phone rings. Panic tells him that it's Mary and also that Angela belongs to a generation which thinks nothing of snatching up phones in other people's houses. He hears her shift on the bed and he lurches backward, desperate, heedless of pain. One ear scrapes the damp underside of the water closet and for a moment the phone's ringing is lost in the beating of blood in his ears. But he tugs until free. The crown of his head strikes the toilet lead-in again. One sharp heave and he sits on his haunches on the floor where he rips the flexible strap from his chest as he stands and in one motion stuffs it like a basketball into the back of the shelf.

He knows his face is flushed, his hair mussed, but he crosses the room trying not to look agitated. Angela studies him from the bed where she's drawn the quilt over her breasts, face framed in hair matted on her forehead, a sweet-natured girl with an open face and a heart to match. She's smiling strangely. When he lifts the receiver, bringing its sharp bleat to a merciful stop, he sees why. A hard-on's blooming in his boxer shorts.

* * *

He says into the receiver, "Yes?"

"Sweetheart?" Mary speaks to him solemnly. He feels edgy with her voice in the room, as well as puzzled by an undertone he can't comprehend. Mary says, "You sound a little—I don't know—far away. Like you're speaking from the bottom of a barrel."

Michael clears his throat. "I just got up."

"The air does that. Soon you'll be snorting and spitting." She starts to laugh, then cuts herself short. "Anyway, hon, can you get back to the city this morning?"

"This morning?" he asks. "Oh God. Is it one of my parents?"

"No. Nothing like that. As a matter of fact, I just talked to your father and they're both turned on about that anniversary thing this weekend."

"What then?"

"Brace yourself." When he says nothing she asks, "You still there? Michael?"

He's looking at Angela huddled in the bedclothes. One bare shoulder peeks out, smooth and pink. When Michael draws an imaginary knife across his throat, he sees he's still got the silver battery pinched in his fingers. He asks, "What's the kid done this time?"

"We need the registration for the Tercel."

"Not the Tercel."

"That's why I called your father, actually, thinking maybe you gave it to him for safekeeping."

He groans. "Not the Tercel." He braces the hand holding the battery against the wall. "How bad is it?"

"We don't know. That's just the thing, we can't do anything till we get the papers. The police won't touch it."

"Autopac?"

"Won't look at it until the police say it's okay."

"She totaled it, didn't she?"

"Look," Mary says, "the good news is there wasn't another car involved. No accident report. You see?"

"Wonderful." First the Honda and now the Tercel. The kid's a used-car salesman's dream come true. "It *is* totaled then?"

Mary sighs into the receiver and a pulsing silence comes over the line. Michael hears a child shouting somewhere down the beach. The sun is already throwing up heat waves from the sand, but near the cottage are long shadows which a dove is strutting through as it feeds. "Just a little bump," Mary says. "A scrape."

"Even scrapes these days cost a thousand bucks. Minimum."

"Maybe. Maybe not."

"Who's going to pay that?"

"The insurance is. That's why we've got it."

"To send my rates through the ceiling?"

"Look, there's no use getting in a sweat. From what I can tell it's not bad. Maybe a fender has to be replaced—or something."

"Or something?"

"Honestly Michael—"

"I know. Keep cool."

"Do that. What's done is done." There's that finality in her voice she uses on clients. "Don't you want to know about Jane?"

She always survives. He asks, "How is she?"

"She'll tell you. Here she is."

He glances at Angela, picking lint off the quilt which has slipped off her shoulder, exposing part of one breast. Michael wishes he could put the phone down and take her in his arms.

"Daddy."

"Peanut." He hears a strange mixture of tones in his voice, concern and offence, and, above all, surprise.

"I'm really sorry about the car. You know?"

She sounds repentant now but was probably high when she cracked up the car. "Well," he says, forcing conviction into his voice, "it's just a car." When she doesn't answer he asks, "You okay?"

"Yeah. A scrape on the forehead. Pissed off more than anything. My knee got twisted or something."

"You had the seat belt on?"

"The cruddy car jerked when I geared down. Suddenly we're smack into one of those divider things at the foot of the bridge."

"Medians," Michael says. "Did you pump the brake?"

"Yeah. But the goddamn thing—"

"And geared down at the top of the bridge?"

"That's when it started skidding. Like I said."

"You're sure?"

"Yeah. The gears wouldn't go from third to second but there was this awful noise, whunkawhunk, and then the car started swerving."

"Listen," he starts to say, then hears the phone hit the floor. He glances around, holding the receiver in one hand. Angela's bra, he notices, is tangled with his shirt. Michael wiggles his toes. He's chilled standing on the cold floor, naked except for shorts.

The phone spits sound. "Honestly, Michael," Mary says, coming back on. "She was trying."

He shifts his gaze to the window. The dove is gone, though Michael remembers seeing one in the same shadows years ago, feeding. It came often, sometimes with a mate, and had a nest in the eaves. He loved listening to it cooing on the roof. One morning he watched it through the window, its head bobbing to the gravel. He stood stock still so as not to frighten it. But then, jusf twenty feet from him, he saw the dove caught by a hawk, wings spread and beating the air to hold it aloft as it lifted the dove in its deadly grasp. The dove's eyes bulged but it uttered no cry as the hawk clamped the life out of it, bore it upward in a sudden swoop. When Michael examined the gravel later he found no blood, only one fine breast feather catching light from the sun.

Mary is waiting for him to answer. "So was I," he says, anger in his voice. "Trying."

"Now you're getting into a state."

"I am, am I?" Saying it he realizes his jaw is tight and his eyes are burning, the first signs that a headache's on the way. He fingers the crown of his head and feels a bump where he struck it on the toilet. "Can you blame me?"

She asks, "You do *have* the papers?"

"Yes," he says.

"In your wallet, I think."

"Right."

"And you'll be here by when—ten? Michael?"

"I don't know."

"Let's say ten."

"Let's not. I'm—I need a little time."

"*You* do? Michael, I'm the one stuck here trying to sort things out for *your* daughter while you're having a nice lie-in at the lake—or whatever it is you do up there."

"Great. Now I'm to blame. My car gets smashed up and because I have a few simple questions for the kid suddenly it's my fault." He's been tapping the battery on the wall for some time, its hard edge making little half-moon impressions in the plaster.

"Can't you think of anything else, Michael? Your own girl nearly kills herself and I'm up half the night talking to doctors and the police, worried sick, missing work, and all you're concerned about is who's to blame."

"We know who's to blame."

"Honestly." The silence she leaves throws him into panic. He doesn't want her to hang up angry, though he's being stupidly hostile and forcing her to do just that. She says, "Look, make a cup of coffee. Sit and think about it for a minute. I'll be here till noon, and then you can reach me at the office."

"Right," he says. "I'll call."

"Do that."

After he puts the receiver down he stares out the back window at the gravel road running down the spine of Willow Point, and imagines Mary looking into the backyard in Woodydell. Branches will have broken off the weeping willow in last night's wind and blown onto the lawn. Mary's right. It's not her problem, it's his. Rotten kid. He shuts his eyes and when he opens them he sees a black 4X4 with smoked windows come into sight, an unfamiliar vehicle on the island. It disappears in the bushes behind the cottage, a cloud of dust settling in its wake. Michael turns and asks Angela, "Coffee?"

"No," she says. "You're in a hurry." She has her jeans on and is pulling a cotton shirt over her bra. She's leggy and graceful, and probably realizes just how sexy she looks tucking that shirt into her tight jeans. "And I should get going."

He stares at the battery in his palm and then down into her eyes. "You think?"

She asks him casually, "What's happened?"

"The bloody kid smashed up the car. My Tercel."

"Jane? The one who's—"

"Exactly. Little miss carnage." He laughs wryly.

"I meant pregnant. She's okay—in her condition?"

"No fear," he says, "you can't kill that one."

"Well," Angela says, straightening her shirt and pulling up the zipper of her jeans. "It's just a car."

"That's what everyone seems to think. Except me."

"You don't have to defend yourself." She smiles, embarrassed for him. "And she isn't hurt or anything?"

"No. Just needs someone to hold her hand."

"So. I should be going." She lifts her bag from the floor and rummages around in it for the keys to the Porsche. "Don't fret so much," she says. "Look at the upside. It's just a car. And your daughter's not hurt."

"Yes," he states flatly.

"That's important."

"I know."

They drop it at that, Angela smoothing her hair with one hand as she prepares to leave, Michael feeling awkward as he waits for her to go. He knows she's delaying, hoping he'll invite her back, but he's tired of this sneaking around. He wants it to end, but if he says anything like that, even hints it, he hurts her. So he busies himself tidying bedclothes and tying his sneakers. Maybe after she's gone he'll go for a jog and work out the knot filling his chest.

Angela stands at the door shifting from one foot to the other. There are silences like this between people when the buzz of insects or the hum of appliances claim the mind, when the unspoken is more important than anything that words can later make good. Michael looks at Angela and smiles weakly. He straightens some articles on the counter and glances briefly into the refrigerator. Pulls the cottage door shut.

He ducks at the elm and follows her down the path to the car. When Angela stands with the Porsche's door open he knows she wants him to embrace her and kiss her, and he feels the queasiness he felt holding Mary in public a decade ago. Women want so much. This is what the guys writing for the glossies never figure out. Their need for displays of affection, their need to say *my man*—something that goes with romance and love and devotion which they learn and men do not. He leans over and pecks Angela's cheek. Looks away from her when she tosses her bag across the seat and slams the door. She stomps the gas pedal and the Porsche's rear end fishtails through the gravel.

Maybe it's over. He wants it to be. In the past months he's slept poorly. "You look beat," Mary says, stroking his cheek when she sits beside him to watch TV. He wants to tell her it's a thing he didn't even start, it just happened—but how can you say that to your wife, *I just started sleeping with another woman*? He said that to Patricia and she tried to kill him. He kicks at the gravel with the toe of one sneaker. He told Angela it wouldn't be one weekend—and it's dragged, miserably, through the summer. He's lost focus, he can't write his newspaper column. Angela. Half the time he prays she'll get lost, and he'll be left in peace to love Mary. The other half . . . His eyes wander along the driveway. He spots a pelican feather in the gravel and crosses the road to pick it up and admire its colors. When he lifts his head he sees the 4X4 parked at the bend in the road fifty yards down, facing back at him. Against its hood leans the man in the camouflage jacket. His arms are folded across his chest and he's watching Michael through those dark glasses sheriffs wear in B movies. Mirrors.

* * *

Michael throws his clothes into an athletic bag and ten minutes later backs the pickup out the driveway, glancing once in the rearview mirror down the deserted road to the point. His hands shake on the wheel as he wrestles with the image of the man in the camouflage jacket. He appreciates mystery, but this figure is not mystery, it's terror, and Michael is a man who abhors violence. He could use a cigarette to help him think. There are students, he's heard, who come after teachers for revenge. In New York, where you can buy a gun on the street, people shoot each other all the time—that guy Goetz blew away some black kids in the subway. Maybe Angela has a boyfriend who's jealous. Former lovers have committed axe murders and afterwards not remembered their crimes. As he drives down the gravel road he glances in the mirror, but there's no sign of the 4X4.

His first impulse—the one he knows is correct—is to go to the police, but he knows also that he'd have nothing to tell them. The cops at Belvu are former schoolmates of Michael's who'd dutifully record his story in their note pads. But what, finally, could they do? Stake out his cottage and neglect their other duties? In the end his story would only embarrass them all. They'd ask awkward questions and start gossip about Angela.

Michael digs through the junk on the dash and finds a piece of Juicy Fruit, his wretched substitute for Winstons since he quit smoking. The gum is not as stale as he'd expected, kept fresh like so much now by preservatives. He flips the foil wrapper out the window and watches it flutter into the ditch.

The hum of tires on cement soothes him, though the pickup bounces along crazily and every joint in the highway jolts his spine. He looks in the rearview mirror for the 4X4, but there's nothing behind him except shimmering pavement and birds pecking gravel along the road. The sun is a smoky haze of orange in the sky. Outside Belvu he passes two kids walking along the gravel shoulder, jabbing each other with bullrush cutlasses they've brought up from the ditch. He finds them comforting. Things can't be so bad if boys still have fun with reeds on a summer day. Belvu comes up on his right. A knot of teenagers hangs around the Shell station this morning, drinking Cokes and chasing a frisbee. They eye him as he slows where the highway bumps over the railway tracks, and one pitches a stone in his direction, a scrawny type with glasses, wearing a military jacket and heavy black boots. Pent-up rage lurks everywhere. And violence. The highway cuts past the high school, where he earned his letter for basketball, and then curves around the general hospital which has a new wing he's never set foot in. Funny, building it on the edge of town like that, as if they knew most of the trade coming in would be the bleeding victims of road accidents.

Past the grain elevators it's open country. Michael has begun to calm down now with the fields stretching to the horizon on all sides, though the image of the guy leaning against the 4X4 still gnaws at him. He fiddles with the radio, a cheap staticky thing that only brings in a few stations. The markets are news again, Tokyo up a thousand points and the Dow Jones ninety. Unprecedented, the announcer says, and switches to a colleague on Bay Street. Everybody's buying, she says, but before she can continue, the signal fades. Michael raps the dashboard with his palm. White noise.

A black pickup pelting towards Belvu from the city swishes past and Michael watches it disappear in the rearview mirror. With ten miles between him and the cottage he can think about the 4X4 without shaking and forces himself through a series of questions and answers. What did he actually see? A man leaning against a truck. Why did it upset him? The answer to this is tricky. Was the guy really watching him? He reflects, gnawing at the gum. The guy wore a camouflage jacket and its military look scared Michael. But then the kid in the Shell lot wore the same jacket, didn't he? Michael looks out the window at fields where farmers have begun swathing. He smells the rich odor of cut crops. The point is, he tells himself, this was the same guy he saw before. Or was it? Michael groans. There's no way to pierce through to the truth. He's guilty about betraying Mary, that he knows. But beyond that? It may be only guilt working on his imagination. The conclusion, though, is obvious— however flattering it's been to have an affair with Angela, it has to end. Having reached this decision, he spits out the gum.

With a crackle the radio comes back to life. Michael hears that the TSE is up a hundred points. Excited, he calculates his gains. His shares of petroleums, worth fifteen bucks each at the start of trading, have made him three grand this morning. He whistles. The transports may not have done as well, but the mines should do better now that gold's on the rise again. Capitalism. He used to rail against it, and now he basks in its golden growth. In total it could be as much as ten thousand in profits. So what's a scraped fender? What's a crummy Tercel, for that matter?

He keeps the speedometer at fifty-five and eases back on the bench seat. This is where he used to light up a cigarette and ride on nicotine, but he doesn't need that any more, he's high on profits. Had he taken that credit margin he would have made another couple thousand in profits. Enough to scrap the Tercel outright or give it to Jane as a peace offering. Yes. The BMW he saw at Deals on Wheels was going for $28,500—last year's model but what the hell, it had only been used as a demonstrator, and the way Germans build things they go 200,000 kilometers without needing as much as an oil change. Perfect steering, that solid feel on the road. He liked the paint job, too, it looked gold-flecked in the sunlight.

Morning sun warms him and he sinks farther into the seat. He's made a lot of money this morning, enough to banish silly things like camouflage jackets. For the first time in a long while he doesn't want anything, he's happy just to coast along and absorb whatever life has to offer: the old pickup with its rattling valves and musty interior, the tang of sugary fruit flavor from the gum dissolving between his teeth, the sound of radio music fading and returning through the grid of static set up by power lines running into the city, the play of sun on the hoods of cars whizzing past. Life's a gift. He drifts in a haze of good feelings about the markets, and when he passes a field ten miles from the city rolls down the window of the pickup and sucks in the sweetness of fresh-cut alfalfa. Yes.

Somebody is explaining hog futures now on the local station, and on the CBC a woman with a fruity voice is helping callers with their sex problems. There *is* such a thing as a g-spot, she tells a woman, and when manipulated it allows some women to release g-spot fluid, quite a rush of it, it smells sweet like clover and will wet the bed, good. The announcer laughs in a hearty way. "So if you're not touchy about that," she concludes, "enjoy. Nobody's going to die." That's it, Michael thinks, nobody's going to die. And in a minute he's buoyant. He begins an inventory of the good things that can happen in the next twenty-four hours. Once he's straightened out the car business and comforted Jane, he'll call Stephen and set up a tennis match. His serve is improving since he got that graphite racquet. They'll drink a few cold beers after and sit in the shade. Mellow out over talk about the Jays. Yes, starting today he's getting out of the Angela thing, it's too complicated—gymnastic sex, secret meetings. He's fifty, for godssake. What he wants now is a routine of simple pleasures and ordinary satisfactions. A good glass of Burgundy with a rare steak, canasta and a few laughs with friends who don't make judgments, screwing in his own bed. Tonight will be sweet, he figures, after he's put Jane's nonsense behind them—and if there is a g-spot he figures he'll find it.

* * *

The tennis match lasts two sets. Baseline rallies, overhead smashes, service winners. With his new racquet Michael reaches crosscourt returns that once eluded him and punches crisp volleys to Stephen's backhand. Michael loses the first set 6-4, but he comes back to win the second 6-2. Afterward, he and Stephen sit and drink soda water with lime. What, Michael asks, does it mean to love a woman half your age? Stephen arches his eyebrows and offers, stupidity? Michael says most of the time he feels scared. Stephen runs one finger around the lip of his glass. Of what? In the silence that follows they hear game scores being called out. *Forty-love, advantage, deuce.* When Michael doesn't answer, Stephen speaks for him. Of the young woman in himself— Stephen says—the responsive, vulnerable, and intuitive parts of himself that Michael always denies. In other words, the feminine. Like most men, Stephen insists, Michael is drawn to the feminine—but resists it, too. Stephen says all this with a straight face, looking not at Michael but at his hands, locked over one bare knee, thumbs twiddling, and Michael listens to shouts from the courts and the pock of balls being struck. This Stephen, he thinks, is a good fellow, but he reads too much psychology.

* * *

He asks Stephen, those dreams where I run the guy down, what are they about? They sit under the trees and the blue sky, cooling down. Rage, Stephen says. Michael asks, *rage*? What the hell does Stephen mean? Stephen nods. There's a lot of rage in you, buddy. You curse things, you lash out at people, you pout and sulk. Don't get me wrong, I don't blame you. See, there are two kinds of people, the passive and the angry. The passive accept what's handed to them, a job here, a lover there. Most people lack the character to get angry at what they're given. Pay the overcharge on the phone bill and grumble out of earshot. Run and hide when they're dumped by lovers. Let things happen to them—the same things over and over. Right? Drift toward death, even, with a shrug of the shoulders. But the angry, they're different. They bridle, they rage, they throw tantrums. That's you, buddy. You have rage—pure, volatile, awesome. It's wonderful, but it's scary, too. As your dreams tell you.

* * *

Did I only get involved because the girl's dying? Out of pity? Or is it just selfishness? Michael asks himself questions as he lies in the tub after tennis. He's talked himself into dumb things before—is this another one? That he's slept with Angela because she's dying? She needs him? Looked at one way, it's a pathetic rationalization. A way to avoid the responsibility of that decision. Throw it back on the girl. Years ago Patricia laughed at him when he said he wanted a divorce because Mary loved him. *You mean it was her idea? She initiated things? Don't fool yourself.* These words ring in Michael's ears. He wonders what Stephen would say about this. He decides he doesn't want to know.

* * *

"To make a long story short," Michael says, raising his voice for emphasis, "when I drop her off the kid asks can she take the pickup? She's just smashed up the car, nearly killed herself, set the old man back a thousand bucks, and all she cares about is does she have wheels to go to a concert at the racetrack." He tells this to the shadowed faces around him before sipping cognac. "Now doesn't that just put frosting on the cake?" Michael's words float through a silence which he feels the need to fill before it's obvious no one cares any more than he does about Jane's fiasco with the Tercel. It's past midnight, the tag end of an enervating summer day, and they're lingering over drinks by the Connors' pool. No one even has the energy for canasta. Kelly is sitting next to Michael, leaning forward when he talks, to hear him better, he thinks, and this pleases him. When he described how the police badgered Jane and how later Patricia threw a fit on the phone when the kid called her from the Autopac office, she shook her head in sympathy, though for what, Michael was unsure. Mary sits next to Kelly, closer to Stephen than Kelly and back in the shadows. Something's up with her, she downed a lot of wine with dinner and has been nipping away at a liqueur since, distracted and sulky, odd for her. Like August this year, her mood goes up and down, bright and sunny one moment, blustery the next. Michael drums his fingers on the arm of a deck chair, making a hollow sound. To fill the silence he asks Stephen, "Did you buy that oil stock—Galveston?" Stephen's dropping ice into a tumbler and swishing it with soda, so he misses the question. When he's got the mix right he leans back in a chair and sighs audibly.

Kelly leans forward again and says in a voice hardly above a whisper, "It must have been awful for her. Harassed by the police like that."

Michael turns to face her. "Well," he says. "She brings it on herself. First she's sulky and then she lashes out."

"Just angry that everything seems beyond control," Kelly says.

"Exactly," Michael answers, surprised by the way she put her finger on the kid's psychology. "Like my ex-wife. *She's* pissed off because the girl's shacked up with someone."

"I'd have to go along with her there."

"Really?"

"I may be an old fuddy-duddy, but living together seems a dumb idea. For young people."

Michael laughs. "Fuddy-duddy," he says. "I haven't heard that expression for a decade."

Kelly laughs, too, at herself, and Michael likes her even more. "What I mean," she says, "is the noncommittal attitude of it. Soon as the first thing goes wrong there's a handy excuse to bail out. It's too easy. Nothing's ever worked out."

Michael looks past her toward Mary who sips from a crystal glass, Benedictine, Michael recalls. He says to Kelly, "And this noncommittal thing has something to do with what's happening to our kids—drugs and so on?"

"Of course." Her voice is quiet again, confidential. "Oh sure, outside it's all cool and devil-may-care, that's what they get from TV. "Miami Vice" is vile—vile. But inside's a different story. They have no moral framework, nothing of meaning. Did you know the suicide rate among kids is lots higher than in our day? Eighty thousand teenagers in the States every year." Kelly purses her lips for emphasis and adds, "Lots successful." This is a long speech for her and she sits back and folds her hands in her lap.

"That's a big leap—from living together to suicide."

"It's just one aspect," she says. She sighs and takes a long look at the sky, clear for August, with a big silver moon that gives all their faces an unearthly sheen. From inside the house Michael hears laughter and phrases of the rock music the Connors' kids are playing on the stereo.

He's about to say something about this when suddenly Mary stretches her arms wide, taking in the night, and says, "It's so warm out here." She extends her legs, feet forming a V, and Michael is reminded of what the woman on the radio said about g-spots.

"Lovely." Kelly sniffs the air and looks up. "For August."

"To answer your question," Stephen says, leaning forward so Michael can hear him, "no I did not buy those stocks."

"The coward," Kelly says.

"Damn right." Stephen runs his free hand through his hair. "The only thing I trust is real estate. Land, you know, something you can feel and smell. Tangible. Like a farm."

Kelly asks, "Isn't oil tangible?"

Stephen waves her question away. "Real estate," he insists loudly. "Otherwise you may as well bury your money in the backyard. Stocks, bonds, all that paper is just worthless."

"Not quite," Michael says. He's floating on maybe ten thousand profit this week, almost twenty since the start of the year. "With what's going on in the Persian Gulf, and Ghaddafy stirring the pot, too, the only safe place *is* the market. Blue chips." He sounds a little too much like a huckster even to his own ears, though he does believe what he's saying. In fact, he's noticed a certain element of boosterism since he's been writing the investment column. He says to Stephen in his best down-to-brass-tacks voice, "Besides, the movers and shakers on Bay Street say this bull market is here for the long run."

"If you get cold feet, you can average down," Mary adds. "Or sell before the market turns." She likes tripping jargon off her tongue. First it was real estate, now this.

"Huh," Stephen grunts. His eyes glow in the semi-gloom, and he adds forcefully, "God only made so much land."

Michael leans back and sips cognac. He won't accept that simple-minded thinking but he doesn't want to argue with a friend. Stocks have gone up thirty percent since the start of the year, some more, but people like Stephen are back with the dinosaurs and you may as well leave them there. With this mess in the mid-East, oil and gas are climbing daily. Now the Iranians and Iraqis are shooting again and American tankers are being escorted down the Persian Gulf. Nobody knows what's going to happen next—war maybe—but one thing's for sure, an oil crisis is on the way. Already Texas crude is up ten dollars a barrel and they're talking fifty bucks again, as high as in 1972. Some sharp deals in petroleums will be like gold next year. He blinks and feels pressure behind his eyes. He'll have to stop drinking soon or he'll get that splitting headache.

"1929," says Kelly. "That's what scares me. Soup lines for blocks, men riding boxcars across the country."

Mary says, "I don't think so." She shifts higher on the lounge chair and says firmly, "I have faith in the American way."

Kelly says, "People are sure buying things—or renovating. I read the other day that the renovation business is bigger than the housing market. Two billion dollars yearly."

"Like I said." Stephen leans forward. "Land goes up and down, too, but it's there, it's real." He grins, feeling solid as a rock about mortgages and land titles held by the bank. "One for the road?"

Michael looks up. "Maybe." Then he catches Mary's eye.

"Hon," she says. "I think we should be going."

Suddenly Michael's tired, too. After tennis he got a pain in the back. He's been trying to numb it with booze, but all that's done is start a headache. The stars overhead are fuzzy, but the dark looks comforting, deep and distant. He thinks of it as cool, the touch of cotton sheets on naked flesh. "You think?" he asks.

When they stand Stephen says, "Tomorrow, buddy, you see the big serve, so hit that sack the moment you get home."

* * *

Instead he stands under the shower with his face turned into the stream of water, hoping it will clear his head. Turns both shoulders into the jets coming from the nozzle and feels the back muscles relax. Tennis requires abrupt lurches—and stretching for balls almost out of reach. Spasms develop, knots form. In the steam-filled room Michael towels his body slowly, deep-breathing air into his pulsing brain. Rubs his scalp vigorously.

He's read that massaging prevents baldness, and if there's still a physical feature he's vain about, it's his hair. Brushing his teeth he stares into the mirror. Who is this guy with crow's feet round the eyes and fleshy face who looks like Peter Ustinov and fancies himself Kenny Rogers? Lately he's not so happy about what stares back at him from the glass. Soon he'll avoid mirrors entirely. He spits into the sink, gargles with mouthwash, pats his gut, and wraps a towel around his waist before crossing to the bedroom.

Mary is sitting on the bed in a terry-cloth robe, studying the paper. She looks good, the nape of her neck still beaded with moisture from a shower, legs tucked under Indian-style. She has the business section of the paper spread over the quilt, a pencil in one hand, calculator in the other. Head bowed in concentration, she reminds him of Jane ten years ago at the kitchen table sweating over arithmetic homework.

"Good news?" he asks.

"Great," she says into the paper.

"Galveston up?"

Mary looks at him. "From 5.12 to 5.85. That's three grand in one day. Since we bought it, it's up over five." Her face shows joy mixed with bewilderment. "Can that be right?"

"You bet." He sits on the edge of the bed, crinkling the face of George Bell which smiles from the sport page. Michael takes the business section from her hand, still moist and warm from her shower, a musky message to his body, and studies the columns of figures. Everything's up. "What's it come to?"

"Eight thousand seven hundred and eighty-seven."

He whistles. "Magic number, eighty-seven, eighty-seven." With his free hand he traces 8787 on her exposed pink thigh, angling upwards toward the center, testing.

"We'll be rich." Her eyes are big with excitement. A fringe of wet hair sticks to her brow. Sexy.

"We'll buy Cadillacs," he says. "Pink and mauve and silver

and gold, one for each mood. Beef Wellington and Chateau Rothschild."

"Summers in the south of France."

"Cashews. Bowls and bowls of cashews, because they were too expensive when I was a kid. Even at Christmas." He laughs and she laughs with him. As she leans forward Mary's robe falls open, he wants to reach inside where she's moist and damp. "For my birthday you'll get me Glenlivet and for yours I'll buy ruby-studded panties."

"Rubies!"

"Yes. Which I will chew until they pop off!"

Mary laughs and her eyes bulge with mock concern. "No, really, what *are* we going to do?"

"We're going to smother in greenbacks," he says, moving toward her over the crinkling paper, smelling shampoo and lotion, a warmth radiating from her skin.

"I'm so excited," she says.

He rolls her over suddenly and opens her robe. The cords in Mary's face tighten with surprise. She giggles and wiggles under him. He hadn't expected to be erect so fast. "Doggy," she cries as he reaches in to her, and they roll on the quilt and the newspapers underneath, tossing aside bathrobe and towel. Mary grabs at the bedside lamp, her thin arm and wrist illuminated brightly, then suddenly gone. In the moonlit room her back is white. He enters fast and jerks her by the pelvic bones to take his slack-gutted thrust. Moans. Despite the alcohol, the shower, the lateness, he finishes fast and collapses beside her. Mary's damp hair tickles his nose. "God," she says in his ear, "it's good when it's fast like that." He murmurs and dozes, his mind free-floating from the bond market to the smashed Tercel to the guy in the dark glasses. Then his heart begins to pound in his chest. Thuds. He rolls onto his back and probes his ribs but doesn't know what he's feeling for. No pain, at least. Both hands flex easily and he holds them up toward the window and studies his knuckles in the white splash of light coming from the moon. Beside him Mary is curled into a ball with her face lost in the pillows. He closes his eyes. Let it be.

* * *

An hour later Michael wakens with a pain in his chest, and when he opens his mouth to cry out, his throat fills with panic and he chokes. Then he finds he's rolled onto his stomach, the calculator is digging into his ribs.

* * *

Towards dawn he sits up with a start, repeating to himself the words *tanks, camouflage jackets, that scene*. Patricia used to accuse him of being blind when it came to seeing the obvious and he's come to enough sudden—and embarrassing—realizations since the divorce to suspect she was right. Angela's father is a military man. *The Colonel*, she calls him—not Dad or Bill Shaw. *The Colonel*. He's retired and in business, yes, but military types never cut their regimental ties. A right-wing crank, probably, Bill Shaw, even though his daughter speaks of him glowingly. Michael pictures him—beefy, with iron-gray hair, a good fellow round the officers' mess, likely to stand the boys to a drink, but a holy terror when crossed. Bill Shaw would know how to hire a guy to shadow somebody, how to hire a psycho to terrorize his daughter's lover.

Michael eases back on the pillows. It makes sense. He saw the gunman first on the afternoon when he and Stephen walked to Willow Point, the spring day after Angela came to his office. Yes. Though it's a puzzle he's pleased to have solved, instead of being relieved, Michael feels uneasy. He doesn't have all the answers. For instance, what's going to happen now? And what should he do?

The clock on the bedside table shows 4:22. Mary is snoring, one foot sticking out from the quilt, toes twitching. Michael closes his eyes and tries to wish himself back to sleep. Instead his mind tracks to a dream he had somewhere in the night. He was standing in a hallway with Barb Hegge, his high-school sweetheart. In the dream her lips were glossy orange, and her blonde hair fell to her shoulders like Mary's, not teased as it had been in 1958. Before he could kiss her he woke up. He rolls onto his side.

Dreams. Other people seem to think they're important, but they're all about buried secrets and nasty childhood memories. The few times he's thought about his dreams he's felt bewildered and then guilty. He'd like to forget the past, not relive it. Too much pain back there. No. He'd rather not think about dreams. They trouble him, though, and force him into rituals of evasion.

At one time he used to fall asleep thinking of women he'd like to screw. In the last few years that hasn't worked, so now he finds the way to drift off is to focus on a sound and ride it into sleep. He concentrates. Somewhere in the distance he hears the steady throb of a train and after a while its short dull whistle. He only hears trains at night now. He feels blood pounding through his head. Alcohol. During dinner Stephen refilled his glass with Burgundy and later poured big snifters of cognac for sitting beside the pool. Good stuff as it burns on the way down. Michael's tongue is raw. After a lot of booze it seems as if his skull shrinks and presses in on his brain. Wouldn't that cause cell damage? If it's not the old heart giving out, it's some other organ. The surprising thing, really, is that the body holds up as long as it does—what with coffee, booze, cigarettes. And they're only the worst. Additives in hot dogs and soft drinks lay waste to the guts, too. Even milk, some guy was saying on TV. It contributes to hardening of the arteries.

In the dead of night Michael realizes he's afraid. His body is running down, and with it his time. When he lies on his side, one ear to the pillow, his heart sounds like a giant turbine that throbs in a factory, tremors horribly amplified. He's sure he's going to die without waking and feels the same giddiness as when he starts awake convinced that one of his parents has died. An illusion, Dr. Fayyaz says about this heartbeat fear, common in middle-aged men and in adolescents. Michael can't understand how something he feels so intensely can be an illusion. His heart feels like it's right in his gullet. He starts to gag. He distrusts doctors on instinct, and when they tell him patent nonsense he's outraged. Listening, he's convinced that any heartbeat could be his last, that the body is trying to tell him something—and he knows what it is. Get out of the Angela thing while he still can.

For a while he'd told himself it was scruples that made him jumpy around Angela, morality nudging him to be good—to be true to ideals he had learned from his teachers along with the Apostles' Creed and "Rule Britannia." This is what he couldn't tell Stephen. That he saw himself as the good man who stays faithful as husbands were trained to in the fifties. What a joke! He'd convinced himself of all kinds of nonsense. That he wasn't the type to lure housewives and teeny-boppers into bed with a devil-may-care shrug of the shoulders. The snatch-and-grab type. No, Michael had refused to see himself that way, stupidly arguing that the good life is more than random couplings. He even had a phrase for it—growing up, rather than growing old. He rehearsed for himself many statements having to do with commitment, lectures concerning noble ideas such as moral progress, things which Michael believed in once and told his students with a straight face. A lot of prattle, really, amounting to little more than being scared. Which amounts to fear masquerading as fidelity. It's laughable, the commitment bit, sugaring over terror with philosophy. Michael's been fooling himself. He wanted Angela, but he was scared. Or rather his body was.

Yes, moral conscience has nothing to do with it. His body is terrified. It wants nothing to do with Angela—because lovers demand not only devotion but performance. And the body knows its limits. Knows gentle love is where it's at for guys of fifty who enjoy amiable games of tennis, playing canasta on Friday nights, and reading the sports news with a glass of scotch at the end of the day. The old heart, the harried back, he imagines them debating every urge like the guys in Woody Allen's *Everything You Wanted to Know about Sex*—and shaking their heads knowingly when the erection furnace starts to blow apart from too many demands. Laughable, really. Reading the glossy magazines, with their locker-room lore of seduction, men picture themselves as studs. But that runs out at thirty-five, forty if you're in good shape or lucky. Then fear takes over—and caution. You want to prolong the gift of life, not risk it on something like a passing piece of tail. Yes, the Angela thing is over. Michael bunches the pillow under his head. Sighs. He wants to make gentle love to his wife, and afterwards, with the moon slanting onto the quilt, lie in her arms and talk about which French cities to visit this summer, how much to spend on patio doors, or what to buy the kids for their birthdays. Is that so bad?

* * *

"It's not so bad," Mary says, "wanting the good life." By which she means membership at a club, vacations in Europe, and shopping in New York. "It's not so bad," she says, "liking the boutiques on 57th, it gives you a buzz when the clerks call you *Madam* and bring you tea while you try on Chanel. I like that, I like being treated special, life offers few enough occasions, so why not grab a little attention when it comes by? Feel important. Anyway, no one ever hurt anyone else shopping, so what's the big deal? Why do we always have to be careful with money, careful with feelings, careful we don't show we have desires and whims and frivolous selves—where's the harm, for heaven's sake, in showing that we're human?"

* * *

The river runs west out of the city, and where it snakes through a wooded ravine the burghers of the nineteenth century built their grand homes of stone and mortar: Wellington Crescent, Ravine Drive. Solariums big as entire houses in the north end, wine cellars, servants' quarters. Rambling places sheltered behind banks of forsythia and lilac at the ends of long curved drives.

Houses like this rarely go on the market—they discreetly change hands among the very wealthy. But on a warm afternoon in August Mary reclines on a brass bed in one of them, wiggling her toes as she calculates the commission she'll make selling it. Ten thousand? If they get the full price, fifteen, maybe. But she knows it won't come easy. Places like this are difficult to list. Then they stay on the market forever. Taxes and upkeep scare people off as much as high selling prices. This one they're listing at a half million. It must cost thousands to heat the sixteen rooms in the winter, especially a place made out of stone and hardwood.

Mary likes it though: high ceilings, lots of windows, the master bedroom on a floor of its own. Sunlight slants through the leaded windows and falls on the threadbare Persian carpet where Mary's clothes lie twisted in knots with Fred's. Her bra and his jockey shorts, his blue tie and her white blouse.

Mary does not feel guilty about carrying on an affair in someone else's bed. It's a matter of convenience. Houses for sale sit empty, and agents have keys to their doors. To Mary a key is a magical thing. Made of bright polished metal, each has its unique design, wonderful jagged teeth that slip smoothly into a slot and roll the secret tumblers coated in factory oil until they yield up their surrendering click. Click. A key lies in the palm with the weight of a coin, winking when turned to the light. And like a coin its value far exceeds its worth—a piece of aluminum after all, or bronze, it commands doors onto wine cellars,

Chippendale, and was it landscapes by Lawren Harris in the parlor? Held against the cheek a key is cold, a sliver of ice, but pressed into a lover's hand, warm with promise.

Mary carries many keys in her purse and enjoys the chink of metal as the bag swings into her hip. Car keys with a leather tab bearing the Mercedes star stamped in gold. She still carries the Tercel's keys, too, but why, since Michael bought a BMW and gave the Tercel to Jane, she doesn't know. If Jane locks herself out, the keys would be handy. And Jane is the type who locks herself out, the kind who gets herself into trouble. Mary should give the keys to her—maybe when Jane comes over for a heart-to-heart about the baby. How many weeks has it been now since Jane decided to have the baby—and keep it? It's months, Mary realizes.

Thinking about Jane gives her gooseflesh. When she slides out from under the quilt, Fred buries his face in the pillows. He's short and wiry. His hair is thinning. He jokes about it, asking to borrow Mary's brush when he's washing up afterwards. She likes looking at his naked body. His legs and arms are thin and ropy, his stomach flat and muscled.

Mary slips into her bra and blouse. The bathroom, one of three in this house, is as big as the bedrooms in her Woodydell bungalow. She finds a tissue and blows her nose. In the mirror she studies her complexion, always blotchy after sex. It's a wonder her mother never caught on when Mary came in from dates, her heart pounding under her rumpled bra, warm and damp between the legs. Poor old Mom, plodding between breakfast nook and television in that one-room flat on the coast. It breaks Mary's heart to think of her mother's last years leaking away like that. And the phone calls Mary dutifully makes each week don't help.

The bathroom is all shelves and drawers. Matching silver-plated hand mirrors hang from hooks. A big jar of petroleum jelly sits on a vanity with plastic tubes of shampoo and bath salts in an oversized brandy snifter. A little dish of potpourri beside tissues in a pastel box. Mary lifts the dish to her nose and smells lavender and dry autumn leaves. Inside the cupboard are more secrets. In one drawer, two packets of bandages, three tubes of toothpaste, a dozen plastic-handled razors. Jars of cosmetics. Mary twists the top off one and dips her finger into cold cream. Dabs her cheek and studies the effect in the mirror. Her skin tone is good. No wrinkles in the throat. *Wattles,* her mother called them—an ugly word. In another drawer she finds a second jar of petroleum jelly. For sex? Tylenol with codeine, Dristan for sinus blockage, NeoCitran for sniffles. Rows of prescription bottles with blue and orange and red capsules, dates and names typed in tiny blue letters. Mary shuts the drawer and straightens her blouse in the mirror before leaving.

Other people's houses seem so empty and cold. Electricity ticks in the walls, a refrigerator hums somewhere below. Mary stands at a window and peers down on the driveway at her silver Mercedes and Fred's white Coup de Ville. Fallen leaves are collecting in the gutters. It's been a good summer for weather and a better one for sales, but another year's come and gone. Michael's meeting with students already. One warm evening in June the moon is a little silver slip you catch over your shoulder and the next it's a big harvest orange, raging through the bare elm branches as you store the lawn chairs in the garage for another winter. Mary hugs her arms over her breasts.

One hurts a little where Fred pinched it with his lips. He's quite an athlete. He tells her he plays hockey in some liniment league where he set a scoring record. He arches his brows coyly when he says this, *scoring record.* Around the office he laughs at his own jokes. One day he quipped, "I feel like a man trapped between a dog and a fire hydrant." He wears jackets with big checks. The dandy at heart. He came back from a convention with red suspenders and wing-tipped shoes. He's always late for appointments. No one can stand this—Mary, clients, his wife—but no one can change him, either. *I'm hopeless,* he says, shrugging and shuffling his feet. But that's the face he shows to the world. Things bother him. He got an ulcer some years ago and has to carry Maalox in his coat pocket and swig from it several times a day. He drinks imported beer, too, and smokes Cuban cigars, and cannot keep track of his VISA spending. He asks, *why bother? Go for the gusto,* he says. He's so much on the surface Mary laughs aloud at him sometimes. Once he showed her a thousand-dollar ring he'd bought his wife, Joan, on impulse. He treats the office girls to champagne, strutting about with a foaming bottle in one hand, cigar in the other.

Mary studies herself in the full-length mirror. She has good breasts, maybe a little too big. In junior high you worry if you'll get any, and in high school if they'll be big enough, and after that they start to sag and you wonder what all the fuss was about. Stretch marks on her thighs. Why don't men get them? She turns slowly, appraising herself. She could lose five pounds. Fat bottom, legs too short. She has a bulge around the tummy. Nonsense, Michael says when she tells him she could lose weight, your bottom's beautiful, you're pretty as a partridge. And as plump, she thinks. She worries about losing him to a younger woman. He's surrounded by college girls who hang on every word that comes out of his mouth. What chance would she have against some pretty young thing in a mini-skirt? Mary shivers. She returns to the bedroom and nudges Fred where his bum sticks up under the quilt.

He loves sleeping. It's like death, he says, but with a happy ending. Mary never knows what he's going to say next—or do. That's why it's fun to be around him. He knows the words to all Patsy Cline's songs—hurtin' songs, he calls them—and he sings them around the office.

He sits on the edge of the bed now. In one hand he holds an argyle sock, blue and gray and red. From behind he looks small, the bones of his spine forming a vulnerable ridge as he fumbles on the floor for the mate to his sock. There's a large mole on one shoulder, the kind Mary associates with cancer, and a scar near his ribs, where, he told her, he had one kidney removed as a child. He missed a year of school and couldn't play sports for another, but that's also when he figured out that life was fragile, anyone could be gone tomorrow.

"You're dressed," he says, turning toward her.

"I was having a look about."

"There's wine down there. Racks of it. Red, which I love."

"The paintings," she says, "are really valuable. One's a Lawren Harris, sky and mountains." She motions with her hands. "I don't recognize anything else, but some of it looks like Impressionist."

"These folks are loaded." Fred stands and pulls on his pants. He picks lint off one leg and then the other. When he moves to the mirror, he wets his fingertips and pats a tuft of hair into place. Grins back at Mary from the glass.

"What do you think it'll go for?" she asks.

"Not half a mill. Even in this market." He straightens his clothes and steps back from the mirror. "It's cold, though, don't you think—the house?"

"Yes," she says. "Joyless."

"Four-fifty." Fred takes the Maalox out of his jacket and opens it carefully before drinking. "Four-twenty, maybe."

"Honestly. My dad didn't make that much in a lifetime."

"Think of the commission," he says. He puts his arms around her neck. "We could fly to Paris and sleep on satin sheets. Or San Francisco. Since those Rice-a-Roni commercials I've been dying to ride trolley cars." Mary smells chalk on his breath and feels hairs from his tweed coat tease her lips. She hears the hum of the refrigerator below. Outside a gust of wind flings a tree branch against the bedroom window. She wants to tell Fred how good it feels to be sharing this moment, an ordinary moment in an ordinary day, but a lovely one just the same, but before she can say it, his pager goes off in his jacket pocket and that moment's lost forever.

* * *

Mary takes Valium. One pill before going to bed and two on mornings when she's closing a big deal. She doesn't tell Michael. The pills are tiny and yellow, notched down the center, in case Mary wants to take only half. She never does. The label on the plastic bottle gives the name of the pills, Novodiazapam, and her name, and her doctor's: A. Goldstein. Mary needs the Valium for tension. After work she gets a knot in her neck, a knot she can feel but cannot rub out with her fingers or steam away with hot towels. She tosses in bed. The knot feels like a lump, like cancer. Even the professional masseuse she visits can't move it. But the doctor's pills do. She, too, she confides to Mary, takes Valium now that she's stopped smoking. Tension, she tells Mary, stress. Deadlines, confrontations, screw-ups. Everyone takes something. Don't they?

* * *

On the phone Jane sounds upbeat. She's just bought a jolly-jumper for the baby and yesterday Michael's parents came over with a new stroller—rubber wheels, folding legs, leather seat, retractable canopy. She has bright plastic blocks, too, that telescope together or form a pyramid when inverted. Her checkup at the clinic went great, though she's coy about revealing the results of the ultrasound examination, playful when Mary asks leading questions, teasing. She chuckles at Mary's frustration, she makes a joke about Patricia's stinginess, she hangs up laughing and leaves Mary with a smile that takes her through the afternoon.

* * *

But for their heart-to-heart Jane arrives late. Mary hears the Tercel crunch on the gravel and looks up to see the late summer sun setting on Woodydell. Michael's at his evening class. Mary plugs in the kettle and lifts wax paper off the Danish. Now that she's pregnant, Jane has a big appetite for sweets. Her boots thump across the cedar deck announcing her arrival, but she pauses at the door—to steel herself for their talk?

"Come right in," Mary sings out, too gay, she thinks. If she's eager to please, Jane will take advantage. Mary turns down the volume on the radio over the sink.

The door bangs shut. Jane enters the kitchen and the two women stand awkwardly facing each other before Mary crosses to the girl and gives her a brief strained hug. They part and Jane holds her hands self-consciously over her stomach. She is in her sixth month now. Her heavy calves peek out from a striped maternity dress and her ankles look thick and swollen. "It's the wicked witch," Jane says. And adds, "I look a wreck."

"No." Mary motions her to sit. "No you don't."

"I got caught in traffic." Jane's lips are dry and the end of her nose red and chafed. It's been a rough pregnancy.

Mary asks, "Tea?" When Jane nods she busies herself measuring leaves into the strainer. How did she imagine this might be fun?

Jane drops heavily onto a wooden chair. "Wouldn't you know it," she says. The announcer on the radio has just forecast rain.

"Bad day?"

"That lousy car. Every time I stop at a light it stalls."

"I thought Brad had that fixed."

"The transmission got fixed." Jane says this in a voice filled with suppressed rage. "Now something else is fucked."

"Brad will fix it," Mary says. Jane is fiddling with the buttons of her coat, a pea jacket with leather collar and cuffs. When she doesn't answer, Mary says, "He's good at that. Mechanics."

"Right."

"Well, isn't he?"

"He said something about the carburetor. It won't idle right."

"There. You see."

"Yeah." The finality of Jane's speech hints at trouble—which Mary would rather not know about. She wants a pleasant chat over tea—a chance to talk about pregnancy, a chance to demonstrate her good feelings for Jane. She pours boiling water over the strainer and puts the plate of Danish on the table. "Go ahead," she says. Jane's head is bowed, the part down the center of her head crooked, her scalp an unhealthy red.

When Jane lifts a Danish to her mouth, she says around it, "And if that's not enough, some jerk cuts me off just as I get to Windermere. Like the road belongs to him or something. I slammed on the brakes and knocked my head on the steering wheel. Look." She tilts her face up for Mary to see a welt under her bangs. "Pretty, eh? Goes along with the rest. Ugly, ugly, ugly."

Mary moves back to the sink, glancing quickly out the window at the empty space where Michael parks the BMW. Reflexively she touches the amulet at the base of her throat. She's learned to mutter words over it in times of crisis. "Don't say that about yourself."

"My ass is wider than a barn door."

"You're filling out," Mary says through a smile, "like all mothers do."

"What bullshit. I don't sleep all night and wake up sick and the shitbox won't go and then this jerk nearly kills me."

"Here," Mary says. "I'll take your jacket."

"No." Jane pulls the coat tighter around her shoulders. "I'm cold all the time. You know?" She shivers dramatically. "At night we're freezing, but that asshole landlord won't turn the heat on."

Mary says, "We've got a space heater in the basement. Take it when you go." She's sitting now, too, and picks at a pastry with her nails, flaking bits onto a saucer.

"Can't somebody make him turn the heat on?"

"Take the space heater."

"The taps drip and the paint's falling off the walls as it is. You'd think he'd at least keep the place warm."

"Maybe his first concern isn't your comfort."

"Whose is?" Jane says this as if it were exactly the point she'd been trying to make all along.

When Mary steals a peek at her watch, she sees it's an hour until Michael's class ends. She needs tea to steady her nerves. "Anyway, about the car, we'll get somebody to look at it."

"Don't bother." Jane waves her hand, a gesture she's learned from Michael, who can't stop talking, even when he's eating. Dusk is closing in on them now, the streetlights on Wildwood flickering at Mary through the trees. She feels forlorn. She knows any chance of a pleasant chat has faded, too. Jane is saying, "I was thinking maybe we could sell the thing and buy an old clunker."

"Sell? Your father likes the Tercel."

"Yeah. That he likes."

"Come on, Jane. Your father isn't that bad."

"Isn't he?"

"Whatever you may think, he loves you."

"That's totally obvious." Jane breathes audibly out of her nose. "You know what? He loves that dog more."

"Not true. He's just not good at showing it."

"But he teaches poetry."

"And grew up in the fifties watching Gary Cooper and John Wayne. The strong silent types. You see?" Mary doesn't understand herself. Most men seem to mask their feelings. Michael, Fred, her ex-husband.

"What I see is you're covering for him." Jane taps her spoon on the table. "Everyone always covers for him."

"They love him."

"No one covers for me. They just dump shit on me."

Mary pulls back. Jane's anger frightens her. "That's not true." She reaches her hand to Jane's shoulder. Something's wrong, but Mary's not sure if she wants to know what.

"God," Jane says, "I'm crazy, aren't I?" Her whole body shakes, rattling the teacup in the saucer.

Mary wants to hold her or strike her in the face, she can't decide which. "You're a little upset."

"Pissed off is what I am. God, I'm twenty-two, I should have learned by now not to—not to have any expectations." Jane crosses her arms over her chest and hugs herself. "I should know better."

And Mary should have motherly advice to offer, things she's read in *Chatelaine*, maybe, but all she can come up with is a cliché. "Things don't always work out like we expect."

"Gimme a break. I know I got myself in this mess. But everything gangs up on me. Brad, the car—"

"We'll get that fixed."

Jane throws the spoon at her, not at her, but over her head, into the doorway of the living room. "Stop saying that!"

"What's wrong?" Mary fights to keep hysteria out of her voice.

"It's not the goddamn car."

Mary leans across the table and seizes Jane's trembling hand. "Take it easy, honey."

"I can't."

"Talk to me."

"There's nothing to say."

"About why you're upset."

"It just sounds stupid. I'm a hopeless loser."

"You're not. Now pull yourself together."

"I can't." Jane pounds the table with both fists, sending the teapot jumping across it and spilling tea onto the floor. "Oh, God, I can't go on." Before Mary can stop her she picks up a plate and smashes it once, twice, three times onto the table, spraying fragments of china across the kitchen floor.

Mary stands. She circles the table, she reaches blindly, she grabs Jane from behind by the shoulders. "Stop," she screams. She stamps her foot on the hardwood floor.

"It's Brad," Jane says hotly. She buries her face in both hands. "We got into a fight and he hit me. That's how I got this welt—not driving." Jane pounds her fists on the table. "Oh God," she moans, "he hates me. And now he won't."

* * *

Mary stands at a rain-streaked window watching the Tercel's taillights disappear through mist. She's in Michael's study, book-lined on three walls with the fourth in the process of being refitted with sliding doors. Forster says it should be the guest room and Michael's study should be part of the extension he's building, but Michael says he won't move. He's so stuck in his ways. Mary sighs. When he finds out what's happened between Jane and Brad he'll make a scene, and then afterwards brood through several stiff scotches before saying anything. So predictable. Michael hates bad news. When he senses it coming, he cringes and grows sullen, and in the days that follow he's constipated and tosses in bed. He can't sleep. When Mary wakes in the night, she hears him pacing from room to room.

His children scare Michael. Before their visits he fidgets and drinks too much, and after they've arrived he can't sit in the living room and talk with them. He jumps about, getting ice, straightening books on shelves, fiddling with the radio, anything to put off face-to-face contact. Mary does most of the talking. With Maurice this isn't so bad. He's serious but he's developed a peculiar sense of humor and some poise, now that he's twenty-five and has a beard. He seems to have forgiven them for what happened a decade ago, but Michael's guilt puts them all on edge. His children remind him of the family he wrecked. From what she's heard, that wasn't such a picnic, but time has a way of distorting the past. He probably remembers his kids hunting for chocolate bunnies at Easter and wading through thigh-deep snow with him to fetch home a Christmas tree chopped in the woods. Sometimes Mary thinks of her own awful marriage in rosy terms—before she catches herself with memories of tears and sulks, and the week-long silent treatments she and her husband inflicted on each other. Pooh.

On his desk Michael's left a printout of his latest column:

Better Be a Financial Tortoise!

Sticking to the sober rules of conservative financial management—safety first and always balance possible risk against anticipated reward—may sometimes seem discouraging when you read about so many instant millionaires sprouting up, it seems, almost everywhere, thick as mushrooms on a manure pile. At the same time, hucksters drench us almost daily with a steady stream of get-rich-quick schemes. You probably have to remind yourself that slow and steady will take you and your money further, and that greed is the grease of financial disaster.

More anxiety. It's hard to recognize in these cautious words the bearded radical who marched against the War Measures Act in 1970 and voted for the Communist running for mayor a decade ago. Sad, when she's finally freeing herself of the dime-pinching homilies her mother fed her—along with what her brother called "depression sandwiches," baloney on white bread—that she's stuck with a man who's backing crab-like into retirement. Running scared. He has prune juice for breakfast now and boils oatmeal Sunday mornings when Mary would like to go to the Fort Garry for the brunch special. And all that jogging, which he thinks will strengthen his heart and trim his gut. It doesn't look bad on him anyway, his students probably find it sexy in a paternal way. But he's vain and reads books on dieting and weight loss—which get tucked onto the shelf later to gather dust while he roasts up a chicken and pours another double scotch. Like a lot of men in their fifties, Michael thinks reading about weight loss is as good as diets and exercise.

He's left a book face down on the desk. The passage he's

marked reads: "*Homo sapiens* is a markedly deviant mammal in more ways than braininess alone. We live about three times as long as mammals of our body size should." More fretting about the body. Sometimes Michael hunches over his wristwatch, counting heartbeats. And maybe with good reason. When Mary sees him breathing hard after tennis, face flushed red, she's sure he's a candidate for early heart attack. The other book on his desk is *Illness As Metaphor*. Why is he reading that? Idly Mary turns the book over in her hand, thinking of Poppsy in the hospital bed with tubes in his nose and that hateful blipping machine attached to his arm. No pain, the doctors said, but he died squeezing her hand so hard she had bruises on her wrist for weeks.

Mary raises the amulet to her lips, biting one of its bone edges. Thoughts of her father hurt her. Such a tough man, so brave, but the pain broke him, too, in the end.

Michael's always trying to outrun pain, preferring to dodge rather than take the blows in the face. But that only brings them on. Mary sees the same thing in Jane, a weakness that invites attack. She likes Fred's idea better. *Roll with the punches*, he says. Years ago when her brother was in junior high and Mary a sixth-grader, the school bully beat him up on the playing field. He took punch after punch—in the face, on the arms. Mary felt angry and helpless. She wanted to do something but all she could think of was running for a teacher, and that would have been worse for her brother. So she stood and watched. The thing was, even though he was knocked down, her brother kept getting up, landing a blow for every three or four he took. Later at home she asked him why, and he'd explained it simply. He'd got a cut above the eye and a bruised cheek. But he'd stood up to the school bully, and he was a hero. Roll with the punches.

Mary strolls into the living room. She picks up the spoon which Jane threw at her and places it absently on the mantle between two photographs, her mother seated at the piano twenty years ago, and Mary's official portrait as Saleswoman of the Year, Fred grinning to one side as she smiles into the camera and clutches her prize, a gold key. Blushing. Fred makes her blush, and at heart she knows it's because she betrays something with him, a secret she hides from most people, even Michael this decade and more. She blushes because Fred sees through her. She likes the way he stands right in front of her at parties, fingers hooked in his suspenders, eyes studying hers. He reminds her of boys she knew in high school, with their undisguised eagerness. It's not aggression. He speaks in a soft voice and emphasizes what he says by touching Mary's arms and shoulders. When she speaks, he listens, smoothing that tuft of hair into place—and tells Mary straight out when he thinks she's wrong. Always at parties they end up laughing together in a corner. Michael notices this, though he pretends not to. He laughs at Fred's business schemes. Small-time, he calls them, full of contempt—and jealousy.

But Fred actually likes Michael, and admires him in an ironic way. When she told him Michael had invested a hundred thousand in the stock market, he whistled and said, "Better to play the ponies." Which is what he does. After that he ribbed Michael about the market. "Down ten points," he said once, sitting at the kitchen table across from Mary, and tapped his nose with his forefinger. Michael refused to join them for drinks on the pretext of walking Ruggles and claimed afterward that Fred was a dreamer who didn't understand the first thing about finance.

In truth Fred is downright cunning about money. In his business dealings he buys low and sells high. He knows a certain percentage of transactions will go bad, and he hedges against them. *Taking a beating*, he calls it. With his loud jackets and jock's cologne he seems at first to be a bumpkin, but he's shrewd and crafty, so much so that Mary's never known him to be bested in a deal. He studies financial reports and subscribes to business magazines. Also he reads books which women like, psychology and novels, and at parties chatters with them in the kitchens. The gawky jock, he has a sense of relationships Michael lacks. Fred seeks out the quiet wife flipping through magazines in a corner while Michael goes straight for the men laughing at poolside over beer. Fred refuses to talk about love but he sees marriage as a kind of game to play, where Michael assumes people are frozen into roles which they merely act through. Fred notices clothes and talks to Mary about fashion. He asked once when she wore Giorgio, a gift from Michael, did she think she was a tart? Fred has those sleepy eyes, but he sees through her, the way no one has since her high-school friend, Sharon, who smoked cigars and said between drags, "You got this inferiority thing, Mary-Moo, you want people to like you too much."

It's true. She's spent her life trying to please. First her parents, then teachers, then Bob, and now Michael. And Fred saw it right away. "Be tough with the world and you'll get respect, be nice and you get shat on," he told her once after she cried about a client who reneged on a deal. And when she told him the story about the wind and the sun and the man with the coat, he hooted and patted her head. They went to lunch. "Don't let the bastards grind you down," he said between Bloody Caesars. He fondled, not patted, her hand, and said the touch of her skin was electric. They drank a bottle of Blue Nun and Mary laughed at his impersonation of Brian Mulroney—*Jaws III*, Fred called him. Pulling on her coat, she realized she'd forgotten her weasly client, she realized she hadn't laughed that way for months. On impulse she kissed Fred's cheek, leaving a lipstick mark on his jaw which she wiped off in the car with a trembling hand.

The next time Michael was at the cottage, Fred suggested they work on a condo proposal over dinner. Mary declined, saying she had chores to do. It was a lie. She was afraid. Alone in the house with Ruggles snoring at her feet, she wondered what Fred's hands would feel like on her breasts, and then feverishly baked Michael's favorite cake while she should have been working on the condo proposal. For a week she hugged Michael at odd times and in odd places.

Fred kept laughing and making her feel good about herself. One day he gave her a back rub, massaging out the knots not even her masseuse could dislodge. He wormed into Mary's dreams, a stocky figure whose hot breath on her skin made her start awake repeating the word *electric*. One warm June day they were in an empty house together doing an appraisal and he pulled her into the bedroom by the hand. "Try the bed?" he asked, half as a joke, and they had.

In the intervening months she's grown to like him. He makes Mary laugh at herself. *You're wonderful*, he tells her, stroking the small of her back. He mocks her habit of figuring everything out to the last penny. *Don't sweat the small stuff*, he insists. He corrects her need to please everybody. He sees himself as a teacher, instructing her, encouraging her when she does something good. And she tells him things that make her blush. This is the real betrayal, opening not just her body to him, but her mind as well. That's what *he* needs, to talk and comfort and be loved for his compassion—she sees it in the way his eyes are always waiting when she looks up from her work. He helps her understand why she needs him for a while—and why she loves Michael. He makes her better with Michael.

* * *

Mary waits up in front of the TV, but nods off watching reruns of "Hill Street Blues," and is wakened by Ruggles' barking when Michael gets back. His footsteps on the deck sound like the tread of the murderer whom Renko and Bobby Hill were following through a tenement. Creak, groan. She hears, too, the sounds of a suburban night, the blat of horns in the distance, trees sighing, teenagers laughing. Michael sets his books down on the hall table and comes in through the kitchen. In one hand he carries a paper tube containing a single red rose, and he places this on the glass-topped table near Mary. When he leans over to kiss her she smells cigarette smoke—and sour beer fumes. "Hey, sweetheart," she says.

"Missed you," he says, a form of apology.

She lifts the flower in its paper tube and smells the blossom. The bloom is already off. "Sometimes," she says, "I wish you'd come home instead of sitting around bars half the night."

He straightens and sighs. "It's not even twelve yet." He glances at his watch for confirmation and continues, "And it's not as if it's just fun when we go for drinks. The class needs it in a way, and the students loosen up because the bar is the great leveler." This sounds like a rehearsed speech and Michael looks embarrassed.

The tip of Mary's tongue rests on her upper lip. In a minute she will say the wrong thing and regret it. At least there was no smell of perfume or that flush that Michael's cheeks get when he's aroused. She was drinking soda water while she watched TV, and she has a sip now, but it's flat and uninviting. "You missed Jane," she says.

Michael crosses to the buffet where they keep the liquor. "She took the check, I see."

"And the space heater. Their apartment's cold."

He raises the scotch up to the light, then takes a long drink and holds it in his mouth before swallowing. "It's been a vile day," he says. He sits beside her on the sofa, pushing papers away. "And I'm sorry you had to be here alone."

"It's all right. I started off wanting it that way."

He snorts. "I take it she was miserable."

"Wretched," Mary says. She takes the glass from his hand and sips. The taste of burnt wood flares in her throat. "First she cried, then she beat her fists on the table."

"Jesus. She used to break things. China, glassware, once a vase Patricia got as a gift. She didn't break anything?"

"What's broken is the girl's spirit. That Brad. First he gets her pregnant, and then he tells her he won't marry her, and what's worse he's moving to Calgary."

"Now? Not even the Newfies are going to Alberta any more." Michael shakes his head in wonder. "He'll never find work."

"It may not be work he's trying to find."

"Exactly. A little breathing space."

"Honestly. Now Jane has nowhere to go. Paying the rent is out of the question. She can barely buy food with the little cash she gets from us and Patricia."

"I suppose *she* wouldn't have her?"

"What do you think?"

"No." Michael snorts again. "So I suppose we'll have to take her back."

Mary shifts the rose from her lap onto the table. There is silence in the room and in darkening Woodydell, not one car swishing by on the street or one voice coming over the houses from far away. She says, "Either that or she moves in with her friend—Peggy?"

"Sally." Michael gets up to freshen his drink. He sways across the room with an uneven gait. "Lordy-o," he says from the buffet. "I was hoping for your sake that this phase was over." The neck of the whiskey bottle clinks on the tumbler, a ringing sound, so he holds it steady in both hands. "What do you think of having the kid under the roof again?" He looks up, thinking that these days they hardly have a roof.

"I'm not ecstatic at the idea." Mary coughs into her hand, then looks out the window. Across the way the lights suddenly go out at the gays' house, plunging that side of the bay into darkness. "But we can't refuse her—in her state."

"She look bad?"

"Awful."

"Poor rotten kid." Michael looks out the window, too.

"That isn't the worst of it," Mary says. "She and Brad got into an argument about abortion and he hit her."

"Christ. Someone should knock him around a bit." They both know he isn't serious about this. Michael settles beside her on the couch again and puts his feet up on the table, reclining against Mary's breast. "But she went back there?"

"Oh yes. Brad apologized for what he'd done right away. Good as gold, according to Jane."

He sighs wearily and says, "I guess she's coming back here, then. I guess there's nothing else for it."

"It might not be so bad," Mary says. "Jane can cook. She'll help around the house." Mary runs the fingers of one hand through Michael's hair abstractedly, something he loves.

"Um." He settles back and closes his eyes. "And pigs can fly." He pronounces each word carefully to avoid slurring. "What about us, I wonder?" he asks, sounding as if he's about to fall asleep.

Mary wonders about that, too. In the past few years life has been good to her. She's worked hard and has a job that brings her satisfaction and money in the bank. She enjoys playing the ponies, and last week she stopped in at the Squash Racquet to arrange for a trial membership. Now there's Jane to worry about again. Shouting matches. Guilt.

And Michael. Over the years their affection for each other has grown, though sometimes she wonders about the way they've drifted lately from passion to ritual to routine. On her shoulder now he grunts, tipping into sleep. Fred will be out now, too, even sex can't keep him from his shut-eye, he says, laughing gently at himself. He reminds her of a boy she knew in high school—Nick, whose last name she's forgotten—he was tanned summer and winter, and his skin was snake smooth and cool. His father owned the Chevrolet dealership and on weekends he got the Cadillac with the big fins and leather seats in back. Mary's bare bum stuck to the leather and came free with a smack. Football player, Mary thinks, and a Cadillac, the guy was another Fred— she has a soft spot for goofy athletic types who throw money around. Poppsy was such a tightwad, doling out allowances on Friday night, grudging each bill as he passed it over. And where did it get him? A long time dead. Mary hears Michael's steady breathing. He looks beat.

She closes her eyes and sinks back in the sofa, relieved to be alone with the night and her thoughts. So much is changing. In middle age you think you should be on top of the world, but everything keeps shifting, the people you love, your sense of self. Imagining you can be in control is the mistake. You're tossed about from one thing to another by desire, greed, duty, lust. In college they said you grew through experience into a personality, something definable, something in control of its destiny, more or less. All Mary's professors talked about choice, free will, and doing the right thing. Nonsense, she thinks now. Everyone's a slave to drives they don't understand or even know about, repeating the same old mistakes. No one learns anything. You're tossed from one crisis to the next and make up your life as you go along. There's no willpower or destiny. And personality is an illusion, too. Mary hears a car swish by on the road outside. The air has density to it now, a density that says winter is on its way. In a few weeks the birds will gather for the flight south and she and Michael will rake leaves into green plastic bags. Sweaters. Gloves. Another year. She looks for taillights dancing through the trees. They remind her of the rows of lights on the big fins in the fifties, angora sweaters, doing the Cha Cha at Riverdale High, boys in leather jackets combing their hair back in ducktails, their secret parts down there like hard stretched rubber in your fingers and the way their mouths went dry on yours suddenly and they gasped. Nick Kontos. The girls made fun of his name behind his back. Married and divorced, he's living now with a woman he met in Hawaii on a business trip.

She remembers the greenish glow of the radio dial tinting the car's interior and Nick crushing her so she couldn't breathe. Such urgent strokes and then finished so soon. Some hard breathing and then nothing, that's sex. And life, too, when you think about it—all over before you learned how to do it right. It seems a cheat somehow, those mayflies come and gone in one day, the summer sun muscled out by the clouds of October, but what can you do except take it as it comes and make the most? Mary shifts on the sofa and takes Michael's hand in hers. "C'mon, big guy," she says, "time to go to bed."

* * *

Michael wakes with a start. 2:14. The bedroom window is open and the blinds rattle against the frame when the breeze teases in through the screen. Michael's stomach is in a knot. He probes it with his fingers. He should get up and take some Eno, burp the bad gases away, try to settle himself. He'll be awake now for a good hour and has the choice of tossing and turning in bed or maybe easing himself back to sleep with a scotch and hokey dialogue on the Late Show. But he doesn't want to get up and stalk the cold floors until dawn. He breathes deeply and closes his eyes. Why can't he sleep? Stephen claims he drops off within minutes of hitting the pillow and is out until the alarm goes at 7:30. Angela falls asleep in chairs. Mary snores gently through the dark. Even Fred, who, Mary tells him, has to carry around Maalox, sleeps. Only Michael lies awake studying the ceiling. What's wrong with him? What wakes him in the night and won't leave him in peace?

* * *

Now Michael is receiving hate mail. In late July he found a typed note in his letter box at the college: YOU PIECE OF DOG SHIT. The characters were faint and unevenly spaced, punched out on an old-fashioned typewriter. Reading the note Michael felt sick to his stomach, the way he had on the school ground when some secret everyone else was in on buzzed around his panicked ears. He chucked it in the trash. Teachers are used to harassment: notes shoved under their office doors, late-night phone calls. He convinced himself the note was a prank, a student's grudge that would be exorcised once the message was sent. But a week later an ordinary business envelope arrived with another note: YES, SHIT. This message was printed in block letters, reminding him of his first-grade teacher's perfectly formed characters. He put the envelope in a desk drawer and brooded about calling the police. Of course, he didn't. But the following week he avoided the mailbox. Then one morning a package came Special Delivery, a shoebox wrapped in brown paper and tied with string. He opened it at his office desk. Inside was a turd wrapped in toilet paper and an index card with this message: MICHAEL SAMUELS = DOGSHIT. He put the top back on the shoebox and sat for an hour, turning the index card over in his hands. He made a note of the date, 15 August. Because it smelled, he sealed the box with tape and put it on a high shelf in his office. It was then he flashed to the mystery gunman, it was then he knew he should call the police.

He'd had to get them in on a case like this once before. In his first year of teaching, Michael had been pestered by a student, a woman of forty with stringy blonde hair. Elaine something. She had been deserted by her husband and was getting a degree in social work. Michael felt sorry for her. He talked to her after class. That was a mistake. Elaine pursued him. She waited outside his lecture theater and tagged along with him to his office where she spent hours pouring out her life story: her husband had run off with a cocktail waitress, she had no money, a man down the street followed her from the bus stop. Michael nodded, he looked sympathetic, he tried to ease her out the door. When she persisted, he helped her arrange meetings with a psychologist, but she skipped those appointments and instead started showing up at his door on days when they didn't have classes. Michael employed ruses. He hid in the Common Room when he spotted her outside his office, he had colleagues tell her he was gone for the day. But she persisted. She sent him poems, thinly disguised erotica. He dodged. But one day, when he came out of the college, Elaine was waiting for him in the parking lot. She screamed at him and beat her fists on the roof of his station wagon. She had a knife, a paring knife with a green handle. She flashed it over her head. Said she'd kill him unless he'd go to a motel. Michael threw his briefcase at her. He bolted into his station wagon and drove to the police station. When the police sent him their final report, Michael discovered that Elaine's first baby had died a crib death and that she'd spent a year in a home for the mentally disturbed. In a quarrel she'd stabbed a city bus driver in the hand.

* * *

Michael shakes, thinking about this, as he climbs the steps to his office with the morning mail. A subscription notice from a local arts magazine, two bound midyear reports from mutual funds, and a plain envelope with his name scrawled in red ink. He sits at his desk with a cup of coffee before opening it. Inside he finds a printed letter.

YOU THOUGHT I'D STOPPED. YOU WERE RELIEVED. YOU HAD THOUGHTS OF GOING BACK TO YOUR LITTLE PIECE ON THE SIDE. I KNOW ABOUT THAT. YES. YOU'RE A MAN WHO ISN'T HAPPY WITH ONE WOMAN. FOR YOU A WIFE AND FAMILY ISN'T GOOD ENOUGH, YOU HAVE TO WRECK THEM. YOU ARE A SHIT. BUT THIS TIME YOU ARE IN SHIT. AND I'LL SEE YOU CHOKE IN YOUR OWN BLOOD. I'LL SEE YOU ROT IN HELL.

Michael reaches for the phone. Now he has to call the police. If it goes on longer he may not be as lucky as last time. He reads through the letter again. The paper is drugstore typing stock. Maybe he shouldn't be handling it. The things they can do with forensics now. His eyes stop at *your little piece on the side*, and he remembers suddenly the interrogation he went through when the cops were putting together a profile of Elaine—artists' sketches, sheets of sworn statements, endless explanations. Under the police microscope Michael had started to feel dirty and guilty. How much will they want to know about Angela?

As he sips at his coffee, he flips on the plastic radio propped on a bookshelf. He's missed the news but catches the sports and weather. The Jays are holding a two-game lead coming into the dog days. A hockey coach charged with indecent exposure in Buffalo pleads guilty. The Ontario Attorney General is prepared to investigate the mysterious circumstances behind a jockey's death. Weather mild for September. Michael looks out the window. On the quadrangle below boys in bright rugby jerseys are throwing a football, their voices cut off by the sealed windows which the college had installed along with air-conditioning last winter. Everybody's renovating. At one time the college took pride in its stone and wood appointments, but now the Council wants wall-to-wall carpeting and sealed tripane windows. He looks up. Fluffy clouds overhead. A good day for a run.

Michael lifts the receiver and dials Angela's number. He should go to the cops, but there's one more angle to pursue first. Colonel Shaw. Gunmen. Hate mail. These might be pieces of the same puzzle. He should talk to Angela before dragging her into a mess with the police. On the third ring her answering machine comes on. Michael says grave things, trying not to sound melodramatic, then he specifies a meeting place.

* * *

One day he's talking to Angela on the phone and he tells her about his dream, about the car and the man in the wire-frame glasses. He asks, why do I want to run someone down? Because, she says, you're afraid of death. Isn't everyone afraid of death? Yes, she says, but some accept death while others fight it. So it's a case of victims and survivors. If you are a survivor you understand that the death of someone else, because it is not your death, is a triumph over death, your own death—even if your understanding is only at the unconscious level. In dreams, say. He doesn't get it. He hears her click her tongue over the line. It's left-brain thinking, she explains, not right. The logic of psychology, not math, she explains. If someone else dies, then you don't. This is a comforting idea to the ego—or whatever. So you picture someone else as victim and yourself as the deliverer of death, and thus in a small way you control death. He's skeptical but intrigued. He asks, why do I dream about running down girls, then? Think about that, she says. What are they that you aren't? That you no longer are. Young. It's simple, she says, destroy kids and build up your own ego. Say to yourself it's not the old who die, but the young. Michael pictures Angela's blue eyes, the smooth skin on the backs of her hands. Who is the teacher here, who the student?

* * *

What about sex? he asks another day, remembering what Stephen said. Am I sleeping with you to defy death? No, Angela says, to know it. To take death into yourself.

* * *

Lunch is at a downtown place tucked between a shoe shop and a dry cleaner's, Astoria Pizza. Angela has picked a table against the back wall and waves to Michael when he hesitates in the doorway, adjusting his sight to the dim light inside. He steers between men in business suits drinking beer. At one time this place was called Couscous, but it never caught on with the white-collar types. Michael liked the okra dishes and the tang felafel left in his mouth, but nobody was into health food in those days, so the balding Libyan proprietor went under.

"Hi," he says, putting a hand on Angela's shoulder. He appraises her skin tone while he takes his coat off. "How are you?"

"You know," she says. She's wearing blush to highlight her cheekbones. "Now they're sending blood samples to Paris." Angela's blue eyes swim up to him. "*You* look harried."

"Harassed." She's ordered a beer for him, and he gulps at it greedily. "Thanks," he says.

"Such a mysterious message." She says this while ducking her head down to drink. "I love a mystery."

"You won't when you hear what it's all about." He sighs and drinks again. Nothing is ever easy. Angela plays with her napkin as she waits for him to settle. "I'm getting hate mail," he says. "Letters. Other things."

"Poison-pen letters?"

"That's a bit old-fashioned, isn't it? Dorothy Sayers?"

"Sorry," she says. She takes his hand in hers and squeezes it. "It's been very upsetting."

"I am sorry. What other things?"

"At first magazines which I didn't order. *Gun and Stream* kind of thing. *American Mercenary*. There were phone calls, too, but I didn't notice at the time, didn't think it was serious."

"And it is serious?"

"A turd wrapped in toilet paper."

"My, my." Angela bites her lower lip. "Human?"

"What difference does that make?"

She slides her school ring slowly up and down her finger. The color of the stone changes with the light, garnet then ruby. "This. You don't know who's been sending this stuff, correct?"

"Maybe." The draft beer tastes of wild flowers. Michael savors it before swallowing. "That shoebox with the turd is still sitting on my shelf," he adds. "It's beginning to stink even though I sealed it with tape. I'm sorry to be troubling you with this."

"Not at all. It's fascinating." She leans forward after she says this. The imitation candles in brass holders on the wall throw pale light which emphasizes the dark pockets under Angela's eyes. She looks tired but not sick. "You think it's a student?"

"Could be. Some creep festering over a bad grade. You know the sort of thing. Someone needs an A to get into medical school and blames me when he doesn't make it."

"Or she."

"How's that?"

Angela looks over her shoulder. At the table on one side men in suits are passing papers back and forth. The table on the other side is not occupied. Angela says in a hushed voice, "Most hate mail is sent by women—it's embarrassing to report."

"Women?" Michael strokes his beard. "Sounds strange."

"Veiled crime, criminologists call it. All very sneaky. There are some famous cases. Blue-hairs in small-town New England. Wives of executives passed over for promotion."

"Stranger yet."

"The strange part is a lot of cases involve dog shit. Smeared, usually, on paper or clothes."

"You think?" This description doesn't suit the fleshy-faced Colonel Shaw. Michael plays with his beer.

Angela shifts to let the waitress set a platter of pizza between them. When the waitress leaves, she tears off a piece and chews thoughtfully. "I'm hungry all the time," she says, "since I got this blood thing." She smiles at him briefly and continues, "You wouldn't predict that, would you? Hunger, I mean."

"I don't know. After we buried Uncle Charlie the whole family sat down to roast beef and potatoes, and later the men drank whiskey and the women tea and the aunts fixed cold cuts and cheese and rye bread. Death and hunger. There's some connection."

"I guess," she says.

When she's finished one piece of pizza she wipes her mouth

and Michael decides to take the chance. He leans in and says in a conspiratorial voice, "I thought it might be your father."

"You're kidding? The Colonel?"

"Why not?" Michael outlines Colonel Shaw's motive before explaining about the gunman and the mysterious 4X4. Her eyes widen when he describes the military outfit, when he mentions that the 4X4 appeared following her night at the cottage. She was enjoying the mystery aspect of Michael's story, but the suggestion that she has something to do with it starts her fidgeting. "So," Michael concludes, "that's why we had to talk before I went to the cops."

"That doesn't sound like the Colonel," Angela says. "As kids he put us over his knee. No pussyfooting around, you know?" She rolls a napkin between her fingers. "No, not the Colonel's style at all."

"So he hasn't said anything to you?"

Angela wipes crumbs from her lips and stares at her plate. She tears off another piece of pizza but says before she starts eating, "Tell me about the letters."

"One, really." From his coat pocket Michael produces the folded paper and passes it across the table. "I threw out an earlier one."

"Too bad." Angela reads. "Um. *Choke in your own blood*. That's ugly. Whoever's sending these has a sick mind."

"Exactly. It scares me."

Angela turns the note over in her hands. She looks at the blank side, then holds it up to the light. Finally she reads, "*You're a shit*." She gives him a penetrating gaze. "Do men say that to each other?" She's enjoying herself again, tracking down clues like the amateur sleuths in her detective novels.

He thinks of situations where he's been angry with his brothers. "I'd probably say *you're a bastard*—or *asshole*. But I don't know. This seems kind of crazy, reading back through phrases like this. Like astrology or something."

"Astrology?"

"Unscientific. Guesswork."

"I'm just trying to help."

"You're confusing me. I came here thinking it was your old man, but you've done such a great job of muddying the waters that my head's buzzing. I can't think who else it could be."

Angela shakes Parmesan over the remaining pieces of pizza. "Notice this," she says. *"You're a man who isn't happy with one woman.* A man wouldn't write that. He wouldn't say *a man* that way. But a woman would. Follow me?" Angela's lips purse as her eyes focus on the note again.

"Where did you get all this stuff?"

"From a course in criminology. Very illuminating."

"One course?"

Angela nods and lets a long silence pass before she asks, "What about your ex-wife?"

Though he hadn't thought of Patricia, Michael is adamant in answering, "That was a long time ago. Ten years."

"But why not her?"

"I haven't seen her in six months."

"Well," Angela says, "present or past tense may not be important." She takes the last of the pizza and eats it in three quick bites. "The important thing is, what's her life been like since then? Is she happy? Does she see a man regularly?"

"What's that got to do with anything?"

"Don't be so touchy." Angela reaches across the table and takes his hand again. Cool fingers. Her painted black nails give her a roué look that contrasts with her porcelain complexion. He finds it irresistible. "Some wounds don't heal," she tells him. "And women think differently than men. They fester. They want to get back, but feel powerless in a way that men, who are used to nice clean schoolyard scraps, can't understand."

"That's crazy," he says. But he's not so sure.

"Hell hath no fury."

"Well, Patricia vented plenty at me. She attacked me with a knife. She meant to kill me."

"You said. But that didn't take away her pain."

"Maybe," Michael says. He drinks his beer and waves his hand when Angela orders baklava for herself. Gas bubbles percolate in his stomach, the aftertaste of grease mixed with fear.

* * *

But while Michael's running later his mind circles back to the riddle like a tongue probing a cavity. Could Patricia be seriously sick? He mulls this over as he crosses the grassed yards of his Woodydell neighbors and climbs Wildwood Street in the falling light. In autumn the sky seems never quite the same from one moment to the next. Bright when he looks over his neighbors' chimneys toward the river, it turns violet as he and Ruggles turn north to mount the grade to Windermere.

He takes the asphalt loop around the park at half gait, saving himself for the home stretch. His lungs are beginning to protest, but the legs are still strong. He wants to push himself today, past pain to the high of exhaustion—he remembers it from high school. His legs seemed tireless then. He'd play a full game and then be able to dance in the crêpe-papered gym after. Like children's deep sleep, that won't come back again. Snapping towels around locker rooms, dense with steam and filled with jibes about condoms and girls. He scored forty-two points against Teulon—where he first saw Patricia—in the provincial finals.

Patricia. A farm girl with a big stride and a wide mouth, she dressed like no schoolgirl. She threw her clothes together the way kids do now, boots, blue jeans, and a black leather jacket, her hair a tangle of curls—as if stopping before the mirror on the way out of the house hadn't occurred to her. Michael liked her unkempt look. She wasn't dirty, but she was untamed. On her parents' farm she rode ponies bareback and helped her father pitch hay. She had big hands. She raised sheep, which her father thought foolish, tending a flock until she graduated from high school. During their marriage she hankered for a pet dog and fed neighborhood strays their table scraps. Could someone who cared that much for animals send hate mail to her ex-husband?

Panting, Michael pulls up at the war memorial and wipes his brow with his facecloth. He feels his heart pumping in his throat. Ninety-six beats to the minute according to that chest gauge when he did a trial run. At rest seventy-eight. He was sure he had it under seventy but these high-tech gadgets don't lie. Seventy-eight is high. He's in bad shape. Someone who doesn't smoke and who exercises should do better. Michael places one hand on his chest. He pictures blood and muscle exploding into the chest cavity, a frightening image which reminds him that two of his uncles died in their early fifties and his mother's father at fifty-six—all from heart attack.

He's running along Crescent Avenue now, up the gentle slope back to Point Road where Ruggles gets into a duel with an Irish setter behind a hurricane fence. Their barking upsets Michael and he shouts as he crosses to the far side of the street, his voice unexpectedly loud in the evening air. Even this early the houses seem secretively dark, their lamps throwing light on the plants and paintings inside—it's amazing how many of Michael's neighbors have cheap reproductions on their walls, Whistler's Mother, Gainsborough's Blue Boy, their taste beaming from over the mantle. But the lives inside are veiled. A father could be beating a child behind that aluminum door with the stylized flamingo, a wife could be poisoning her lover under those hanging ferns. We know nothing of each other, Michael thinks, glancing both ways at an intersection before loping past the stop sign. We pass on the street, we share an extension ladder, our kids play on the same teams. All surfaces. Inside we're embezzlers, adulterers, and murderers. Whose black heart isn't capable of dogshit in a shoebox? Michael's brain pounds with bloody thoughts as he climbs the grade toward the home stretch. Under the veneer of cheers at the ball park and advice on applying Tanglefoot lurk lusts and furies, thwarted ambition, love denied, sexual perversion. Rage. Violence. When Patricia stood above him with that knife, she meant to kill. Last week a teenager in Scarborough shot three classmates in the head and turned the gun on himself. We pretend life has order, the way it seems to in Victorian novels: virtue triumphs and morality wins out. But in our lives? There the daily fare is chaos, rage, lust, and madness. Gunmen lurk on beaches. Teenagers take baseball bats to a pensioner, a father blows away his kids with a shotgun. The surprising thing is not that somebody turns on somebody else every now and then, but that the mail isn't filled with shoeboxes of dogshit every morning.

Michael's knees jar now as he drops down Riverside past brick houses with curved drives along the Red River. His mother wanted to buy one of these places when they moved from Belvu to the city, but his father insisted on the split-level neighborhood across the river. Like so many of his generation, the old man's warped by the depression. Once he'd plucked a branch from a hawthorn bush in the backyard and struck Michael across the legs when he lost the grocery money. Not hard, his heart wasn't in it. But the lesson took root. Michael still feels awful if he doesn't have cash in the bank. He needs reserves and has many different bank accounts—savings, checking, T-Bill, so he won't get caught short. In nightmares he drops his wallet on the street and the wind blows bills along the sidewalk as he scrambles on hands and knees to recover them. Funny, since his stocks have done so well, he feels like a balloon going up over the city on a gust of warm air, but he still has those nightmares, waking at four with numbers on his lips. Lately, too, he's had nightmares about gunmen in watchcaps. Does someone really want him dead? Angela insists it can't be the Colonel, so who then? He can't imagine Patricia hiring a thug just to gain belated revenge.

She might send hate mail, though even that he doubts, but machinations with guns? Not after ten years.

Pain cuts into Michael's side as he jolts down bumpy Chester, an unpaved street running tangent to Woodydell and rutted by fall rains. Spasms flash down his spine. Almost home. He can push hard to the finish now. His mind careens. He remembers few run-ins with students over the past decade. Crazy Elaine moved to Calgary where she reunited with her husband and has a little girl now, she writes to tell him. Family. Why can't he get along with Jane? He pictures her waddling pregnant up the driveway, his baby making a baby, making him a grandfather. Could time really have gone that fast? Nature. It's pushing him out. Before he gets comfy there will be grandchildren, another generation. They grow up too fast. Just a year ago, it seems, he was helping Jane do homework, and now her breasts are matronly, her pelvis distended to drop the baby. She keeps to her room upstairs, where she reads magazines about infants and books of a strangely religious bent. She's got a new boyfriend now, a Jesus freak or something. When he passes in the hall Michael hears through her door not the thumping of rock music, but Jane chanting along with cassettes she got somewhere about natural childbirth.

He takes the dike along Wildwood, running Woodydell's perimeter to complete the circuit. Dry leaves scrape underfoot, autumn, and he breathes ghosts into the chill air, winter coming on. The homosexuals, Lenny and Albert, have their lights on, proving to the neighbors the normality of what goes on inside, he guesses. What does go on? In school there was a soft boy, Sheldon Busby, who was awful at games but a good ballroom dancer. Pansy, they called him, Pansy Busby, but no one had heard of gays then and they called each other cocksucker, not really knowing what it meant. The kids all know today with "Boys in the Band" on TV the other night and AIDS discussed in classrooms and Gay Liberation holding an all-gay film festival during August. Suck and fuck, the kids on the street called it. They know everything now. A whiz kid hacked into GE's computer last week, a group of high-school kids in California made a million bucks on the stock market, and street urchins under sixteen work as hit men for the Mafia, immune from the law. He feels sorry for kids growing up in the sewer that the country's become. His grandchild.

Ruggles is barking at squirrels now, chasing them high into the trees becoming denuded of leaves. Michael follows one as it leaps from branch to branch. The sky is darkening over Woodydell. Birds flitter through the bushes before bedding down for the night. Another day salvaged from cats. From death.

Running has cleared Michael's mind. He's not going to the cops, he's decided. Better to let well enough alone. What's to be gained by raising a fuss with the police? What profit in stirring up Angela in her condition? And then, he hasn't actually seen the guy with the rifle since Angela was at the cottage. What he has to do, Michael's decided, is get his priorities straight and act on them. That means easing out of the Angela thing. Only then will his troubles end—murderers with rifles, hate mail, guilt.

Coming around the bend near the private school, a car dips its headlights at him. He should be wearing fluorescent flash patches, but when he set out there was still light in the sky. Darkness sneaks up on the unwary this time of year. It breathes around him in the pines that shelter the school buildings from view. School. So long ago now. Miss Watson gave him licorice for his finger painting in the first grade and he beat out Charles Hancock for the public-speaking shield in the eighth. Tracey Boileau kissed him behind the hockey arena. Shorty Alexa tore his shirt fighting over marbles—and then they fought about that. He hated the Kozar brothers down the street.

The last five hundred yards of the run is downhill. He feels wobbly in the legs but his chest has expanded and, though burning, fills with triumph. He's pushed himself hard this time. If only he could manage it every day. Funny how the body floats that way, brain high from oxygen depletion. It soars like a balloon and flies free and makes him aware of how good life is. If it weren't for the hate mail and the gunman he'd be at one with the world. The thing with Angela will settle soon. Jane already has. It actually feels good having the kid under the roof again, hearing her pink slippers pad across the floor when he's watching TV with Mary and drifting off over a glass of scotch. The house ticking with young life. She shows them little outfits in catalogues and magazine articles on the breast-feeding debate, wondering what Mary's opinion is. She blushes a lot—he'd forgotten what a child she still is—and she's lost that hollow look around the eyes. From the study he hears her and Mary laughing at "SCTV" reruns. He can't remember the kid laughing much when she lived with them before.

In a minute he'll be home. Already he can see the roof of the house through the trees, lights ablaze in every room except his study. Mary will be at the kitchen table with the form chart. Tomorrow's Derby Day and she's talked him into spending it at the track. If he wins twice more than her, he'll have the better record for the season. Jane he'll find in front of the TV watching "Crime Story" and drinking soda water. Lately she's been looking through books of baby names. Solomon Michael, she thinks for a boy, and Alison Jean for a girl. Solomon?

Up the back steps and into the kitchen. He sits on the floor unlacing his sneakers, feeling his face flush with blood. Mary says that his jogging is bringing on heart attack, not putting it off. He pats her on the bum. Not to worry, he assures her. What would she do without him, little real-estate sharpie, have to take up with one of the Aramis cowboys she meets at conventions? He can picture them planning trips to Hawaii and selling Amway when real estate goes sour. No, he won't keel over on her. But he'll go all out to the end. That's just the point, he figures, push yourself to the limit and come out on top like the high rollers on Wall Street do.

Inside he starts to sweat, trickles running under his armpits and down the center of his back. Good. He leans against the wall and feels his lungs filling with air. The old ticker chugging away, thumping on and on to that good solid beat.

* * *

In the shower Michael fingers the fat around his waist, *the pouch*, he calls it. It doesn't bother him now as it did when he was turning forty and thought it would scare off women. Somehow it's had the opposite effect. Maybe women feel they can trust fat men. Maybe they want to mother them. Michael fingers the cords around his spine, the muscles running down to the groin. He pinches the pouch again and feels the greenness of bile rise suddenly to his mouth, but when he leans his head over the bathtub drain, nothing comes up. He lifts his head. Stars. Water clouding his eyes. From the far end of the house he hears the blurred noises of the television, the rumble of Jane's voice. He leans over the drain again. Forces one finger back in his gullet, then two. His free hand is propped against the mosaic tiles beneath the showerhead. Michael spits, then steels himself for one determined effort. When he forces his fingers down this time, his gorge goes into spasm, his guts rupture, like the guts of a caught fish ripped out when the fisherman yanks out his lure. Reddish stuff spatters the white tub, drips from his lower lip. Michael spits. He turns his open mouth to the showerhead. *All right*, he says to himself, *all right now*.

* * *

On TV the "Crime Story" lawyer, finally driven mad by the gangster who murdered his father and beat the rap by turning state's evidence, stands in the center of a plush living room with a pistol pointed at the gangster's head. Both men have greased-back hair and wear the baggy pants of the fifties. The lawyer's hand shakes, but just before he squeezes the trigger, the cop with the pitted face barges into the room, revolver trained on the lawyer. The gangster looks up and smiles, a weasel's smile, and this image becomes a freeze-frame.

"Ah cripes," Jane mutters. "They always do that." In the blue glow from the set her face looks white and pinched.

"Keep you dangling?" Mary sips Benedictine from a stemmed glass. "Like in soap operas?"

"It's maddening," Jane says. "Just once I'd like to see a gangster get what's coming to him. Good old-fashioned justice."

Michael looks up from his paper. He's sitting in the wing-back chair. Relaxed after his shower, a glass of scotch at his feet, he's studying the form chart. Mary's sure to bet on The Big Cheese, a winner last time out, but carrying twenty pounds more tomorrow. "Old-fashioned," he says, "but not good."

"Why not?"

"It's giving in to the same ugliness as the gangsters."

"No way," she answers. "Anyways, what's wrong with an eye for an eye?" Rage flares in her speech. Since moving back she's worked hard to please, but her pain keeps breaking through. Frustration.

Mary looks up from her fashion magazine. "Don't take it so seriously. Enjoy the acting, enjoy the sets." She asks Michael, "How about those old cars with fins?"

"Cadillacs. All the flash drive Caddies."

"What bugs me," Jane says, "is this kowtowing to the law. Everyone knows that cops are on the pad, that politicians are bought and sold by the Mafia, that the whole society's crooked. So why all this pretence about doing the right thing?"

"Wait a minute," Michael says. "Our cops do a pretty good job. I feel pretty comfy."

"Hah," Jane says. "This whole country's a mess and one place to start cleaning up is in our own backyards—schools, for instance."

"You've been watching too much TV," Mary says. "American TV."

"Exactly," Michael agrees. "That TV violence doesn't touch us." He rolls the amber around his tongue before swallowing. "Junkies may be stabbing folks in New York and gangsters shooting each other's faces off in Chicago, but we're okay here in snug Woodydell. We've got it pretty good."

"*Smug* Woodydell, you mean." Jane leans over his shoulder and squints at his notes on the newspaper in his lap. "What's that?"

She's had a bath, too, and smells of baby powder. Michael puts his arm around her waist. A child growing inside. His baby making a baby. "A strategy for beating Mary," he whispers, just loud enough for Mary to overhear. "At the track."

"He thinks." Mary laughs, a trickle of liquor on her lower lip. "Only the last time he was so sure of himself, I beat his pants off."

"Two lucky wins is not beating the pants off me."

Jane asks, pointing at the form chart, "What's PP?"

"Past performance." Michael runs one finger along the columns. "This final figure is the odds. What Mary doesn't mention is that though she's won two more races than me, I'm way ahead in cash terms. Almost a thousand bucks. She bets sure things, see—"

"Our deal," Mary interjects, "was who won the most. And right now that's me."

Michael laughs and has another swig of scotch. Good burning taste all the way to the stomach. "Well," he begins, intending to explain to Jane how to bet the ponies. "See—"

But Mary interrupts. "Sweetheart, Jane's been thinking about what she's going to do after she has the baby." Mary pats the sofa as she says this, signaling Jane to sit next to her. "She's thinking of doing a course at the college."

"Is that so?" Michael takes the paper from Jane.

"In real estate maybe."

"Maybe." Jane sits heavily beside Mary on the sofa and sips from her Coke. "Also I met this guy taking agriculture management."

"What's that?"

"Farming, Pa, only they throw in stuff about geography and environment as well as courses on livestock and book-keeping, too."

"So it seems like a real course."

"It *is* a real course."

"Farming?" Michael has to turn in the wing-back chair to look at Jane. Outside it's dark. Headlights from Wildwood Street splash into the trees when cars make the turn near Riverside.

"Or real estate," Mary says, giving him a look that means he should lay off Jane.

Great, Michael thinks, now his kid is throwing in with the hippie holdovers. "Do you know what that life's like?" he asks. "Getting up before dawn every day—there's no weekend on a farm, you know—mucking through cow dung and chicken shit for a measly living, the water pipes freeze every winter, the pump goes on the fritz and the guy who fixes it charges a hundred bucks to track mud through the carpet. Isolated, lonely, boring."

"It might be fun."

"Fun? Both your mother and I lived that way as kids and were only too happy to kiss it goodbye on the run, thank you very much."

"Actually, I've been talking to Mom about it," Jane says. She's holding Mary's hand in hers and the other over her swollen belly. "It's not so bad. On the farm you set your own pace and do things in your own time. Nobody's your boss." She glances at Mary, who nods once quickly, and continues, "And things are cheap. Fuel and stuff. You grow your own food."

Sure, Michael thinks, if you already have a place. The scotch is wearing off fast, the floating feeling turning into a downer. He asks, "Do you know what a farm costs these days with the Germans buying land at a thousand bucks an acre and more?"

Jane has an answer for this, too, and says sweetly, "Right now nobody's living on Grandpa's homestead."

Michael takes a deep breath and lets it out slowly. She has been talking to Patricia, and either doesn't know about the weeds growing through the floor and the pathetic rutted road which turns into bog at the first drop of rain, or won't admit to them. He should argue with her, but what's the point? The kid's made up her mind, and from the way they're cuddling on the sofa, has talked Mary around, too. A city girl, Mary's always had a fantasy about a country place with sheep and horses. He's lived on a farm, pumping water, walking on cold floors. But there's only one way to put the back-to-the-land fantasy to rest, and that's to cart the slops around for a while and smell the chicken shit. He says to Jane, "Peanut, it's your life. But you've got a baby to think of, too."

"That's just the point," Jane says warmly. "I can raise her away from the city. Away from all this pollution and noise. Crime."

"There's no crime in the country?"

"It's a more healthy place to bring up kids. More simple and—well—Christian."

Michael recalls her dough-faced boyfriend. His religious zeal must be rubbing off on Jane. Michael's not sure what's worse, punks or Jesus freaks, and he says, "You girls have this all worked out."

Mary says, "We talked." She casts a knowing glance at him over her glass of Benedictine and adds, "No conspiracy, though."

In a way he wouldn't mind if it was. He spends too much time worrying about Jane, so it's nice to see someone else taking charge of her for a change. Also the kid's idea isn't totally ridiculous. Everybody today is talking about self-sufficiency and subsistence economies. He clears his throat and studies his paper. Columns and figures, order and clarity.

"Talk to your friend again," Mary says to Jane. "Then we'll look at all the courses and see what we come up with."

"Especially the real estate," Michael says. The kid could learn a lot from Mary and not have to go traipsing off into the sticks with a baby on some hippie mission for God.

"*All* the courses," Mary repeats. "And next time we'll talk, not pick at each other."

"I wasn't picking." Michael drinks the remainder of the scotch. Burn without buzz, the pleasure's been drained out of it, too.

"I'll take the cassette player upstairs," Jane says.

"Do that." Mary pats Jane's hand and gives her a knowing nod. "We'll see you in the morning."

"Goodnight, Pa."

"Goodnight, peanut."

Jane's pink-slippered feet pad along the hall—then silence when she hits the carpet in her bedroom. Michael gazes abstractedly out the window at tree trunks silhouetted by the streetlights on Wildwood. Woodydell is still at this hour, a suburb cloaked in midnight, but it's his place, silent and familiar. He's happy to sit and listen to the harmless thumping of his heart.

Mary uses the remote control to find the late news. Fiddles with the volume. He puts his paper aside and looks at her, slippers propped on the hassock her mother sent as a housewarming gift, eyes intent on the flickering screen. There is a calm at the center of Mary that he longs to drift into like a foundering ship escaping a storm. She looks up at him and smiles. "You *were* picking."

"I know. Just to hold my own."

"Against your own daughter?" She laughs. "You're some case."

"You laugh?"

Michael gets up for a last scotch. Maybe he can find that place where he floats again and ride it to bed. Maybe Mary will be up to something later. While he's pouring Benedictine in her tiny glass, the market news comes on. "Look," she says. "The Dow is down again."

"Again?" In the past week he's been occupied with other things, and this is news to him. He turns to say so but she cuts him off by turning up the volume. The announcer says the index has fallen one hundred and seven points in ten days. Michael whistles. That's the biggest drop since 1974.

"But still way up from a month ago," Michael says.

"Right."

"But you're worried."

Her eyes turn to his. "It doesn't look good, does it?"

"A little fluctuation," he says. For all her sales success, Mary lacks the brashness to be a good player. To ease her mind he adds, "One day up, the next down. That's why it's called a market."

"You're sure?"

"Nothing's sure. But we're okay for the short run." But is this true? Michael's broker is a white-haired man near retirement who confided to Michael that he lost a bundle in the sixties' recession. "We've got bonds, we've got cash. If stocks start to fall we can always get out."

"Let's hope so," Mary says and sips Benedictine while the announcer runs through the day's gainers and losers. As he goes down the list, Mary's face gets tighter and tighter. She tips the liqueur glass to her mouth but her eyes stay riveted to the set. She's figuring their gains and losses, Michael guesses, going over the numbers in her head. He sips, too, and breathes deeply to calm his heart. After a while reruns of "Maude" come on and then there's nothing to do but go to bed.

Three

The market stumbles through September, up for a week after the British government announces the sale of BP and down almost two when a U.S. frigate is attacked by Syrian bombers in the Persian Gulf. Promising reprimands, the pale and shaky President forgets part of his speech on TV and looks helplessly into the camera with watery eyes, and the Dow plummets another forty points the following morning. When gold soars to five hundred dollars an ounce, Michael panics. The TSE has dropped almost ten percent since its high in August. If the bottom falls out he could lose thousands, plus the house—mortgaged for a leverage loan—and even the cars. He calls his broker who tells him to sit tight and wait out the correction, but prices continue to fall. Shares of Dome Petro drop as Shell and

Amoco drag takeover proposals out of the boardrooms and into the courts. Daily Michael studies the business section of the paper. He and Mary stay up to watch the market report on the late news. They sell their shares of Galveston the day the Blue Jays lose the final game of the season to the Tigers—but they sink the proceeds into T-Bills before the Cardinals and Twins square off for the World Series. What else can they do? Leave it in the bank where it collects five percent interest?

On the Friday before Thanksgiving the Connors invite Michael and Mary for dinner. For the past few years the two couples have been visiting each other on alternate weekends to share a meal and play canasta. They play in teams, women against men, and listen to old LPs, the Everly Brothers, the Mamas and Papas, as they shuffle and take tricks between peanuts and cold drinks. But this Friday, Stephen tells Michael over the phone, is different: he's bought a pool table and has laid in, he laughingly reports, champagne to christen an era of eight ball in his basement.

The evening is warm. Michael stands in the yard waiting for Mary with a bottle of Rémy Martin clutched in his hand. Some hardy birds hanging on after the first frost twitter in the trees. He scans the sky. By this time most years the geese have begun their long journey south. The moon is a slice of silver over the gays' house, lit up as usual, figures moving from room to room. They seem always to be having people over, barbecuing in the backyard once the weather breaks in spring, and playing badminton on the lawn over summer. Shouting, laughter. At first Michael felt threatened by them, but now he feels strangely possessive. He puffs into the air and looks for traces of breath in the moonlight. It's warm for this time of year. Another greenhouse effect? At Willow Point, where they're going for Thanksgiving dinner tomorrow, the trees will be bare and the beach deserted, though these thoughts of absence are comforting to him, not disturbing. Twice recently he's fallen asleep in a chair on the deck and has wakened stiff and cold, wondering if this is some sign he should take note of. Maybe he's started the soft decline into senility.

On the walk over he asks Mary, "You get the goose?"

"This morning," she says. She smells of shampoo and the shower, good smells, and he takes her hand as they mount Wildwood Street. She adds, "Fred and I were in the north end and stopped on Selkirk." She drags the toe of one shoe along the grass bordering the sidewalk. "It's a big bird," she says, "but it's mostly fat."

"Like me." Michael tugs at his belt. Lately he's been packing it on. Booze, rich food. And the exercise program has not really worked. Not even fretting about hate mail or brooding about Angela burns much off.

"Including the steaks I spent over fifty dollars."

Michael whistles. "The Rémy was over sixty. I remember it at fifteen bucks."

"When houses in Woodydell sold for twenty grand." Mary laughs and squeezes his hand. "We're starting to sound like old fogies."

Michael does not laugh because this makes him think of his parents, living on less than a hundred thousand in the bank, which brings them an annual income of ten thousand, maybe less. There's old-age pension and social security, too, but it doesn't seem right, skimping and saving the way they did, to see their last years pinched by inflation, years when they should be traveling and spoiling their grandchildren. He asks Mary, "Where'd Jane get this idea about a farm anyway?" In the side of his vision he sees her patting stray hairs into place. When she shakes her head, he adds, "Watching too many of those 'Twenty Years Ago Today' TV specials."

"How do you mean?"

"Oh, the roots of rock and roll, Woodstock. That stuff. It's turning a generation into back-to-the-land couch hippies."

"Jane is not a hippie," Mary says. When they turn at Windermere she slips her hand onto his elbow. "She's quite conservative."

"She swears like a trooper."

"Not since this new boyfriend. Anyway, that was all show, the tough girl act. She really wants a color TV and Royal Doulton china—and she's scared she won't get them."

"I had to work for stuff like that," Michael says. It bothers him that his kids take so much for granted. "I have to bust my ass to get on top and the kids just waltz in and take over."

"Oh pooh," Mary says. "Don't be irrational."

By which she means she never is. He breathes the night air, tasting again oaky scotch on his palate and the vinegar pinch of the black olives he was munching while Mary dressed. Down Windermere the pulsing streetlights throw a moonscape pall over the neighborhood. Michael half expects a threatening figure to emerge from the shadows, and he glances quickly over his shoulder. Nothing but the arms of tree branches, swaying in the breeze. Still, he feels something like dread. Maybe it's a memory trace of the time before Woodydell was developed, when odd things occurred beneath these trees—murdered babies, crimes of passion. He looks at his neighbors' windows, reflecting greenish light from the streetlamps hovering above. Blank.

Mary tugs his arm again and Michael suddenly wants to tell her about the hate mail and the mystery gunman. He dislikes secrets. But he weighs the consequences and keeps silent. Instead he asks, "Who is this new guy of Jane's?"

"Arnold something. He came to pick her up in a beat-up van, and he wore work boots. I think he's a Bible-thumper."

"Really?"

"Just something Jane said when we came home from the track."

"The track?"

"About betting being a sin."

"God. She's so simple-minded."

"Not really. She's young and judgmental. But that will pass. Like acne and heavy-metal music. All in good time."

Michael's happy to hear her confiding tones. "And you're so sensible," he says, pulling her shoulder against his in a rough hug, feeling her blonde hairs twitch his nose. "So you think we should help Jane out?"

"With the course at the college, yes." Mary puts her arm around his waist and they walk like young lovers. "Maybe even the farm."

"I don't want to, you know. Give the kid more money."

"Then why don't you say so?"

"I have." Leaning forward to whisper, he smells that perfume again. When did she start wearing lily of the valley?

"I mean why don't you thrash things out with Jane—instead of always leaving them dangling?"

"You know me."

"Only too well. The artful dodger."

"I prefer to let things slide."

"Someday you're going to have to face things and act, Michael." Mary pulls away from him as they start up the Connors' walk. Her eyes are bright with moonlight when she says to him, "You can't keep running scared forever."

* * *

Inside, the Connors' house smells of lemons and roast beef. "I thought you said pizza," Michael says to Stephen as he throws his jacket over the back of a chair and passes him the Rémy Martin.

"You can't keep him away from that gas barbecue," Kelly calls from the kitchen. She pokes her head around the archway and says, "He's talking now about moving it into the garage for the winter." On the table an open bottle and two glasses wink champagne. Kelly is at the counter that divides the kitchen from the dining room, squeezing lemons over lettuce. "Isn't that just like a man," she adds, "thinking that the dozen times he barbecues a roast balance off the thousands when he's got his feet up watching football."

Stephen turns to them with an affected harried-husband look. He places the cognac on a side table where bottles of red wine stand ready. He brings two more champagne glasses to the table and pours into them before topping up the others. "Well," he says, "if you're game, there's just enough time to try that pool table before the roast's done." He reaches his glass over to Michael's, clinking it, and adds, "Here's to the canasta players."

* * *

After the champagne toasts the women decide they don't want to play eight ball, so Stephen and Michael take the open bottle with them into the basement where Stephen racks and then breaks. The three ball drops, making Stephen stripes. He moves around the table deliberately, studying the angles of shots. The room is paneled and lined with bookcases. Michael runs one finger along the spines of some novels while he waits for Stephen to shoot, noting that his friend, though quiet, is chewing his lower lip. He has something on his mind, but he's not the type to come right out with it.

Michael looks around. A few photographs hang between the bookcases, Stephen and Kelly on a hiking expedition many years ago, Kelly with hair down to the middle of her back hippie-style, another of Stephen with one arm around his father, a small dark man, the two of them leaning against a 1959 Ford. Stephen's father, Michael recalls, played semi-pro ball as a young man. "Well," he says, "the Jays took gas again." Losing three to Milwaukee and then four in Detroit, they blew a two-and-a-half-game lead going into the final week.

"Batting," Stephen mutters. "Their bats just died." He's missed the five ball to the side pocket and is inspecting his cue.

"Those macho dudes from the Caribbean." Michael leans over the table. "Bell comes up and every time he's swinging for the fence. All he thinks about is home runs when safe singles start rallies just as well."

Stephen shrugs. "He did it all year, he wanted to do it again."

"You have to put the team first," Michael says. He, too, has missed his shot, and he rests the cue against the table as he picks up his glass of wine. "A little less macho and a little more brains might have won it all for them."

"They'll be back next season. Older and wiser."

"I'm not so sure. Teams come and go, what with trades and free agency and injuries. That was probably the Jays' last shot at the series this century."

"I like them," Stephen says, ever the optimist. "Besides, sometimes change is good. Look what it did for the Expos." Neither of them likes Carter, and they delighted in Montreal's showing without him, so they nod agreement about this as Stephen leans in to shoot. When he scratches off the cue ball, Michael lines it up at the far end of the table and sinks the six. Good sound, stone striking stone. There was a parlor in the Belvu barbershop where Uncle Charlie took Michael as a kid, and thirty years later, the pock of billiard balls and Uncle Charlie's gruff laugh come back to him when he smells after-shave. He chalks the cue, considering his next shot.

"I had a beer yesterday—with a friend of yours."

Michael hears the conspiratorial hush in Stephen's voice but is busy lining up the four ball in the end pocket. College politics, Michael thinks, somebody trying to parlay a handful of conference papers into a full professorship. "Who would that be?"

"Angela Shaw."

When Michael looks up, his eyes and Stephen's reflexively shift toward the stairway. They can hear words from Mary and Kelly drifting down and the thump of feet padding across the floor. Michael imagines their wives sipping champagne and picking at the olives in the salad. Over the years they've become great companions. They enjoy beating Stephen and Michael when they play canasta.

"A lovely girl," Michael says finally.

"A spectacular girl."

The four ball heads for the pocket after Michael strikes it, but as it nears the end of the table, curls wide. "A little bit of a tilt there," he says. "I noticed it earlier, too."

"I'll get a book," Stephen volunteers. "Prop it up."

While he's busy jamming a small volume of poetry under one of the legs, Michael sips champagne. The bubbles tickle his nose and he sniffs and then pinches his nostrils between his thumb and forefinger. "But otherwise," he says, tapping the tip of the cue on the molding, "it's a great table."

"The guy said they sell more of these than any other model."

"I can see why. Good roll, nice feel."

Stephen makes a gentle tapper into the side pocket and stands at the wall drinking, the game momentarily suspended.

"Tell me," Michael says, pondering a mental image of Angela and Stephen huddled over a table somewhere, "do you still think I'm an idiot?" He feels odd about Angela and Stephen getting together. A little resentful. But relieved, too, that Stephen has met Angela, someone he can confide in.

"I never thought you were acting the idiot," Stephen says. "Things happen. *That's* what I thought."

"So," Michael says, "now you know the whole story."

"I don't know much at all, actually." Stephen licks his lips after drinking and sets his glass on a shelf. "She did say something about being sick."

"She told you that?"

"Yes. About a blood condition, or something."

"She's dying."

"Good Lord. She never said that."

"Let me tell you," Michael says, "it's got my head turned

around. The betrayal was bad enough. The guilt. Christ, then she tells me she's dying. I can't take this stuff any more. I've lost the resilience, the stamina." Michael shakes his head. He wants to make this all clear but he's talking around what's at the root of it. "Tell me," he asks, dropping his voice, "what do you do when things get you down?"

"I run," says Stephen. "Nothing like a good sweat to empty body and mind."

"I do, too," Michael says wryly, "but not the way you mean. So far I've been running away. And drinking. Brooding and drinking and counting the cracks in the ceiling at four in the morning."

Now Stephen shakes his head. He stoops for the bottle of champagne on the floor and pours first into Michael's glass, then his own. Michael tastes the tartness in his mouth. Above he hears Mary burst into laughter and then Kelly's voice saying, *Right up the front of her bathing suit!* Water lines surge when a tap is opened. Stephen asks, "Whose shot is it?"

After Stephen nubs the cue ball, Michael puts his glass down and leans over the table. Four in the side, he isn't fooling with that end pocket any more. He enjoys that good solid *thunk* when the ball hits the bottom of the webbing. Ten in the far side. Twelve off a double bank. He moves around the table and sights the black. Eight ball in the side. Game over. When he takes his glass back he says to Stephen, "It's eating me up inside. I can't sleep."

Stephen nods in sympathy but doesn't say anything.

"What I mean," Michael asks, "is how do you shake off the blahs? Say if you wake up in the middle of the night with something turning your gut inside out?"

"I drink hot milk. Though to tell you the truth, that doesn't happen too much. Maybe take a walk. Once I went for a long drive in the country and ended up too tired to drive back. I slept by the roadside until dawn. That was years ago."

"I've been watching the late movie. But it's not working."

They stand in silence for a moment, looking at the green felt of the billiard table, listening to the sound of someone flushing the toilet upstairs. The voices of Mary and Kelly sound closer, as if they're moving toward the basement. Stephen strokes his chin and Michael probes his stomach as if trying to loosen a knot.

"Sometimes I wonder if I'm just drifting," Michael finally says. "Do you think I've made a mess of things?"

"I don't think it matters." Stephen has crossed his arms over his chest, but still holds a glass in one hand. "Or rather, it doesn't matter what you've done in the past."

"No judgment, then?"

"No judgment."

Michael nods. "I used to think you were a moralist."

"Far from." Stephen has the champagne bottle by the neck and is pouring for them. "But I care about you."

"Moralists want to improve you. Do you think people improve?"

"They learn things as they get older, maybe they avoid the errors they made earlier in life. The really big mistakes."

"I don't think anyone improves." Michael looks at the floor and then around the room for a place to put the cue. He leans it against a bookcase. "Not one whit. And when we offer advice, it falls on deaf ears. And after a while on stone hearts."

"Have some more champagne," Stephen says. He clinks his glass against Michael's. "And cheer up," he adds. "Your eyes are starting to bug out that way—like a toad's."

"You know what else I think, Stephen?"

"What?"

"I think I've spent most of my life trying to understand things and it hasn't made a damn bit of difference. We don't understand life, we pass through it."

"If you're going to get philosophical on me, I'm going upstairs to play canasta with the women." Stephen smiles to let Michael know he's not serious.

But his warning isn't necessary.

"I am becoming a bit pathetic," Michael says, sighing. Idly he fumbles with the spines of books on the shelves. He has let his fingernails grow too long and one snags on a frayed spine as he muses over Stephen's library, and he bites it off with his teeth. "But she is a wonderful girl," he says finally. "She graduated at the top of her class. She's on the university golf team. A project she did for a design class has been bought by a firm in Toronto. We talk for hours, you know?"

"She thinks you brood about things. Her, for one." Stephen twirls his wine glass by the stem as he speaks. "That's why she talked to me. So I could reassure you. She seemed to think you wouldn't believe her."

"That's what she asked you to tell me?"

"That she means it when she says she doesn't want anything from you. We had a drink at the student pub. She told me about her trip to Central America last summer. I liked her candor and the way her face lit up as she talked." Stephen looks from his glass to Michael and back to his glass again. "Nothing threatening."

Michael wishes this were true. The meeting between Stephen and Angela has changed things. He'd been pretending that nothing was happening, that things with Mary were the same as always, but with Stephen in the picture now, his betrayal feels real. It frightens him. Michael coughs into his hand. Stephen doesn't seem to have anything else to say, and when he shifts from one foot to the other, Michael adds, "It was all pretty innocent, you know. We talked. We walked a lot. I had the feeling she needed someone to confess to. I was more a father to her, really. And it's over."

Stephen looks as if he doesn't believe this. He sighs and nods, waiting for Michael to say more. But Michael is staring at the blank basement window and wondering if he should tell Stephen about the hate mail, the gunman. While he's trying to decide, Stephen says, "I hear the women coming down."

The door opens at the top of the stairwell and Kelly's voice rolls down to them, ". . . so we decided to spend our cash while we've still got it." The clatter of heels on the steps and a moment later Mary and then Kelly come around the partition into the room. Kelly says to Stephen, "I was just telling Mary they should come south with us after Christmas."

"Great," Stephen says, looking from Mary to Michael. "We're flying to Guaymas in January. The sun, snorkeling, tequila sunrises, and the most joyful sound of all, the chink of dollars being converted into pesos."

Michael asks, "Guaymas, that's Mexico, right?"

"The Pacific coast," Kelly says in a bright voice. "Not really very much south of California."

"But a totally different feeling," says Stephen, anticipating objection, "from either California or Acapulco. Still pretty much unspoiled by urban blight, considering."

"We've never been," says Mary. She likes lying in the sun near warm water, but she asks, "Isn't it kind of—well, Club-Meddy?"

Stephen says, "Depends where you go. What kind of package."

"The sun," Kelly says, "just sinks into you down there."

"This time we have to find a place with tennis courts," Stephen says. "Or at least golf. I don't mind sitting with a book for a few days, but that gets boring. I start to drink too much. Get sunburned." Stephen turns and says to Michael, "You'd like it."

Michael tans poorly. He gets headaches if he drinks in the sun—and a flushed face. But he likes to watch that little switch in Mary's gait when she walks on the sand in a bathing suit. He asks, "What about the water? Montezuma's revenge?"

"Stick to the bottled stuff," Stephen says. "That's what I do."

Mary says, "He's getting that look. Like what could go wrong." She hooks her arm into Michael's and gives it a tug. "Come on," she urges him. "It'll be fun."

"I like the idea," he says.

162

Kelly says, "The week right after New Year. Do the family thing with the turkey and then take off for the sun." She says to Michael, "The food is super. Fish, which I know you love, cooked in hot sauces and served on rice. Mussels, clams, scallops. You sit on a balcony overlooking the ocean and watch the moon rise as you drink coffee and liqueur. All laid on with the price of the hotel."

"Speaking of food," says Stephen, "we should get at that roast." He tips back the remainder of his wine and smacks his lips. He says to Mary, "Get the big guy to cash in some of those stocks and let us know. First week after New Year."

* * *

In bed Mary asks, "So what do you think about Mexico?"

Her voice probes Michael's alcohol-soaked brain. Burgundy, cognac. Later, in the living room where they talked about Baby M, Turkish coffee. Michael feels it tightening his chest. He's buried his face in the pillows. He needs to lie perfectly still until he drops into sleep. "Mexico's okay by me," he says.

"Seriously." Mary flounces, straightening her nightdress under the quilt. Each movement registers in Michael's skull.

He opens his eyes. Turning on his side, he looks directly out the window into the stars. Funny. He likes to have the blinds up so he can ease into darkness, but Mary likes them down to block out the morning sun. He'll pull them when he gets up to pee in the early hours. Outside the wind has come up and is shaking the elms in the backyard. By morning the lawn will be covered with broken twigs from the golden willow. Sometimes he fills a whole garbage can after a night's blow. A nuisance, that tree, dropping branches all year and snowing the yard with leaves in fall, but Michael feels a sentimental attachment to it. It reminds him of an old man with knobby knuckles, hanging on. The moon which was a slice of silver earlier is brighter now with winter iridescence.

In a month, there will be two feet of snow, and ice to scrape from the windshield. "The sun part sounds great," he says. "But how much will it cost?"

Mary sighs dramatically, hinting that he should forget about cost, and says, "The exchange rate is ten to one or something. So even things that seem expensive are actually cheap."

Though she calculates her commissions to the last dollar, Mary is often vague about money. She goes shopping with a hundred bucks and returns with a book and a scarf and eleven dollars change. She's a spendthrift. But Michael doesn't mind. She doesn't hassle him about his scotch and he says nothing about her spending. There are more intimacies in marriage than those of the bedroom. Michael's dry tongue sticks to the roof of his mouth. He'd like to drift off, but Mary says, "Anyway, that's not it, really, is it? Money?"

"How do you mean?"

She strokes his cheek. "You know."

For a moment he thinks she means Angela—and he stops breathing. "I don't," he finally says.

"You're scared."

Miserable is what Michael feels, a heaviness that descends on his chest. His heart pounds the way it does after a long run. Though he would dodge out of the next few minutes, he can think of no way—not even silence—to avoid what's coming. He says balefully, "Everybody's scared. The oceans are drying up, the whole planet's on the run, for godssake."

"True. But not everybody's as old-fartish about things as we are. Things like traveling."

"But we've got one of the finest beaches in the world right out the front door."

"It's been a curse in some ways."

"In what way?"

"Too easy to fall back on."

"We don't fall back on it. We *like* it."

"It's been wonderful. But maybe we need to do something different. Maybe we need a change."

Michael closes his eyes. So that's what this is all about. Green shafts of light pass along his lids and mark the pulsing of blood in his temples. "You think?"

"It's just that other people aren't stuck." When Mary stops stroking his face, the skin tingles where it's been touched. "Ten years ago you always took chances. That's what I loved about you."

True. Ten years ago Michael enraged his children and parents as well as ruining Patricia's life by taking a chance with Mary—and the heartache was almost more than he can bear to recall. "We've drifted a long way," he says, "from Acapulco."

"Guaymas. Not really." She pinches her mouth into a look of thoughtfulness and closes her eyes. "Change is change—you can use it or get swept up by it. But you can't fight tidal waves, sweetheart, only ride them. So the best thing to do is grab your surfboard and make the best of it."

"Surfboard!" Michael laughs. Where does she get these ideas? He touches her face now and says, "This is a good lecture, honey. But I'm truly whipped."

"Right," she says. "I'm talking too much." When she rolls onto her back Michael closes his eyes. Silence. He hears a siren wail out on chilly Pembina. Then it fades into the south end of the city, an ambulance probably, rushing to someone's bedside. Things could be worse, Michael thinks. Heart attack, stroke, death. He listens for Mary's breathing and tries to imagine sleep as a black hole he's slowly sliding into. After a few moments Mary says, "You would like it, you know? Mexico."

* * *

Michael dreams of walking along the beach with gulls wheeling overhead, the sand wet and squeaky underfoot. There are vast spaces around him, an emptiness like fog into which he'd like to walk and disappear forever. He sits on rocks watching waves wash up the shore and smells dead fish, dead fishflies, and human refuse on the beach. When he wakes he feels lonely, troubled. He sleeps again, and this time dreams that he and Stephen are arguing as they play eight ball. Shouting. When Michael picks the cue ball off the table, he sees that Stephen is cradling a rifle in his arms, and that he's wearing a black leather jacket. Michael tries to say something and wakes abruptly, thinking, *totally out of place.*

* * *

At 4:50 Michael is awake. Pounding in his head, pressure on his bladder. He slips out of bed and, dodging the corner of the dresser, starts momentarily when he sees his reflected shadow leap forward as he crosses in front of the hall window Forster installed to give the back of the house more light. He splashes cold water on his face and rubs both eyes with his knuckles. The taps are cold to the touch, the metal drug cabinet glints moonlight as it swings open on its hinges. Taking four aspirin daily, *Newsweek* claims, reduces heart attack, but he takes it for his joints. He drinks two glasses of water and runs his tongue round the inside of his mouth, tasting bacteria built up from food and drink. He should brush his teeth but he'll do that first thing in the morning when he won't disturb Mary.

Back in the bedroom he stands in the bay window, also a recent Forster addition. It looks into the backyard—though, jutting out, it also gives a perspective of the Yims' bedrooms. All is dark and silent there. Everyone's asleep. It will be difficult for him to slide into that black hole again tonight, Michael thinks. Behind him Mary sleeps, her breathing light and steady. He used to dream about her, sexy scenes where he cornered her at parties and put his hands on her breasts. Now he has nightmares about gunmen and blood.

On the lawn outside he sees in the palette of moonlight

falling between the houses the tennis ball he tosses for Ruggles
to fetch. It's getting soaked by dew and rain—and, soon
enough, snow. Why is it dogs are so happy doing the same
thing over and over? Ruggles drops the slobbery ball at
Michael's feet and waits for the next toss. And the next. A
human wouldn't do that. Not even a child. After only a few
months a child gets bored with repetition games. "Throw me
again, Daddy," Jane cried, bouncing in his lap, but one day she
turned three and that game ended suddenly. Then she started
to be unhappy. She'd learned to want more than repetition, and
that marked the beginning of unhappiness.

This saddens him. He feels chilled and pulls on a sweatshirt.
During their days in the Furby Street apartment he often sat up
half the night in the wing-back chair waiting for sleep to come.
Guilty. Behind him Mary stirs, and he looks to see if she is awake.
One breast spills out of her nightgown, large pink nipple. She's
great in bed. But is she happy with him? Her face tells him
nothing. She looks angelic, but for all he knows, she could be
screwing the tennis pro or one of the neighbors. Watching her
sigh into the pillows, he wonders if she's capable of betraying
him. Yes, he thinks, but it's not likely. Mary, too, has had enough
of that heartache.

Out the window he sees something dart across the street into
the caraganas bordering the Yims'. Fences are not allowed in
Woodydell, but low hedges in backyards are. A cat probably. He
hates them. Sneaky mean creatures, their piss permeates carpets
and lingers in basements. He'd kill them, he says to himself in a
half whisper, and with a two-by-four stud. Why does he think
that? He'd never deliberately injure an animal—though he
remembers Uncle Charlie chasing a tangerine cat around his
Belvu yard one summer day. With a two-by-four? Yes. A cat
which had pounced on a baby chipmunk Uncle Charlie had been
feeding and had tamed into eating from his hand. "Sneaky
bastard," Uncle Charlie screamed when the cat dived under the

woodshed. The baby chipmunk was dead, Uncle Charlie was weeping. After, he told Michael, "Never trust a cat." Also, "Mikey, you want too much from this world, and when things don't work out, you go off in a huff. Learn to take life easy, learn to let go."

And now he remembers, too, a day years ago when he glanced out the window and saw a neighbor's cat with a baby robin. The cat sat on its hind legs toying with the bird, letting it loose, then pouncing again. Michael ran to the back door. He searched for something to throw. On a ledge near the door stood a beer bottle he'd used for mixing bug spray. When he opened the aluminum door the cat bolted, making for the hedge, bird in its mouth, but Michael got off his shot. He was hurried and threw out of reflex, but he struck the cat in mid-stride. It flipped over and lay still. The baby robin hopped under some bushes. By the time Michael crossed the yard, the bird had scurried out of sight. The cat was dead. Michael rolled it over. A single drop of blood clung to its tongue.

He's cold and looks down at his feet, expecting them to be blue. His toes are large and bony. Angela laughs at them. She says he should cut his nails more often, that his toes cramp up in his shoes. Some wonderful kid she is, worrying about him when she's dying of a blood syndrome. That doesn't stop her having appetites. At the Swiss Chalet she eats half a chicken with fries and gravy and cleans up his leftovers, lips greasy with hunger. And she loves him in a way he finds disturbingly expert, holding a twist of hair back with one hand while the other guides him to her mouth. She likes coming on top where she rides him into exhaustion, in her eagerness showing no restraint while his old heart beats wildly and his back goes into spasms. Also she likes kissing him after he's been at her down there, kissing the wild musk of her other lips, kissing herself, really. Strange how we make love to ourselves, Michael thinks—with mirrors, with lovers' mouths. Maybe there's something to the Greeks' story about how humans were first hemaphrodites and then were split in half by God and made to wander the world searching for the lost half. To find oneself to love.

Groggy and hungover, Michael feels his thoughts expanding toward nonsense. The dark lawn outside seems to rise toward the window. Ruggles running after tennis balls. *Here boy, good dog.* Bringing back not balls but dark sticks, branches of black bark in his slobbery mouth. Totally out of place. Black bark of elm. Its branches loom suddenly and Michael's heart surges with blood. A man with a gun leans against black bark. His bark is worse than his bite. A voice says, *dogshit, totally out of place,* and for a second Michael feels the seductive release that comes just at the moment of sleep—and then he starts awake again, heart thumping.

He glances at the clock radio. 5:20. No light yet on the horizon. *Totally out of place.* What was that all about? Totally out of place. Isn't that what the kids say, totally awesome, totally radical? He wiggles his toes. Cold. As ice. As death. If he gets back in bed he'll toss and wake Mary, but if he stays up he may tire enough to sink back into the tide of night. He can sit in the wing-back chair and wake with the first light coming in at the window.

He studies the slip of moon high in the sky over the private school. How long did it take the astronauts to get there? He recalls sitting round the TV with friends and listening to the crackle of Neil Armstrong's voice. *It's very pretty out here.* Nearly twenty years ago, when he was at his first teaching job, and only a decade or so after Sputnik. Now there's change for you. Looking back from the moon, man saw his planet for the first time, saw that it was one. What else had Armstrong said? *Tranquility* something, *Tranquility landing long,* it was a joke between the astronauts in the module and the men in the landing craft. He used to know these things and quote them to his students. One world. One human race. From the vantage of the moon it's clear that if you drop an atom bomb on Hiroshima it affects the entire planet, that the fallout spews on everyone. Somewhere in a world his grandchildren will inhabit there will be one global language and one culture. Coke machines in Missoula and Madagascar and felafel at the corner store. It scares him, yes. He was born into a town where the first TV arrived to a fanfare in 1956, and now the rock groups Jane listens to simulcast their concerts to all corners of the globe.

But Mary's right, only fools insist on hanging on to the past. You can't fight change. Not even the final change. He supposes in his muzzy state that the origin of conservatism is dread of death, is gut fear of the final blue condition. It's a fitting thought for the watershed point of a chill night in October with the leaves almost all down and the teeth of winter glinting in the air. Michael wiggles his toes. If he slides in under the quilt Mary will keep him warm. He may even fall asleep before dawn creeps over the window ledge. He pulls the shade. *Sweet dreams*, he whispers in a husky voice to himself. Sweet dreams.

* * *

Odors. At Willow Point, where the winds sweep down the lake from the tundra hundreds of miles to the north and the air seems dense with oxygen, smells are raw, they affront the nose. When Michael stands at the trunk of his BMW, rummaging among packages on Thanksgiving Saturday, the odor he catches on the noon breeze, an odor blowing from the lake, settles in the back of his mouth. He tastes it. Vile. He tilts his head and asks Ruggles, "What's that?" The dog cocks his head sideways, recognizing his name, and barks. Does he recognize the stench of dead fish? Michael tucks French loaves under one arm and lifts plastic bags of vegetables with the other: cauliflower, yams, potatoes. He ducks for the elm coming around the deck and stops before the door of the cottage. The potent smell of dead fish. Michael feels queasy. He sets the packages at the foot of the door.

But he doesn't go down to the shore immediately. Instead he stands with both hands on his hips, surveying the lake front. It's been weeks since he's been here. The water is calm and steel gray this afternoon in October, and smoky clouds stretch from horizon to horizon. The bushes and trees around the cottage are bare of leaves, so Michael's sight line down the beach is unimpeded, and when he steps clear of the honeysuckle to the east of the cottage, he can see all the way up to the point where gulls wheel over the rocks and deadfall. Shorebirds dot the sand, their cries hovering on the air.

The rotting carcass lies on a ridge of sand ten feet in from the water. As he approaches, Michael tucks his chin down and breathes through his nose. The smell is truly awful—sulphur, burnt oil, the residue of cordite. It's coming from a big yellowing carp, maybe twenty pounds. Ruggles claws in the sand at a distance and yelps but won't go near. Strange, since dogs love to roll in rotting fish. But it is revolting. The body is bloated and putrid. Its eyes have been pecked out, by gulls most likely. Up close the smell fills the air, a cloud of putrefaction. Michael stops two meters off and blinks. He'll have to get the pitchfork from the toolshed. The fish is too big to move by hand, and even if it could be done, the poisonous odor would permeate his clothes and skin.

When he returns with the pitchfork Ruggles has disappeared. Smart dog, Michael thinks, swallowing hard. A rotting fish should be taken far away and buried under the sand, but he has little stomach for carting the carcass hundreds of yards to the rocky stretch near the point where there are no cottages. He stoops, sliding the prongs of the pitchfork into the sand underneath. Bugs and beetles scuttle past his feet, dribble off the carcass as he crosses the stretch of beach in front of his place towards the Barsbys' to the east. A retired couple, they shut up their cottage in September and won't return this season. Still, Michael feels faintly criminal leaving the carcass on their property instead of burying it—and he looks over one shoulder as he dips to unload the reeking body. He flings it under scrub willows and retreats, the stench of death lingering in his nostrils.

Inside, he opens a bottle of scotch and holds his nose over its fragrance before pouring into a tumbler of ice—not too much, he has chores to do. The goose is in the car with the cranberry sauce and a half-dozen bottles of Chablis. He's turned the oven on already and should get the bird inside before Mary arrives from Belvu with the cake she's bringing from the bakery. Later he'll start cooking yams in a sauce of sherry, brown sugar, and walnuts, a favorite of Mary's he makes every Thanksgiving.

On the deck he stands and looks toward Belvu, a smudge of blues and browns in the middle distance. A few fishing boats are out in the harbor, but the season is over. On Saturday afternoon the fishermen will be in the pub at the Belvu Hotel lamenting the catch or bitching about the marketing board's quota system. He thinks of a joke he heard lately: "What's the difference between a fisherman and a 747? The 747 stops whining when it gets to Hawaii." He wonders what's keeping Mary. If he gets his chores done he'll go for a short run after she arrives and burn off some of the muzziness he still feels from last night. He can't take it like he could a decade ago. Though that bothers him less and less. The bleary pleasures of hangovers are for younger men. He enjoys falling asleep in an armchair during a doubleheader and waking at two in the morning chilled and stiff but ready to tumble into his warm bed with Mary. The pleasures of getting—but not being—old. He wants to be fresh for each new day now and finds himself making coffee most mornings in a dreamy haze of thoughtless goodwill.

He makes one trip to the car for the goose and a second for the wine. Still no sign of the dog. Michael stands at the cottage door and whistles, then retreats inside to unwrap the bird and put it in the oven. He rolls up his sleeves to wash the yams. When he cleans and separates the cauliflower, a tiny green worm falls from between two florets and he feels queasy all over again. He stands at the door to get some air. Where is Mary? She was behind him when he left the bakery with the bread. He looks down the road toward Belvu while sipping scotch.

He shouldn't drink before running but he finishes the scotch and takes the binoculars onto the beach while he waits. Looks toward the place where he and Stephen saw the guy in the watchcap. Nothing there today. Almost all the birds have gone south. He spots yellow legs to the west and snipes scooting among the rocks. To the east Michael sees that the gulls have moved closer and are feeding at the water's edge. One dark-headed male is the center of attention. It flicks a stringy piece of something—fish?—in its beak and snaps at the thing when it lands. The other gulls watch. It must be gristle because the bird can't tear it apart. It rips at it with its long beak. Snaps once, twice. Through the binoculars Michael can see the gull ripping again, then dropping the thing onto the wet sand. Another gull moves in to have a try, but the dark one scares it off. They flutter at water's edge and strut about before the dark one returns to its prize. Snap. Flick. The other gulls skirt around watching and waiting, moving stiffly, mechanically along the shore, watchful but affecting indifference. Michael adjusts the binoculars but he can't tell what the gulls' prize is. After a while the dark-headed one grows bored and flaps off. A battle for possession begins among those left. Michael scans the beach. The warblers are gone. So are the pelicans. Along the shore some marsh wrens peck in the gravel. A few crows linger in the trees. Otherwise the beach is deserted.

The last time Angela was here they walked to the point in the rain. He feels hollow, recalling their bleak afternoon together, an afternoon when he made it as clear as possible that they had to bring things to an end. They made a deal. He would visit her if she wanted, but no more affair. He would be just visiting. Angela's sneakers left prints in the sand, tiny marks that the wind had obliterated when they returned.

She is brave but sad. When Michael holds her now, he feels how much weight she's lost in just the few months he's known her. Her arms are thin, the pockets under her eyes have become deep bruises. Sometimes she has trouble breathing and holds one hand over her chest, unable to speak. The treatments they're giving her now affect her eyes as well as her lungs, so she asks him to read to her. The *New York Review*, *Rolling Stone*. She thinks that the President's position on Central America stinks. If she had her way she'd join CUSO or one of the church organizations and work in Nicaragua with peasants. They are the real victims, she tells Michael. And also that she fights with the Colonel about this—and then makes him treat her to mushi pork and vermicelli fried noodles at her favorite restaurant.

It's strange that she still has her appetite even though last week when she called him she was flat out in bed. He toes the sand. It's hard to accept death. He doesn't know how she accepts it, but he does know she has more courage than he does. He'd be a wreck.

He hears a motor and looks up, thinking that Mary's arrived from Belvu, but it's a boat out on the lake, plowing through from the point. Whoever is driving throws one arm up in greeting, and Michael waves back, raises the binoculars, but cannot identify the boaters. Kids wearing leather jackets, huddled behind the windshield. It must be cold on the open water. Probably boozing with nothing else to do on the last weekend before the ice winds blow down from the pole and petrify the lake for six months. If he were their age he'd probably be doing the same. There's only so many summers.

He looks down the beach and spots Ruggles loping toward him. Whistles, waves both arms. When the dog runs up Michael tosses the binoculars aside and tackles him. They wrestle to the sand, then disengage and snarl at each other. Bark. Michael tackles the dog again, burying his face in warm musky fur.

Wonderful dumb beast, Michael thinks. Wonderful because

life-sustaining. For Michael knows he's a shameless man. He's betrayed everyone who's trusted him. He's lied and cheated and probably done worse to wring from the world his portion of pleasure. The small portion he's coveted so much. In high school he broke a boy's nose over a girl. That wasn't the last time he used his size to get his own way. And he's shameless in other ways, too. He cheapens himself to get public attention. To be loved. He's delivered pain to Patricia and his kids in order to get Mary—a selfishness which comes back to him in hot flashes of embarrassment and shame. And now he's betrayed Mary.

But he loves this dumb dog.

Yes, there's that to be said for him. With people he's a washout. He can't seem to get the hang of loving—and being loved. Always power colors the way Michael treats people. He has to be on top, he has to win, so he humiliates strangers, and uses his friends, and hurts his family. It's true. He has betrayed everyone who's ever loved him. Once he sold a cousin's love letters and laughed about it in the schoolyard after. Left to his own devices Michael would destroy everyone around him—including himself. But with Ruggles he's pure giving. For Ruggles has no power, and that saves him. Yes. He listens to the thumping in the dog's stringy chest. Then he hears the Mercedes pull up and they run to greet Mary.

* * *

"We were wondering what kept you," Michael says. He's poured a glass of water to drink as he changes into his jogging gear, a sweatsuit and the black and red high-tops.

"I stepped into the church." Mary has opened a bottle of wine. "The Anglican? Across from the park?"

"Seriously?"

Momentarily, Mary looks guilty. "Seriously. It's a gorgeous building. It must be turn-of-the-century. So much stone."

"So much cheap peasant labor, you mean."

"Gargoyles," Mary says. "Unusual for the prairie."

"I think it's pretentious."

"But solid, too. Stone and mortar." Mary holds the wine to the light and nods appreciatively. "In the nave you look up and sense the enormity of things. Awe, you know? Anyway, it *is* Thanksgiving, and sometimes I feel the need for something spiritual." Michael was raised an atheist but Mary was sent to an Anglican girls' school.

"Religion?"

"Just the ritual. No dogma, thanks."

"That's what they all say—at first. If you're not careful you'll be joining Jane and the Jesus freaks." Arnold, it turns out, is a born-again Christian who's putting pressure on Jane now. The kid's been attending meetings and talking a lot about a group Arnold belongs to. What next?

Mary sips wine. "Try this." She passes him the glass.

"Good," Michael says. "1978."

"A little treat."

Michael pulls his laces snug. Today he wants to go two-thirds speed to the point and push to a sprint on the way back. "Lovely," he says of the wine. Though it looks expensive.

Mary takes back the glass. "The church," she's saying, "was filled with that holy silence you get in Catholic cathedrals. Really very moving. Today I felt like giving thanks, and that was the place to do it. There were candles up front and someone had put cornstalks and wheat sheaves on the altar."

"Not farmers, judging by this year's prices."

"An organ was playing. Haydn. You know what that does to me."

"You'll be converting soon." Michael's begun limbering his back, touching his toes. Mary's face blurs in his vision.

She asks, "Don't you feel that sometimes? That there's more to life than—than cottages and booze and money?"

"We've always got each other."

"We do." Mary smirks over the wine glass. "And Ruggles. But I meant besides that. Things you talk about at school. Inner things. Don't you feel there should be something to thank for all the good things we've got?"

"Your lucky stars?" Michael stands near the door, trying to ease out but sensing Mary wants to talk. She's been brooding lately. He's found magazines about marriage and teens open on the coffee table for him to read.

"That's just the point. It's not the stars."

"What then?"

"I don't know. But all this can't be an accident."

"The scientists say so." Michael fidgets. He's beginning to sweat. "All random coupling, they claim. Radiation, the primal fireball, the big bang. You know the story."

"Pooh." Mary stands with one hand on her hip as she pours wine. "Such nonsense." She sets the bottle down with a crack. "I've heard it and I am not impressed. Random coupling? The big bang? These are the bad puns of horny men."

"You think?"

"I know this much, no woman would claim creation was a gigantic case of the cosmos getting its rocks off."

He says defensively, "All this took millions of years."

"Even so. It's too complicated to be random. The right gases mixing at just the right temperatures. Everything lining up for the perfect moment. What do they figure were the odds of creation?"

"In the dozens of zeroes." Michael shrugs and adds, half under his breath, "But that's not the point."

"And what is the point?"

"That it happened." He looks down at his high-tops, scuffed from running on city streets. "And that things run down. Are you going to blame that on God, too?"

Mary shakes her head. "The blame for that falls squarely on us. Poisoning our water, killing the animals who share the globe.

My God, we've made a balls-up of this planet with toxic waste. This morning an oil tanker spilled millions of gallons on the French coast. That's random and arbitrary action for you. That's self-destruction. Like the impulse to destroy what's closest to us. Those we love."

Earlier Mary looked guilty, but now she seems to be accusing *him* of something. Does she know about Angela? Michael feels hot. He places first one and then the other hand on the door knob. "Not today, though," he says, trying to laugh it off. "Today I destroy fat cells." When he opens the door he catches a whiff of dead fish. He closes the door quickly, leaving Mary with one finger raised, looking like a schoolteacher about to make a final point.

* * *

Through the window Mary watches Michael run past the cars and down the gravel road behind the cottages. He looks big and awkward—jogging pants sag around his bottom and chew into his legs with each stride. At fifty his running is little more than plodding.

Mary sets the timer on the oven. The goose will be cooked by seven, but she'll have to drain the grease on the hour until then. She lines up the spices she'll need on the shelf above the sink, labels facing out, and sits at the table to draw up a list of menu items with preparation times. Order. Mary loves order. When she was a girl she kept a list of books she'd read, Nancy Drews, a series of natural histories on small animals—wombats, martens. Later she wrote the names of boyfriends in a diary and pasted movie stubs and dance tickets beside them. From the time she was fifteen she filled out Poppsy's income tax return. In 1962 he brought home five thousand dollars. Mary thought then that when she graduated from college she'd be happy to earn ten thousand a year, twice what her father made and a comfortable income in those days. Poor Poppsy. He sent her to a good school but he never had much for himself. He never wanted anything enough.

Unlike Fred. *The good things of the world don't just arrive gift-wrapped,* Fred says. That's what she likes about him, his directness. He's a literalist. He takes her to a roadside tavern which makes its own beer, and where the sun slants through the trees and dances on a pond in a garden. Smiling, joking. He loves the simple things—skipping stones over water, betting the ponies. She hasn't seen anyone enjoy life as much as Fred. He takes things for what they are. He doesn't brood over what's past. He brings flowers to the office, he sings his Patsy Cline. There's a simplicity about him Mary loves. As she loves the kick Fred gets out of cocktails—always Tanqueray gin with an olive—and the way he falls dead asleep after sex. No pretense.

Mary gazes down the deserted road. Michael's circuit to the point and back takes him twenty minutes. She crosses the room to the bay window overlooking the lake. When she was at school she used to sneak out of her dorm and go skinny-dipping in the ocean. She'd like to do that now, she'd like to lose herself for a moment. The water will be cold but what the hell, she loves the shock of ice and the way her muscles warm at the fire after. She tosses her sweater onto a chair and slips out of her slacks and socks. She feels wicked and daring and grabs a towel off the rack near the door and runs for the lake. The gravel underfoot is sharp, the air cold. The water takes her breath away, but she dives immediately, forcing her head under, knowing her body will adjust if she works her limbs. The lake is ice. She stays under to the count of twenty, feeling her ears fill with the sound of churning water. When she comes up she treads furiously and breathes fast. Ghosts in the air above her head, and two curious gulls that swoop by, dipping for a closer look. Mary's nipples have stiffened with cold. She strips off her bra and flings it onto the water. She laughs and feels the kind of high she remembers from smoking pot, the top of her head coming loose. Release.

She fills her lungs with air, whoops once, then wiggles about and comes up with her panties. Lace. She tosses them on the water, too. She plunges and swims back toward the shore. When her feet scrape bottom she stands quickly and sprints for the cottage, grabbing the towel off the sand and clutching it to her breasts.

Inside, she stands by the oven warming herself and toweling between sips of wine. The Burgundy tastes sharp in her mouth, but she gulps it back. She feels good, legs tight the way they get after exercise, head light from oxygen. She's been going to the Squash Racquet Club and feels her muscle tone returning. Wrapped in a towel and holding the glass of wine, she moves to the bay window. Michael claims you can see north for fifty miles. Today is overcast, the lake calm. But the weather changes quickly. At dawn there was a breeze coming off the water and rattling the shingles, and by dark there could be a fall storm on the way. Sleet, snow. Looking out at miles of sky and water Mary thinks that life, too, is constantly shifting, though the life they live in Woodydell—Green Machines, gas barbecues, the golden handshake—has the rap of being dull and boring. But that's not true.

In fact, things shift very quickly, even in Mary's life. Because she is no longer so sure of herself as she once was, so sure that the patterns of her living, her loving are the right ones, not for everyone, but just for herself. Mary is not good at guilt, but she does have a Protestant's attachment to order and clarity. She wants things to fall into place the way cards fall into place in a game: your queen takes my partner's ten but my ace trumps your queen. My trick. Funny, that's the word prostitutes use to describe their men. *Trick.* This is a further confusion to the already confused business of love. Of sex, really, though Mary would rather avoid that idea. Too raw, too direct. Why does it bother her? Fear of the flesh? Too working-class for a girl sent to Miss Dahlstrom's to study art history and the Romantic poets along with show riding and the way to dress for trousseau teas?

Whatever it is, it nags her the way confusion about her fling with Fred does. It troubles her, though she cannot say why.

Of course, Fred says they can continue to meet, to pursue their affair as they have in the past, but Mary knows it has to end. Casual sex is okay once—maybe twice. Yes, she was thrilled and aroused. For years, maybe, she'd been bored without really knowing it, and Fred's easy love was good for her. He boosted her spirits, renewed her. Kelly says she looks five years younger. Even Michael's noticed, asking her why she's wearing a new scent. Scary. She hadn't meant to change things with her little fling, but she sees now that they change by themselves.

Mary's orderly mind makes distinctions. She knows it's dangerous to go from making love to sleeping with a man. You only share sleep with the man you love. So she can't sleep with Fred. That's why she's invited him and Joan to this Thanksgiving dinner. She wants him to see her and Michael together, she wants him to witness their love.

* * *

Michael makes the turn at the far end of the point slowly. He gets scared out here. He's alone and winded and would make an easy target for an ambush. Victim. His heart beats wildly when he thinks this, and he has to force himself to be calm. He peers into the trees. Nothing. Squirrels scuffle in the underbrush, but otherwise he's the only living thing on the point. No gunman. No panic.

* * *

Michael walks down the shore with one hand on his stomach. He feels flushed, his face is hot. At the beach he vomits behind the cottage, but otherwise things are the same as in Woodydell. He likes the solid feel of a wall pressing back on his extended palm as he leans forward. The walls of the cottage are cedar siding. Here plants grow around the foundation, plantain, crabgrass, thistle, dandelion, all dead now, all brown and shriveled. Though it does not hurt him, the vomiting terrifies Michael. One more sign his body is breaking down. Or worse, signs of a disease eating away from within. Death. He tells these things to Dr. Fayyaz. The doctor smiles. It's nothing, he says, really nothing, and shakes his head. If you only vomit after running, the doctor tells Michael, stop running. He fingers his pencil mustache as he says this in his singsong but elegant English. How can Michael stop running? Maybe he should see another doctor, an American who understands exercise.

* * *

Mary stands in the kitchen wearing a chef's apron. Sliced tomatoes over mozarella garnished with peppers and parsley wait in a silver platter on one side of the sink, Michael's homemade cranberry sauce in crystal dishes on the other. The Caesar dressing has been mixed but not beaten to the creamy consistency Mary likes. Romaine dries on a wooden rack. The wine glasses are on the table and Mary's counted the silver several times. After she prepared wild rice casserole and Michael the yams, they washed the utensils and flatware. She hates stacks of dirty dishes piled about the kitchen, but Michael would leave them there with food hardening on surfaces, with grease congealing—as he leaves the newspapers scattered about the living room. Mary's put the carving knife and fork on Michael's bread plate. The French loaves sit on the counter still smelling of yeast and ovens. They need to be sliced and placed in wicker baskets under cloth but that can wait. Did she put out the butter? The corkscrew? She takes a sip of wine and runs the back of her hand over her brow. Her hair's still damp and exudes the fishy pong of lake water. She smiles, thinking of the way the water surged into her ears, the way her nipples stiffened—and she checks her lists one last time. Parmesan cheese. Salt and pepper. The first time she and Bob had his parents to dinner she forgot to put out salt and no one said a word through the entire meal. Was that really twenty-five years ago? She sticks her head into the living room where they're discussing the PTL scandal.

"Now Jim Bakker claims nothing was going on between him and Jessica whatshername." Fred laughs after saying this, dotting, Mary sees from her vantage point, Kelly Connor's sleeve with a spray of rum and Coke. He was nervous about coming, guilty, so he's been drinking steadily since they arrived.

"Hahn," Fred's wife, Joan, says. "Jessica Hahn."

"He can deny it forever," says Stephen, joining in. "But he got caught with his hand in the cookie jar, didn't he?"

"I feel sorry for him," Fred says. He arches his eyebrows and smiles at Mary from across the room. "His bedroom invaded by the tabloids of the nation."

Kelly says, "Actually, I think it's pathetic." She doesn't look at Fred, but at Michael sitting across the room. Stephen is in the overstuffed chair by the fireplace, leaving the recliner near the bay window for Mary when she comes in from the chores in the kitchen. "Both Jim and Tammy looked downright pathetic on TV, telling all America they forgive each other."

"Though what Tammy has to be forgiven for, I don't know," Mary comes in with. "Unless it's wearing too much makeup."

Joan laughs at this, a brittle sound that catches everyone but Fred by surprise. She asks Kelly, "What do you think of Jessica?"

"Jessica is a hard article," Kelly responds, her eyes flicking from Joan's to Mary's and back to Joan's. Like the other women, she's wearing a sweater and slacks in case the weather turns suddenly ugly. Michael, too, has on a sweater and Stephen a denim shirt. Only Fred is wearing a jacket and tie, which he's loosened off his open collar. Kelly adds, "Jessica's a hustler."

"But a likeable one," Stephen adds.

"She's gutsy—in a working-class way."

"A woman has to be," Mary says. "These days."

"Yes," Joan agrees. "I like Jessica because she sticks her chin out, defying TV-land to think itself superior."

"You don't want to sentimentalize her, either." Stephen leans forward in the light and smiles at Joan. "She's more a working girl than a working-class hero."

"But a smart one," Mary says. "She's using the system."

"Yes," Joan says. "She's negotiating movie rights now."

Fred comes back in with, "The flesh is weak. That's the real story here. Jim Bakker rails about it on TV, but he's the one seduced by lust. I feel sorry for him." He sits back on the sofa and looks up at the ceiling. "I really do."

"What's sad," Stephen says, "is the money to line the Bakkers' pockets comes from dirt farmers who can't make their mortgage payments and little old ladies living on cat food." Backlit by the fire, he looks sinister.

"Heritage Village," Joan volunteers. "Or whatever."

"That's right," Mary says. "There should be a law against it. Soliciting on TV." She looks from one guest to another. Why hasn't Michael offered another round of drinks? He's being unusually quiet on the far side of the room.

"Bet your socks there would be," Stephen says, "if it was the Communist Party doing the soliciting. Or a religion not approved by the Bible-thumpers in the White House."

Fred looks like he has more to say about the PTL but he drinks from his rum and Coke instead, and then drums the arm of the sofa. Mary looks away from his eyes when they search out her face in the warm room, but she knows they will have to talk later.

Kelly asks, "Is anyone straight any more? All you see on TV these days are businessmen on trial for swindles."

"Get ready for a lot more of that," Stephen says. "It's bad enough when the economy's going great, but the knives really come out when things turn bad. And you can bet that's on the way."

Fred nods. "This psychic on TV sees a crash coming this fall."

"Listen," Michael says. "My old man's predicted a crash in the fall for the past twenty years."

Fred laughs and throws his head back. "Is he psychic too?" Funny the way he's balding, Mary thinks, with hair over the ears and around the collar but none on top. He doesn't try to cover it up, though, by combing long strands across from the sides. If he's going bald, he'll look it.

"It's not just con men," Joan says. "Public officials have their hands in the till, too. It's disgusting."

"True," Mary agrees. "Everybody these days turns out to be dirty. For weeks we watched the Sinc Stevens circus on TV—well, I watched it, anyway—showing this toad to be immoral and unrepentant. And what's the upshot? His cronies might throw him out of the cabinet. *Might*. They're all in it together and one as bad as the next. When did we last elect an old-style man of integrity in this country? A Lester Pearson or a Tommy Douglas?"

Michael says, "Pearson and his crowd were just never found out. Kept the dirty laundry in the closet." His face, too, is in shadows, masking what could be a jibe at people with something to hide. Mary shifts on her seat and looks into the fire.

In the silence Kelly leans forward and touches Mary's arm. "Don't say that. Not about Tommy Douglas."

"Well," Michael says, "the thing about politics is the people we elect don't actually run the country. The guys with real power are on Bay Street."

"I refuse to believe," Kelly says sharply, "that politicians are in bed with organized crime. The Kennedys? Jimmy Carter? Even Nixon and Reagan seem above that." She looks directly at Fred when she says this and then scouts the room for support.

"Still," Stephen states, "*Newsweek* claims hundreds of incidents of illegal activity occurred in Reagan's White House. Influence-peddling, lobbying scams, corruption under every rock. And what's behind it? Good old-fashioned greed."

"Good," Kelly says, "only if you're from Rosedale or Westmount Heights." Her voice insists on finality, and for a moment silence falls over the room. Mary listens to the hiss of wood burning and the crackle of the goose in the oven. Everybody is slightly drunk but tense. The Connors have just met Fred and Joan, and it looks like Kelly and Fred don't get along, though Stephen, as always, wants to, and Joan seems pliable enough. It's Michael who troubles Mary. He's brooding. She would like him to take charge, lighten the mood, but he seems in a dreamy haze—which the wine is only deepening.

"You take this stock-market business, now," Fred says, firing things up again. "Don't tell me there isn't collusion there. Buy-outs and takeovers. The Wall Street barons tune these things as finely as a good piano. Pirates like Boesky drive share prices up and the average guy figures he better get in on the action, too. All a big con. After the little guy's plunked his savings down, they fix it so the prices crash and guess who gets caught holding the bag?"

Kelly asks, "Well that's greed, too, isn't it?" She holds a wine glass in one hand, the other clenched tightly in her lap.

This is what Fred wanted, a chance to show off his knowledge. "Not the same thing at all," he says. He turns sideways to look Kelly in the eye. "One's the stuff free enterprise is built on, making a buck. Nothing wrong with that, as far as I'm concerned, the old profit motive."

Kelly states levelly, "When folks in the suburbs get in on the action, they're just as greedy as the big guys. The principle's the same, only the sums differ. Both want to cash in on the work done by other people. If they get their fingers burned, then nobody led them down the garden path as far as I'm concerned. I have as little sympathy for yuppies as for Jim and Tammy Bakker."

Mary stands suddenly. Her mother told her never to let guests fight. "Well," she says brightly, "we can agree on that, then." She pauses, hoping Fred won't blunder in headlong, face flushed with booze and excited by Kelly's challenge. "What struck me about the Jim and Tammy thing was how the money poured in *after* the exposé. All those people felt sorry for them."

"Yes," Joan says. "It's a shame." She must not drink much, Mary thinks. After only two glasses of wine she seems quite drunk.

"Vicarious living," says Stephen. "If your own life is pinched and dull, you can live through the adventures of TV people."

Joan says, "Some woman paid ten thousand dollars at an auction to have dinner with Tom Selleck. What must her life be like?"

Stephen says, "Not all bad. She has ten thousand more than we do to spend on dinner." He turns suddenly to Michael. "Speaking of which, big guy," he says, "are you going to carve that bird, or what?"

* * *

After dinner Fred tells Mary, "It's like being pecked to death by ducks." He's talking about the holdups at the condominium project. They are standing together on the deck in the silvery moonlight. They're worried about the lease-up on the condos. First, a concrete machine broke down in the midst of pouring foundations. Three days passed while parts were rushed in from Cleveland, three lost days in the short prairie summer. Then a prefab wall collapsed on the construction crew, injuring three and killing one. Another day lost to the funeral. Inspectors with clipboards arrived, reporters nosed around the building site— everyone moved slowly, deliberately. Then came two days of torrential rain. Lightning in the vicinity. The crews were sent home at midday. When the weather cleared the electricians threatened to strike and work slowdowns followed tedious negotiations. Rental units, projected ready for August occupancy, were delayed once, then twice. In the office the phone rang constantly. Two tenants backed out of their leases—they needed places to live. Fred swallowed Maalox, Mary, Valium. They studied their lists of contacts and made phone calls into the night. This is their first condo project, their reputation is at stake.

* * *

When Mary comes in off the deck Michael is down on one knee explaining something about fireplaces to Kelly. He has one arm up the flue and his face twisted sideways to look into Kelly's eyes. His voice rises, then falls abruptly as he stops speaking. When he stands, there is a black smudge of soot the size of a silver dollar on one cheek and a spot like a clown's on the end of his nose, but he doesn't notice them. He's explaining—flues, convections, air currents. Kelly smiles coyly, nodding at what he's saying. Mary joins them. Standing to one side, she has difficulty not laughing herself. But Michael talks on and on, his hands describing arcs in the air to match his explanations, his rumbling voice rising and falling with the rhythms of the wind outside. When Mary approaches with a tissue, he smiles, happy to double his audience, and is surprised when she dabs at his face; when she laughs like a conspirator with Kelly, he looks like a child who's stumbled across a secret of adult life but doesn't know what to make of it. Suddenly Mary throws both arms around his neck. "Oh Michael," she says into his ear, "you're such a guy."

* * *

In bed Michael asks, "Why does Fred come on so strong?"

Mary's brain, fogged with wine, is dropping toward sleep. "He's nervous," she says and rolls to face the wall. The moonlight bothers her on nights when she wants to drop straight into sleep. "Then he babbles to cover up."

"He was bloody rude to Kelly."

"She held her own I thought."

Michael snorts. "Calling her a bleeding heart."

"She implied he was a money grubber who reacted like a spoiled brat when things didn't turn out his way."

"She was saying that about yuppies."

"Which she thinks Fred is. Wrongly."

"And what was all that with his wife?"

"She enjoyed herself. She drank enough wine."

"Only because he kept making a fool of her. Did you notice he put her down every time she tried to say something?"

"You're imagining things." Mary sighs and turns her head. She smells the lake on the pillow, left there by her hair, and the memory cheers her—the taut feel of her breasts and thighs coming out of the icy water. "Mostly you're imagining women need sheltering when they argue with men. That's chauvinism, you know. We dish it out, but we can take it, too."

Michael sniffs. "And all that shit about the market. He only does that because it bugs me. Because you told him everything."

"He needs to know financial stuff. He's my partner."

"Well, he's bloody well not mine."

"Michael. Relax. You've had a few drinks."

"Oh great. Now every disagreement we have can be explained away by how many drinks I've had."

"That's not what I meant." Mary sighs. "Anyway, I agree with Fred about the market. Everyone seems to." She puts one hand on Michael's back. It's hot under his nightshirt. He's been jumpy all night, brooding beside the fire, worrying about things he keeps secret. He's such a child. She adds, "Even you."

"First thing Monday I'm selling. The old man was right about stocks and shares. I'm starting to panic."

"Good. I mean that you're selling."

"What do you think? The oils?"

"I don't know. Gold, maybe?"

"Oils are so fucking volatile. Every time the Ayatollah craps they jump up or down."

"Oh, honey, you decide. I'm really very tired." Michael resettles and she stares out the window, then falls silent listening to his heavy breathing. After resisting, she drops into a grainy sleep troubled by the word *volatile*, spoken by a voice coming, it seems, down a long resonating culvert.

* * *

By late afternoon on Thanksgiving Sunday Michael has recovered from hangover and has gone on his weekly pilgrimage to his parents'. Jane is out with Arnold, and Mary, finished estimates on the condo project, pulls on an Irish sweater and rattles Ruggles' collar against the back door, her way of rousing him from sleep in front of the fireplace. Outside a puff of wind shakes the branches of the weeping willow and tugs the hair on Ruggles' back into tufts. They take the walkway east toward the river and the private school.

Mary's stride is easy. Despite her hangover she feels okay. In the light of day the condo business doesn't look so bad—eighty-five percent leased up. The prize suites overlook the Red River. The view is great and tenants can be downtown in ten minutes or at the new racquet club being built up the street in five. The young MBAs want that now, health and fitness as close at hand as their office towers and their brokers. At $850 a month for one bedroom and $975 for two on the river side, she and Fred should clear nearly twenty-five grand between them for what might amount to a few hours' work. Now that's making money.

She's feeling good about how things worked out with Fred, too. After dinner at the cottage last night they stepped out on the deck together. Fred was sneaking a drink of Maalox. Too much wine, he said, burping, and held one hand over his stomach. With his back to the lake, his face was obscured. In the moonlight splashed on his shoulder, Mary could just make out the checks in his sport coat. "This is a great place," Fred said. "Quiet." His eyes were lost in shadow. Mary could tell from his voice he was embarrassed by his behavior inside. He wasn't pushy by nature, but when nervous he came on too strong. He'd let Mary down. He'd come out on the deck to apologize, but like most men, he didn't know how, so instead he stood shuffling from one foot to the other. "At night," Mary said, "all you hear are the waves rushing up the beach." They listened. It was true. The sound of water striking land swallowed up the wind, the cries of night birds. And it was hypnotic. "Under that spell," Mary said, "you can't help drift off." She had brought a glass of soda water out with her and she sipped from it as they listened to the lake. Finally Fred said, "You must be happy here." She knew then that he had seen what she had meant him to—and that he accepted it. After a while he said, "And it's really cozy." By which he meant a good place for a couple to grow old together. They left it at that. When they went back in, Michael was explaining to Kelly Connor the intricacies of installing a zero-clearance fireplace.

Mary cuts past Woodydell's gymnasium and follows Ruggles toward the private school. Their neighbor, Feniak, is crouching on his deck with a tape measure in his hands, planning more renovations. Last spring his wife of twenty years left him and their teenage boys just weeks after contractors completed the upstairs addition she'd been pushing him to build since the boys started school. There's an equation here that Mary would like to ignore, something involving renovations and divorce. Feniak waves when Mary passes. With his tape measure and carpenter's pencil he's the image of suburban happiness. All he needs to complete the picture is a glass of spritzer and a porterhouse broiling on the barbecue—though she heard he tried to gas himself in the garage when Heather left, and spent months in therapy getting over the separation.

Ruggles dashes toward the dike bordering the private school. When they top its crest and step into the open, the wind cuts Mary's face. It brings tears to her eyes. She stops to let

Ruggles pee against a tree and stoops suddenly to gather a handful of leaves—which she throws in the air. Ruggles leaps at them as they swirl upwards in the currents and then, caught on a gust, disappear over the pines ringing the school grounds. Free, Mary fancies.

She's felt that way herself lately. At the office she hums along with the radio while doing paperwork—tunes Katie gets on the AM stations. Mary prefers classical, but finds she now knows the words to songs by Madonna and Barry Manilow. She's as happy as she's been since school. She looks forward to each day's tasks, to working out at the Squash Racquet Club, to flying to Mexico in January. Last week she found a Chanel suit and on the same day Michael bought her a dozen red roses. She finds she's no longer alarmed by predictions that a housing crisis is imminent, that property values will fall by twenty percent if the prime rate climbs another point. It never happens. And as Fred says, anyway, why sweat it when you can't do anything about it? If the system collapses it takes everyone down with it. Can you prepare enough for that? Have enough cash in the bank? Better to take things as they come, plug along with willpower and determination but also certain knowledge that nothing you do changes much in the large world. Fly to Mexico over New Year, drive a new Mercedes, order cashmere sweaters from Harrods. At home she's begun decorating the rooms in the addition. She's chosen red blinds and green paint for her study. In jeans with her hair tied back, she puts Mahler on the stereo and sings through the lieder as she paints the walls. Forster's got the windows in now and is hanging the doors. Sometimes when she stops to dip her paint roller she hears him accompanying her in his rumbling bass.

Like Fred he drinks imported beer, and when he stops for lunch he opens a can of Heineken. "My father," he tells Mary, "used to say *work is work and schnapps is schnapps*, but I don't hold with that." He laughs, revealing a mouth of gold fillings, and places his large hands on his knees to listen to Mary. She wants hardwood floors upstairs even though Michael thinks carpet would be adequate. Adequate, she's learned from Forster, is not good enough. She wants this house to last. Forster tells her they don't build them like they used to. "Not worth salt," he says, pointing out how the lumber yards shave a quarter inch off the floor joists now, so they're less than two inches thick, instead of somewhat over, the way they came forty years ago. "Junk," Forster says. "These houses won't last."

Mary and Ruggles have circled back to the river where the dog is sniffing for squirrels. Through the bare trees sunlight glints off the water. They scramble down the dike and cross the open field which takes them to the riverbank. Mary's joints are stiff and her calf muscles ache each time her feet meet the ground. They get that way from dancing—which she's taken up again after thirty years. She takes classes on Tuesday and Thursday nights. Mary loves pulling on the tights and the soft dance shoes which thump on the wood floor as she follows the teacher's commands. The first half hour they do stretching exercises, and after twenty minutes or so Mary feels something inside pull loose from her chest and she floats on a wave of well-being sustained by pop songs booming out of a ghetto blaster. In the last half hour they work on technique. The instructor is a young gay who alternately shouts *liftliftlift* or chants *good work girls* as he claps his hands in encouragement. After, she does five minutes on the rowing machine and then sits in the jacuzzi, feeling the bubbling water massage her thighs and calves.

At school thirty years ago their dance teacher was a Swedish girl with raven hair and porcelain skin. Eva something-or-other. Mary thinks now that she must have been in love with Eva without knowing it. Girl-for-girl love, the kind that flourishes in schools like Miss Dahlstrom's. The tingling feeling she got staying after class to talk with Eva comes back to her when she's changing in the locker room of the racquet club and breathes the odor of wet towels and sweating bodies. Eva had been to places like Thailand and Patagonia and hinted in her broken English at swarthy men, at moonlit nights, at love affairs. The girls hung on her stories. She had long legs and muscular thighs that bulged her tights. Yes, it was infatuation. Eva was sexy and mysterious. She glided among the girls in the locker room like a large cat, touching the necks of her favorites. Thirty years later Mary still imagines that her exercises can make her body hard as Eva's as she thumps and bumps across the floor of the Squash Racquet Club.

To have that body. She wonders sometimes if she's taken up dancing to impress somebody. Fred? He said to her once, "You've got a great ass, you know? Heart-shaped." When she threw him her fiercest look, he added, "That's where valentines come from," and shaped his hands in the air to illustrate. "I bet you thought they symbolize romance. If you do, ask yourself why that valentine is always pierced by Cupid's arrow." The ring of his laugh stayed with Mary a long time. When she tried the idea on Michael, he stroked his beard and muttered something about reading too much Jung before returning to whatever he was brooding about.

If he'd only stop brooding, Mary thinks. That's the problem with teachers. They lust after permanence more than most people lust after gold. Surround themselves with the young to prove they aren't growing old themselves. Phys-ed teachers are worst, dashing about the playing fields with teenagers, demonstrating that they're still twenty-two. Mary sees them at the private school, blowing whistles on the sideline and trying to outrun time. And the English teachers like Michael are bad, too. They lust after the changelessness of the great works which they read to their students, searching for a world beyond regret and pain.

Ruggles is making for the water down the slippery riverbank so Mary picks up a stick and flings it back into the field. He's a pretty beast but stupid. In a moment he's forgotten what was so interesting along the river and is bounding in the stunted fall grass. Lately Michael's taken the dog over. That's like him. At first he wasn't keen to have him tracking up the hardwood, but once he noticed other people liked Ruggles, he became the dog's best pal. Laughable, really, like Michael's other transparent faults—drinking too much and then feeling guilty about it, brooding. Needing attention. After they first moved in together she was surprised when he called her to the couch to read aloud bits from the *Guardian* or recount boring details of his day at the college. She was used to her dour husband, who grunted if she asked him questions and fell asleep after dinner in front of the TV, as indifferent as her own father had been. But Michael's needs are those of a child. *Scratch my back,* he says to her—not *please* or *would you*—and has his sweater up blocking the TV before she answers. At first she thought he was honest, but now she thinks he's just rude. And he orders drinks from her, he loses track of his charge cards, he leaves the Saturday papers scattered on the floor for her to pick up.

She loves him, though. There's something about him that just hooks women. It's not anything flashy—the opposite, actually. She noticed its effect on the girls taking Michael's course with her more than ten years ago. In his presence they seemed attentive suddenly, like birds listening to a sound that no one else could hear. At first Mary thought he wasn't aware of this. He blundered along under his shock of hair, behind his face of gray beard, rolling his eyes as he talked about poetry, about walking the Lake District. But his eyes would fix on yours suddenly and he'd say, "My mother has a brooch like that." Unsettling, such remarks out of the blue. Enchanting, too, singling you out that way, looking into your eyes. Was it all part of a pose he adopted to seem vulnerable and vague? He's capable of that, of seduction by default, leaving a space for a woman to move into rather than thrusting his attentions upon her.

But he *is* vulnerable. At home he has a guitar which he plunks away at sometimes, the tip of his tongue sticking out of his mouth. The sounds he makes are horrible. He lacks a sense of rhythm and strikes the strings like a man shaking fire from his fingers. But when he's done he looks up at her with a schoolboy grin, beads of perspiration on his brow. "I'll play something," he says, strumming a few chords, "and you sing along." His voice is grainy and off-key, but that doesn't stop him. Once they sang "Dreams" by Roy Orbison and it sounded okay. They made love in front of the fireplace after and for a week guitar music filled the house.

Crossing near the wooden gymnasium on the way back to the house, Mary sees that Feniak has gone inside, and farther on she steps off the walkway to let a young couple on bicycles past. The woman is wearing a helmet and has a baby carrier attached behind her. Red triangular pennants on steel whip rods snap in the currents they create. The faces of the whole family are flushed with air and exertion, the child's little more than pink cheeks framed by a helmet and a blue scarf. Mary recognizes them as a new family who moved in across the park to share the suburban dream—birds in the trees, little league, private school. She wishes them well. It doesn't always work out. Just ask Feniak.

Near home Ruggles dashes ahead of Mary and disappears around the corner of the house. It's starting to look good now. The stucco exterior is bright, and the double windows along the west side open the house to the summer sun and the green of the park. In a few weeks they'll be able to move the furniture into the new rooms. Mary still hasn't figured out how to maneuver Michael out of his study into the addition. If only she could offer him something as an incentive. But all she has is her love. *That* he needs. He says to her, "You and me, babe," and winks like Bogart in those movies he stays up to watch on TV. He's kidding, but he's right, because the truth is, he does need her. And it's his need that holds Mary to him. She loves where she is needed.

* * *

As she swings into the backyard, Mary notices the door off the deck is open. Jane is home. She complains about cold in her room but leaves windows open and forgets to close doors. "Hell-lo-oo," Mary calls as she hangs up Ruggles' collar. Jane answers something inaudible from the living room, and when Mary enters from the hallway, she sees that the girl's clothes are in piles around her feet. Mary asks, "What are you doing?"

Lately Jane's stopped wearing makeup. "Sorting things," she says. She's put panties and socks in one stack, sweaters and skirts in another. She's either cleaning up or moving out, and Mary's heart skips once thinking how upset Michael will be if Jane's leaving again.

"Housecleaning? Laundry?"

"Arnold wants me to move in with the group. They've got a free room in the house."

Mary's ideas about group homes come from the sixties— drugs and free love. "Just what kind of Christians are these?"

"I've told you before," Jane sighs. "The Friends of the Risen Jesus." She picks up a single red sock, looks around, then shrugs and drops it on one pile. "And before you get ideas, I'm moving into the house—not Arnold's bed. Things don't work like that with the Friends."

This is a barb directed at Mary and Michael, who lived together two years before getting married. A sin, Jane has taken to calling it. Mary asks, "Just how old is the oldest person in this house?"

"Old enough." Jane points. "Can you throw me that blue denim shirt?" When Mary passes it across, Jane folds it down the middle and then in half and bunches it with other items on a teetering pile beside the stereo.

"Jane," Mary says. "This is not a good idea."

"It is a good idea. And it's mine."

"You don't know what you're getting into."

"I told you—one room on the third floor."

"You don't know anything about Arnold."

"Wrong." Jane's voice is insistent. "Wrong wrong wrong." In her eighth month, she's awkward. She turns slowly to face Mary. "For starters I know he cares about me—and about my baby. That's a damn—a darn—sight more than I can say for some."

"If you mean your father, that's just unfair."

"Also Arnold was raised in the country. He's decent, and clean, and above sin. And he wants me."

"So you're charging off to live in holy bliss."

"No one's charging off. Do you see anyone charging off?" Jane's green eyes blaze.

"I simply meant—"

"I'm living with the Friends. Arnold is one of them. Period."

After the long walk Mary's mouth is dry. She wishes she'd stopped in the kitchen for a drink, but asks, "What about the course at the college?"

"Things change, eh?"

"And the farm and raising the baby in the country with no one to dictate what you should do with your life?"

"On the back burner."

"The whole lot?"

"Until I take Jesus as my personal savior." Jane says this without irony and grunts when she lifts a stack of sweaters onto the couch. "Until after the baby."

"That's it? Your hopes for a career, something to fall back on? All that talking about women needing to call their own shots? Swept away by a Christian fanatic?"

Jane flinches when Mary says *fanatic*. She thinks of her recent conversion and the fervor which has followed as rational, as adult. "That's it," she says petulantly, and turns her back on Mary with a flounce to continue sorting clothes.

Mary would like to strangle her, and she suddenly remembers something Michael said after an argument with

Jane—with kids the only way you can win is by killing them, and you can't kill them. She asks, "And Arnold's friends don't mind about the baby?"

"*Go forth and multiply,* they say." She smiles. "That's a quote from the Bible." Jane's proud to instruct Mary. "They taught me to see the beauty of life and the sin of destroying even the tiniest thing." Her smugness suddenly turns into self-righteousness. "And to think how close I came to sin. To abortion."

"I'm not sure about that."

"It's a mortal sin."

"Mortal?"

"Yes." Jane looks at Mary with eyes glazed by certainty. "There's a quote in the Bible about it."

"The scripture," Mary says, remembering her mother's favorite maxim, "can be quoted in defence of the devil himself."

"You're wrong," Jane insists. "It's murder."

"It's not." Mary's voice matches Jane's, brittle, pugnacious. "How can you murder something that's not alive?"

Jane looks away, refusing to be drawn in. She's learned that much from her new friends. "I won't argue," she says sweetly, lifting the pile of socks and panties off the floor. "But that's only one of the reasons I can't live here."

"Disagreeing about abortion?"

"It's not disagreement when you won't accept the facts." Jane puts her armload of clothes down and lifts both hands from her sides in mock exasperation. Her print maternity dress binds on her belly. "Another is this sinful life you and Pa lead. Betting on horses—and drinking. The hours you keep, the language. The way you throw money away. Is it right for a mother to bring up a baby with this stuff going on?"

Strong talk, Mary thinks, for someone who just months ago was living with a boy and making babies out of wedlock. But what can she say? She has no stomach for a shouting match with Jane—or worse. Silent, she crosses to the kitchen and pours water in a tall glass. She glances out the window. The wind has come up and blown away the sun. The lamps in the Vermas' are on and she watches Mister and Missis moving back and forth, setting the table for dinner. She wishes Michael were home. When she returns to the living room she finds Jane packing her clothes into cardboard suitcases. "Good heavens," she exclaims. "You're not going today?"

"Uh-huh. The sooner the better. Don't you think?"

"Certainly not." Mary stands in the archway between the living room and kitchen. How will Jane get along with a houseful of strangers, where will she get money, what will she do when the baby comes? Has she thought of these things? She should talk to Michael before leaving. "What about your father? Don't you care what he says?"

"He'll say the same thing as when I moved in with Brad— which is all he's ever said. Which is all anyone ever says. It's a mistake. I'm too young to know what I'm doing. What does he ever say?"

"You might at least give him the chance."

Jane sits down suddenly, pushing aside one of the suitcases on the couch. Her face is a mask of pain. She takes a deep breath, puffing her cheeks and turning red. "Jesus," she wheezes between gasps, "it feels like labor."

Mary's voice rises, but she remains frozen at the door. "That can't be—there's almost a month to go."

"Three weeks." Jane grits her teeth and rocks on the couch. "It feels exactly like the book describes."

"Probably just gas." Mary hopes so. Where is Michael? "This is what I mean," she says. "You need somebody around when you have the baby. Someone like your father."

Jane has both hands over her face and is breathing deep, as she was taught to. When she takes her hands away her face is calm again. The pain has apparently passed. "No," Jane says. "I don't want anything from him."

Silence while Jane breathes and Mary listens to the thumping of her heart. She moves to the sofa and passes Jane the glass of water—which the girl accepts with a brief smile before drinking. Her brow is pale. They sit side by side between stacks of underwear. Over Jane's head there's a framed photograph of Qualicum Beach where Michael and Mary spent their honeymoon. They dug clams and drank a bottle of wine, a happy day when the sun shone and Michael and Mary were crazy in love. Seeing Jane's drained face beneath the photo now makes Mary sad.

Jane sniffs and brings a tissue out of her dress pocket. She blows her nose. "Actually," she says in a voice barely above a whisper, "there is something." And Mary feels sorry, knowing what it is before the girl says it. "Money. Just a little."

"Oh Jane."

"Only a hundred bucks or so. To buy stuff for the baby."

"Like Vitabath and gold jewelry."

"Like a basinette and a jolly jumper."

"If you stayed here you could have my old stuff."

"I want my own things—not somebody's cast-offs."

"I'd like to but . . ."

"Just a hundred."

"Let's see what your father says when he gets back."

"Oh. Gang up with him again." This is a favorite theme, part of Jane's divide-and-conquer strategy. She puffs her cheeks out and releases a long breath before asking, "Can't you just—you know?" Jane reaches over to her. "Please, Mary?"

"OK," Mary says. "Fifty dollars."

"Fifty?"

"And only if you promise to stay until your father gets back." Mary stands and crosses to the cabinet where she keeps her purse. "Deal?" She brings two twenties and a ten back and passes the bills to Jane. When Jane looks up, Mary locks her green eyes, though she knows it's a long shot that the girl won't bolt once she's got the money in hand. "Deal?" Mary repeats.

Trapped, Jane mutters, "All right." She folds the bills and stuffs them into her dress, then blows her nose again, a sound Mary associates with pain and helplessness, not the rage she sees in Jane's eyes. Mary sighs. She drinks off the water and takes the tumbler into the kitchen where she rinses it under the tap. Outside the streetlights are on. The Vermas are sitting down to their meal, the backs of the two boys' heads to Mary, the parents facing her. Quiet descends on Woodydell but not on Mary's heart. She listens to Jane moving around in the living room. Clothes rustle, a spring sags. After a while Jane snaps the catches on her suitcases. Sniffing. Then silence.

When Arnold arrives Jane helps him carry the suitcases to his van. She leaves without saying goodbye.

* * *

Mary and Michael sit beside the fire with snifters of cognac. Through the living-room windows they look into the yard from time to time, distracted by the scraping of branches against the house. The light coming from their neighbors' houses and from the streetlamps is distorted by water on the glass. At sunset the wind died and it started to rain, plastering branches of the ornamental crab against the walls. Their eyes return to the fire. They have been fighting—Michael insisting Mary should have forced Jane to stay, and Mary blaming him for not being there to deal with the girl himself. They shouted. Stamping one foot, Mary asked, what else could she do? Michael clenched his fists. Why didn't she phone his folks' place? He could have driven back to deal with the girl. When Michael found out about the money, he accused Mary of taking sides against him with Jane, and Mary fled to the bathroom and locked the door. Michael stood outside. He coaxed. It was Jane he blamed, not her. He banged the walls with his palms. He swore he loved her, but went away, as she commanded. He sat in the living room and studied *The Globe and Mail*. His feet turned cold so he built a fire.

Eventually Mary came out, tearful and angry. She poured drinks and joined him in front of the blazing logs.

The past half hour has been one long silence punctuated by brief denouncements of Jane. They have decided that Jane's moving is a good thing. The brat, the little witch. The move will certainly be good for them. They have decided, too, that Jane is rotten, mean, calculating, manipulative, low, and ungrateful. Not that they wouldn't have her back if it came to that. They're furious with Arnold, but feel sorry for the baby. Neither can forgive Jane, Mary because Michael's been taken for granted, Michael because Jane has betrayed Mary's trust. Again.

Michael is on his third snifter of cognac. He stands. His mouth is dry, he says, and he needs a glass of water. From her chair near the fire Mary hears him run the kitchen tap, then open the cupboards. Then what sounds like a plate smashing. She calls, "Sweetheart?" He's clumsy and always breaking things. An interval of silence follows, then she hears another crash, the sound of china breaking. Mary stands. When she gets to the archway she sees Michael at the table with a dinner plate raised over his head. Two others, maybe three, lie broken at his feet.

"Michael!" she screams. He turns to her and grins, a strange grimace—wickedness, joy. The blue gums above his capped teeth show before he sets his lips and brings the plate down on the edge of the table. Shards of china leap from his fingers, fly through the air, and skitter to the corners of the room. Pieces roll across the table and spin on the floor. "Michael!" Mary screams again, horrified, transfixed. She turns to leave.

"Wait," he calls. When she turns, he says, "It's fun." He takes a plate from the cupboard and passes it over. "Try." Something about his look intrigues her—she'd like to feel that reckless, too. Free. Her hand trembles as she takes the plate from him. Mary raises the plate and brings it down on the tabletop. It strikes with a thunk. She holds it up, still in one piece. "Like this," Michael says, raising his hands high and bringing them down fast. This time she feels the plate break away from her fingers, the crunch of china smashing against wood. It *is* fun. Mary extends her hands for more. They smash one, two, three plates, then Mary takes a platter and, watching Michael's motion, swings in time with him. When both plates smash in the same instant, they laugh together and then salute each other with high-fives, like ball players. In minutes pieces of dishes litter the floor and a fine powder fills the air. Mary sneezes. When Michael steps to the cupboard for the butter plates, his shoes crunch across china, grinding small pieces beneath his heels. Fragments are embedded in the tabletop. Mary laughs, pointing at them, and Michael laughs, too. They have a competition, who can produce the most noise, the most pieces. When they get down to the saucers and cups they move to the living room and hurl them at the brickwork around the fireplace, shouting encouragement, shouting praise for good shots. They work hard. Mary laughs so much her amulet swings wildly and bounces off her flushed cheeks. Throwing, Michael pops a button on his shirt. They collapse on the couch in each other's arms, sobbing, giddy, and warm. They cling together. "The hell with Jane," Michael says in Mary's ear. She feels his arm around her, the insistent beat of his heart. She whispers back, "The hell with Jane."

* * *

But nothing is ever that easy. On Friday morning of the next week Jane phones to say she's at a hospital. During the night she got cramps and then blacked out, so she called an ambulance. She tells Michael this tearfully over the phone. In the background he hears the squeak of rubber wheels, a baby crying, and the voice of a nurse reminding Jane she's tying up the line. Michael pictures the room and smells it, too—antiseptic masking the stench of sickness. He hates hospitals. People go there to die. It turns out the kid's calling because she needs a hundred and fifty dollars to pay for the ambulance—which his Blue Cross would have covered if she'd been living at home. Also, she tells him, she's got some stomach disorder—the source of the cramps—that can only be remedied by expensive drugs. "How expensive?" Michael asks. Two years ago he gave Jane a hundred dollars for birth-control pills and found out later that she'd bought a new sweater with the cash left over after she'd spent the thirty at the pharmacy. Jane whimpers into the phone and Michael looks out the window where wet flakes of snow are beginning to fall. Winter, another year running down. Where are Arnold and the Friends at times like these? Michael pictures a circle of hippies in jeans and sweatshirts chanting on a hillside, a ridiculous image, but the one his mind automatically conjures up along with the words *occult* and *pyx*. Did they come from a TV program about Moonies? But these aren't Moonies. "Please," Jane is whining over the phone line—strung out and helpless. His rotten kid.

What can he do? After he scribbles the hospital's address on a pad and says goodbye, he tosses the receiver from one hand to the other before resting it in its cradle. He'd like to pitch the phone through the window. His day is ruined. The jog through Woodydell he'd planned. Maybe his weekly visit to Angela. Now he'll be driving through snow-panicked traffic instead of floating around the park on the high of exercise. He checks his wallet for cash and discovers yet another annoyance—he'll have to stop at the instant teller. Damn kid. He dials Mary's office number.

She comes on brightly, a voice that inspires confidence in a day looking dim. Michael smiles to himself. Mary must have been expecting a client, because when she recognizes him, her tone changes to the breathless excitement of a child with a good report card. Before he can tell her about Jane she says that she's sold four units of the condo today—so that's already thousands in profits, and she and Fred are meeting two more prospects at the site after lunch. There's a lilt in her voice that takes him back to the days when they lived together, a lilt which gives him courage. He asks several polite questions about her clients and says he's got a lunch appointment and might be late getting home. Lies to cover for Angela. Mary is buoyant. But when he tells her about Jane, she says, "Oh, Michael."

He plays for sympathy. "What can I do?"

"Only what you are doing." She clucks her tongue. "Give her money. Offer to help. You're doing the right thing."

"But it feels wrong."

"Whatever you did would feel wrong. That's the way it is with kids." She speaks crisply—at least his news hasn't dampened her spirits.

"With Jane."

She asks, "You can't shout at her or refuse the money—can you? You can't not help?" She waits for him to think this over, and he looks out the window again. Flakes are building up on the branches of the golden willow. She adds, "Just take things as they come."

"I guess."

"And try not to get upset."

He was drinking a cup of coffee when Jane phoned. Decaffinated, it's not supposed to affect the heart, but Michael's is speeding. He sips from the mug and says to Mary, "The trouble is she won't do what we want her to, what's right."

"She's young."

"But she won't leave me alone either."

"Oh Michael. You never give up, do you?"

"It's not a matter of giving up. It's a matter of getting the kid to see sense." He pauses. "*You* want everyone to agree with you—is that so much better?"

Mary's voice is distant when she answers, "Not agree. Be happy."

"That's all I want, too." Michael notices he's stained his new shirt with coffee. Red. He bought it to bring color to a wardrobe

206

drifting toward monochrome grays and navies. Sensible but dull. He can't remember the last time Mary bought him anything as surprising as the Irish bog hat she picked out at Harrods several winters ago. He says to her, "I'll call you later. After I'm done with the kid." And, before visiting Angela, he thinks to himself.

"I may be out." Mary pauses, calculating, he guesses, how long it takes to drive between the office and the condos and return with signed checks. Maybe stop for a drink with Fred. "But let's go out to dinner. The club."

"You bet," he says. They've gone to the club dining room half a dozen times since Mary joined. Good beef. Good wine. Michael feels good when the *maitre d'* brings the tab and Mary signs—just like the daughters of the rich who live along Ravine Drive. He adds, "Drown our sorrows."

"Oh God, I almost forgot. Did you hear the news?" Mary's voice changes to a wheeze, like something sucked the air out of her lungs. "This morning the market took a dive. A big one."

Panic tightens Michael's chest. "Shit." On Monday he wanted to sell, but his broker talked him into hanging on. So he only sold one small chunk of oils. He's got maybe ten thousand in cash. Otherwise his portfolio has been falling all week.

"It may not be so bad."

"Shitshitshit."

"Not everything's gone down. Maybe just oils—something to do with the Persian Gulf."

"With my luck . . ." Now his own voice sounds strange.

"Your luck has been good." Michael can see Mary fingering the amulet as she says this. "Anyway, it's not a matter of luck, is it? It's a matter of advice, and so far we've done not badly."

"I hate to lose what we've gained."

Mary says, "That's why they call it a market." He wonders if she's conscious of mocking him, but probably she doesn't even remember his throwing the same words at her weeks ago.

Outside the snow has turned to sleet, slanting into the window and running down the glass. If the temperature falls, the roads will turn to ice and driving will be madness. She hears the concern in his silence and adds, "Anyway, there's still time to get out."

This prompts him to check his watch. 10:40. The news comes on in ten minutes, so he can listen while driving to the bank. Between then and now he has to change shirts, check on the dog, and call Angela. He coughs into the receiver and says in a voice intended to convey concern, "I'm holding you up."

His words sound hollow, but not to Mary apparently, for she says pertly, "Right. Gotta run." She adds before hanging up, "And don't worry, sweetheart, don't sweat the small stuff."

* * *

At the instant teller, Michael withdraws two hundred dollars in twenties. He steps out the door of the cramped cubicle and stops in his tracks. A man in a black leather jacket wearing a watchcap stands in front of the sporting goods store across the street. His eyes meet Michael's for an instant. Michael's mouth goes dry. He decides to cross the street and confront the man, and looks to his left for oncoming traffic. When he rights his gaze again, the man is no longer in front of the sports store. He's helping a boy juggle hockey sticks into the backseat of a red Mustang. Laughing a big, happy laugh.

* * *

The BMW springs to life when Michael pulls away from McNally's, where he stopped to buy a Dorothy Sayers mystery for Angela. He's wearing a denim shirt now in place of the stained one, and a new pair of sneakers. White. Footwear the middle class has appropriated from the ghetto kids. The BMW glides south down Pembina Highway, wipers thumping a steady dirge on the windshield as the traffic slows for each light

leading up to Bishop Grandin Bridge. One thing about the
Germans, their radios never work. He flips the dial from left to
right, looking for news. All he can get under the hydro and
telephone lines is dense static punctuated by sudden bursts of
clear signal. This weather doesn't help. He's driving into the
city's east end now, away from Angela and their two o'clock
appointment. At the light where the highway crosses the Trans-
Canada he picks up a clear signal, a voice saying over the
rubbery pulse of the wipers, "Fifty years of good motoring
behind *your* wheel." The man sounds like the nasal teacher at
Belvu High who made the announcements during dances, kids
standing in pairs along the gym walls under the crêpe-papered
basketball hoops listening to warnings about cigarettes in the
washrooms, the boys chewing mints to cover the beer on their
breath, the girls powdery and warm in their perfumed dresses,
Michael's arm wrapped casually around the waist of Barb
Hegge whose soft body bumped his when they waltzed, anticipating the fumbling in the car later, the day-glo green of the
radio dial on their faces. When the announcer's done with the
automobile ad, he shifts directly to the news. The stock market
is the lead item, plummeting two hundred points in the first
hour of trading, a record for the TSE, matching the fall of over a
hundred on Wall Street. Full report to follow at twenty past the
hour. A second boatload of Tamils has been denied entry to the
port of Halifax. The captain of the U.S. helicopter squadron that
sunk three Iranian speedboats in the Persian Gulf claims he acted
on direct orders from the President. Again the lead item before
the sportscap, stock markets down sharply in the first hour of
panic trading. Two hundred points, Michael thinks, calculating
quickly, his mind racing. Everything they made since the new
year wiped out. Damn his broker and his ride-it-out advice. And
of course the Jets have lost Olaussen, the Swedish defenceman
injured in the Canada Cup, for the season.

Michael doesn't know this part of the city. Railway yards,

truck terminals, box factories. Cars swish by in the sluice of wet snow, the transport trucks throw sheets of it onto the windshield as they rumble past. The city built a new hospital out here for the burgeoning developments gobbling up the land on the outskirts. This time he has remembered to bring his reading glasses and checks the street signs through the foggy windows—Panette, Dugald, Nairn, all four-lane routes for trucks carting goods to warehouses, abattoirs, and canning companies. What are the Friends of Jesus doing out here? Don't cults live in crumbling homes in the Core? He peers up at a light standard to read a sign and feels a splintery twinge in his ribs—so brief he thinks at first it's a seam of his shirt nicking the skin on his chest. He gives the fabric a tug. Whether that brings on the second twinge or not, he twists sideways when it stabs his rib cage again. Within fifty yards the twinges have become spasms and the car swerves toward the concrete curb—he has to stiffen one arm to keep it on the road. He brakes. He pulls over and snaps on the BMW's flashers. Behind the car he hears the blat of a horn and a semitrailer releasing air to brake.

He has one hand over his chest. He knows what this is. Not heart attack, but a condition older men get that's like it. Chest strain. Cramps, a doctor said on a phone-in show, symptoms similar to heart attack, but actually a minor condition brought on by muscles going through contraction. Like growing pains. Guys his age get them and panic, thinking they're dying when all they've got is a normal reaction of the body to ageing—little spasms of protest to biochemical slowdown. Think of it as the male equivalent of menopause, the doctor said. And don't fight it. Michael breathes slowly, holding the air in his lungs for the count of five before exhaling, head down on the BMW's wheel, remembering the doctor's soft voice, his assurances. *Hang in there*, Michael says to himself, listening to the blood pound in his temples. Hang in there. For a moment it strikes him funny that he's on his way to a hospital and he almost laughs aloud.

Though what he thinks of, strangely, is standing at the window of his barren apartment in the days immediately after he left Patricia, the traffic buzzing below on Pembina, his sparse furniture behind him, a deep and dreadful loneliness in his chest. Tears start in his eyes.

After a few minutes the pain decreases, as the doctor predicted. It still hurts to breathe, but Michael lifts his head. The streetlamps in the distance wear haloes of sickly green and the road ripples before him in a mirage of waves, all running together with the swish of traffic, the rubbery hands of the wipers beating *pump pump* on the windshield. Michael thinks he's going to vomit, so he rolls down the window and sucks in fresh air. Tries to feel his pulse, but he's never got the hang of it—he always confuses the pulse in his finger with the one in his wrist. Don't fight it. He sits rigid behind the wheel, composing himself. I'm going to a hospital, he mutters when he pulls into traffic again, I'll be there in two minutes.

* * *

By the time Michael reaches the hospital the pain in his chest is gone. He parks the BMW and enters through the doorway under the neon EMERGENCY sign. Odors of antiseptic, of pain, of terror fill the cramped waiting room to one side of the reception desk. Jane doesn't see him at first. She's sitting on the far wall between a fat woman bouncing a crying baby on her lap and a short scruffy man with a black eye and a bruised mouth from which dangles a roll-your-own cigarette. The kid is flipping through *People*, legs sticking straight out from her maternity dress, short and stubby, thick through the ankles. She looks beat. Her nose is red, her boots spattered with mud. She looks up and stands when she spots Michael. At his side she whispers, "The people in here." She tilts her head at the fat woman. "That brat squawked the whole time."

After Michael's paid the hundred and fifty for the ambulance, they cross the street to the pharmacy located between a bank and an optometrist's. The sleet has let up, but the wind tugs at the flags snapping on the buildings thrown up opposite the hospital to accommodate its clientele. Everything here will be expensive. While Jane takes two more twenties to the counter at the back of the pharmacy Michael picks up an *Enquirer*. "New Wonder Drug," one headline screams, directing him to an article about AZT, an experimental drug that's had astounding results in curing AIDS and which may do more for human health than penicillin. There's a paragraph on TSP, too, a blood de-clotting agent supposed to stop heart attack.

He puts the magazine down when Jane returns, holding the little blue pharmacy sack in her hand like a bag of penny candy. There must be a washroom in back where Jane straightened her hair and splashed water on her face. At least she doesn't look suicidal now. Since she was in school Jane's eyes have dodged his, and this hurts him—his kid, afraid of life. He puts his arm around her and tugs her roughly to his chest. *Come on. Love me.* He senses resistance but asks, "You get the stuff?"

On the sidewalk outside Jane walks close to him. He feels her shoulder bump his, but she doesn't move away. She might be his friend, he thinks, before this is all over, and the thought cheers him. "Cold?" he asks.

"No." She looks up. "But the snow's coming."

"Maybe. With this greenhouse effect we haven't had a bad winter for how many years now—five?"

"Greenhouse effect? Arnold says that's just a way of covering up acid rain. Toxic death."

The kid's in one of her moods. He was hoping that moving in with Arnold would soften her, but that hasn't happened. Maybe in time. Maybe after the baby. Michael studies the sky. One dense mass of gray with a little light leaking through. Somewhere out there the sun is shining on Acapulco and Guaymas—sand, heat, Mary's footprints trailing down the beach and into the clear warm water. "June, July, and winter," he says, repeating a joke about seasons on the prairie.

"Cooped up for six months."

"Not six. Besides, it's not so bad. There's skiing up north and everybody's into cross-country these days, the land around here is perfect. You always liked the outdoors—skating."

"With a kid?"

Jane's mouth remains agape on the question, showing her stumpy teeth. Why didn't they take her to a dentist when she was a kid? He says, "I thought young mothers were into being active these days. With those papoose things for carting kids around while they're shopping and hiking."

"Snugglies. Yeah, and I read where some silly yuppie froze her kid to death in one last winter."

"Read? In *People*?"

"No. One of your precious *Globe and Mails*."

This isn't going so good. He asks, changing subjects, "You OK?"

She takes his arm. "Now the doctor tells me to *stop* exercising. First they tell me I've got gas and now they say cramps from abdominal exercises. That really bugs me. I wish they'd make up their minds and get on with it."

"I meant all right with Arnold—and his friends?"

"Yes. They pray for me every night."

"That's nice."

"It's more than *nice*, Pa."

"As long as that's not *all* they do. Pray."

"You mean food." Jane flips the hair off her face, looking older than he thinks of her, more worn. "You mean pay the bills."

"Well, now that you mention it."

"You're such an—so cruel. All you ever ask is questions about money. Not even Mother is as bad."

Since moving in with Arnold, Jane refers sweetly to Patricia as *Mother*. No more references to bitches, though she almost slipped up a moment ago. That red hair, that temper. He wonders how the Friends are coping with it. He says, "Oh, I see. And Patricia has a right to questions, does she, that I don't?" Michael feels sweat start in his armpits, the heat of confrontation.

"As a matter of fact she does." Jane has stopped, green eyes blazing now her color's up. "As a matter of fact *she* didn't start sleeping around—having a little piece on the side. Isn't that what you men call it?"

The wounds of ten years ago. They keep eating at the kid, now overlaid with self-righteousness. So he finally says what he'd promised himself he never would. "She did, you know. And before me."

Jane's mouth drops open. As he guessed, Patricia's kept this from the kid—her own short-lived affair with a schoolteacher named Dennis or Dave—he can't remember which—somebody who wore sandals, no doubt, and smoked a pipe. They cross the street in silence. On the other side Jane says calmly, "Anyways, that's not the point, who slept with who, who did what first. Mother didn't just split."

"No, she made me," he says, trying to remember if Patricia really did insist that he pack up when she found out about Mary. Or did he choose to go? The packing he recalls clearly, boxes in the hallway, the clock radio in the backseat of the station wagon. Pain. They pass a man hobbling on crutches towards the EMERGENCY sign and glancing up at the sky every few seconds, as if afraid he won't make it inside before a storm sweeps him away. Michael continues, "The point, as you say, is that all that's in the past."

"Past." Out of one eye he sees Jane flinch and put her hand on her side.

"Exactly. And should be forgotten."

"Buried, you mean."

He doesn't. Uncle Charlie was buried on a day like this, windy in the country cemetery, wet snow blowing in their eyes.

The peace of God, the priest said, *which passes all understanding.* Certainly it passes his understanding. But then who can grasp the meaning of death, the gleaming brown casket with brass handles descending into the wet earth? Maybe Angela, maybe the dying girl he can't let go of. Jane is saying at his side, "What you mean is just pretend it didn't happen, then, how nice for you."

"The way of the world, kid. If you don't let that stuff go, you carry it around inside where it festers, and pretty soon that's all there is. Anger and bitterness and revenge."

She pretends not to hear, shoulders stooped, hands thrust deep in the pockets of the pea jacket as if searching for something. "You could have made it work."

"It wasn't in the cards. Your mother and I fought from day one, her getting pregnant, then having to get married—she was the one who didn't want kids, you know? Oh, the arguments about that. Fights, drinking, affairs, all of that—that crap." They've stopped behind the BMW. Michael sees a flicker in Jane's eyes, maybe she's listening to him, trying to learn something, so he adds in his good father voice, "When you get to my age, you'll see it's best to let the bad stuff go."

"Dump it, like?"

"Just let it go and get on with things."

"Is that what you want to do with me—dump me like you dumped Mom, so you can get on with betting the horses and drinking scotch?" She adds, "Having your woman on the side?"

He hears more than a veiled reproach, something he heard in an earlier accusation but didn't quite get then either. He says, "Sure. That's why I'm here answering your s.o.s." Maybe it wasn't interest he sensed in the kid, after all, but fear.

"You want to know what I think?" Confronting him, Jane's face swells with defiance, defiance and getting the upper hand.

Michael stares back coolly. "What?"

"That all this was somehow meant to be. You dumping

Mother and leaving us in the lurch, then me getting thrown out by you and Mary, getting pregnant by Brad—all so I could eventually find Arnold and the Friends." She stares at him with a look hard as the sound of her voice. "God's will, I guess."

"You didn't get thrown out, you *left* to live with Brad. And this Arnold is no great improvement, if you want my opinion. Where is he today, for instance?"

"He works in mysterious ways," Jane says in the singsong voice she's picked up from the cassettes, "His wonders to perform."

She stares at him impassively and there's nothing he can say short of everything, short of words that would plunge them into fury and hatred. Gently he puts his hand on her arm. "If you want to believe it," he mutters.

"I do." Jane flinches and grimaces again, not from his hand, but from the pain inside, their signal to get her home. They separate to reach the opposite doors of the car, Jane still grimacing as she settles on the seat, the Dorothy Sayers mystery for Angela in one hand, her blue pharmacy package in the other. A few flakes of snow have started to swirl about again, but Michael turns off the wipers before starting the engine. Jane stares straight ahead as he backs out of the lot. At least, he thinks, I'll get to see where she's living, at least I'll get some idea of the pickle she's in this time, poor pup.

* * *

Why, he asks Angela, do I love that dog so much? He has photos of Ruggles tacked to a corkboard over his desk, and more pinned to the refrigerator by magnets. Because he is pure, she answers. Her voice has lost vigor but her eyes remain bright blue. She adds, Ruggles is pure being. He has no knowledge of death. Unlike us. He's completely unto himself—ego, id, whatever. Untroubled by tomorrow, the future, how it all ends. To be that free! We yearn for that. I know I do. So we run in the fields with Ruggles, we touch him, we embrace him and his pure stupidity. Look at TV. All those commercials with retrievers in them. And one more thing. When pets die we're devastated—because we're betrayed. They die, we discover, the innocent die. But can we accept the awful truth?

* * *

The truth, he told Mary just after the divorce when they were living on Furby Street and walking to Lox and Bagels for croissants, the truth is we make pain. Take the way he'd treated Patricia. It wasn't a matter of what was right or what was wrong. You could explain it away if you wanted. He had. To himself and to others. Justifying cowardice. But the whole business—the betrayal, the regret, the guilt, the rage—had nothing to do with right or wrong. It had to do with what you wanted. What he wanted. In his case, Mary. That was the truth of the matter—when you'd cut away all the words, all the talk, all the rationalizations. The truth, Mary said, was that everything dies.

* * *

The spectators' boxes on the lounge level of Assiniboia Downs look over a wet track. Intermittent sleet has soaked the bleachers below and spattered the glass through which the sparse crowd waiting for the next race gazes indifferently at the training ponies and their handlers. Behind the skin of glass Mary's cheeks, distorted by water droplets, look teary. She stands beside Fred, who's drinking beer from a Styrofoam cup. Mary has a plastic glass of rum and Coke which she's hardly touched.

Things have been difficult between them. Work draws them closer at the same time as they're trying to hold each other off. The strain shows on their faces. They can't look at each other. But they're working hard at staying friends—cheerful, supportive, affectionate. They come to the race track ritualistically now, exchanging the clamor of show and place in the bettors' lounge for intimacies renounced in the bedroom.

Mary smiles what she hopes is the brave smile her mother advised for crises while she thinks of the next race. She is not unhappy. One of her ponies has come in already, putting her fifty dollars up. And two of Fred's have made the races exciting, Amber in the third, charging to a homestretch victory, and Sporting Life, which her own Red Dawn nosed out in the first. The track is listed as good, which makes the races interesting, for all but bettors like Michael. He refuses to bet unless the track is fast. No odds in that, he argues—you have to place meaningful bets, and a so-called *good* track—sometimes soggy, others, crusty—creates confusion. He likes to think betting the ponies is a science, something you can control if you know enough about horses, jockeys, and stables. Mary likes the pure luck of it all. Her work is all about prudence and restraint: indemnity, collateral, promissory notes. So when she leaves the office she wants to take risks, to lay down twenty bucks and let the chips fall where they may.

At her side Fred is muttering as he deliberates. His tie is striped red and green, like the house tie Mary wore thirty years ago at school and which she still has packed away in a trunk with her yellowing diaries and photos of the hockey team Eva coached to the city championship. Fred's shaking his head over the choices in the fifth, a race Mary has told him she'll have to miss to get back to Woodydell in time for dinner with Michael. "Look at this, all maidens but none of them's placed higher than fourth." He pushes the form sheet under her nose. "What do you think?"

Mary points. "I'd take a shot at Life Goes On."

"Oh yeah," Fred says, sardonically, not looking up from the form sheet. "Seventh in a field of seven last time out."

"Well, you asked," Mary says. Their warm breath mists the glass looking over the track. Below, hot walkers take the ponies around, collars turned up against the wind. The bleachers which stretch to the south are deserted, the track the flat dun of a beach, the turf oval a thatch of dying grasses. Even the parking lot looks bleak. Washed-out browns as far as Mary can see. Late fall.

Fred sips from his beer and burps. Already he's chewed down half a roll of Tums. "What about Duck Soup?"

Mary runs her nail along the columns of names. "I'm taking Gold Ingot." She means in the fourth, the race they're waiting for, a forty-thousand-dollar race for three-year-olds.

He shakes his head. "I suppose you heard gold was up four bucks?" Mary looks down, numb suddenly with the reality of what's happening on trading floors hundreds of miles away. After he speaks Fred nervously touches the hair above his ears. Last month he bought five hundred Kruggerands, speculating the market would fall. A rise of four dollars means a profit of two thousand for him while she and Michael are going down the tubes with blue chips.

"What's really going on with the markets?" Mary asks. She was cheerful on the phone with Michael, but she felt sick. This sort of thing wasn't supposed to happen, the broker assured them. But it was happening, wasn't it?

"Program trading is what's going on. Once a share starts to fall the computers kick into automatic selling and the whole system collapses." Fred gestures with one hand. "It's like dominoes."

"You think it's 1929 again? The news guys keep making these gleeful comparisons. Black Friday, they're saying."

He puts his hand on her arm lightly, then withdraws it and runs his fingers over the glass. "It'll be okay."

"Easy for you to say, sitting on those Kruggerands."

Fred snorts. "That's where you're wrong. You guys will come out of this all right, not me. Michael's job is safe, right? So what if you take a bath on the markets? You write it off by declaring bankruptcy—and get on with your comfy lives. A good lawyer and a sharp accountant will get you back on track before the next VISA is due. You won't even cancel the symphony tickets, never mind miss a trip to Europe. But for guys like me it's different. If this thing bottoms into a depression, it's goodbye housing market and goodbye Fred. I'll be back selling hay rakes and baling wire—if I'm lucky." His laugh is forced. He gulps his beer.

"The governments," she says, "will step in."

"We hope."

"The Tories won't let their buddies go under."

"You believe that, I've got some property in Alaska for you." He laughs again, all those fillings flashing silver, and shrugs. He refuses to let things get him down. "You still heading for the sun?" he asks.

"Heavens, yes. Get away from all this."

"I went once. To Jamaica." Over the public-address system the track announcer reads the names of the horses as they move into position at the gate. Mary and Fred turn their eyes that way, looking for Gold Ingot's blue and white silks. "Funny thing," Fred continues, "I have this one memory of that holiday, standing waist-deep in warm sea water with a bottle of rum in one hand and a big white moon overhead. Just that one clear picture, but every time I think of it I want to go back."

"Vacations are like that. Snapshots. For me two weeks in Ireland are a picnic overlooking a gorgeous bay in Donegal." And there's something comforting about it, too, she thinks. Michael wore bulky Irish sweaters and drank too much Guinness, and the water was dazzling and the tea thick as tar. Mary turns to Fred, and in her mind's eye she sees their affair freezing into this moment, two rigid bodies in business suits looking out a rain-spattered window.

"You Irish?"

"My mother's family somewhere way back."

"We could have great vacations together." Fred's words are lost in another blur of announcements, the horses coming to post, the flurry of feet moving to the windows. The light from outside is pale in Fred's face. He's waiting for her to say something.

"Fred," Mary murmurs. "You don't even like me. I wear expensive clothes and go to the symphony and fuss over everything. I make Michael turn sports off TV so I can watch opera."

"Maybe. But it sounds like you're saying you don't like me."

"We knew it had to end. It never should have started."

"Well, I don't regret it."

"Nor do I."

"It's almost comic, but this is real tragedy, you know?" Fred looks at her out of sad eyes, and she thinks, it's true, the losses of the heart go unrecorded, the pain of small defeats. Fred straightens the knot in his tie with his strong flat hand and shrugs. "And I do like you."

"Yes. But you don't want me."

The bell rings and the seven ponies pound by in a flurry of mud. Gold Ingot's blue-and-whites are somewhere in the middle of the pack as they go into the first turn. Mary and Fred become alert. Their eyes follow the sweep of flanks and silks around the rail, at this distance a white picket fence, the horses toys for kids to play on at supermarkets. Mary wonders what it would be like to ride one. Some of the girls at Miss Dahlstrom's did equestrian, but she was terrified the few times she got up on the wide quivering backs of Chevron and Malahat. Helpless. Down the backstretch, the announcer tells them, Snow Dancer leads by a length, Gold Ingot holding third. Someone to their right is yelling the name Bigfoot. The crowd is sparse, mostly drunks, bookies, a few deliquent teenagers skipping classes. At the clubhouse turn Gold Ingot's second and in the stretch all Mary can see is a muddy blur, horses, jockeys, one quivering mass of flesh hurtling toward the finish line. Even from above it's impossible to tell one silk from another. She doesn't know how the track announcer is so certain when he calls *Gold Ingot,*

Gold Ingot at five-to-three. Two winners in one day! Mary feels a surge in her chest, her heart thumping wildly, as if she's just finished a workout at the Squash Racquet Club. She asks, "What were you holding?"

Fred riffles his stubs through his fingers. "Guess." The old smile, tinged with a little irony—winner in this, loser at that, it says—the kind of irony people share when they've put sex behind them. On the way to the cashier Mary places her hand on his arm and he pats it once, twice, and leaves his warm fingers pressed on hers as they take their position in line to cash in.

* * *

Driving across the city from Jane to Angela, Michael races through calculations. The TSE is down four hundred points—can that be possible, four hundred? But they're saying four hundred, so that's what, twenty—no, more like thirty thousand he's lost. And counting. The sleet has turned back to rain again and Michael wipes moisture off his brow. The windows are steaming up. Some of his big holdings are volatile energies which will be plummeting—Equity Silver, Husky, Northstar Resources. He should have sold, and he never should have let Mary talk him into taking that line of credit. The thing about her, she's so excitable, so keen to make it—and fast. What they're facing now is a margin call and they've got nothing in the bank to cover. First the BMW will go, and since he doesn't even have the Tercel to fall back on, he'll be puttering to the college and back in the pickup, dented fenders, rattling valves. What else can be liquidated? The house is mortgaged to a hundred grand and Mary has to have a car for work, so they can't sacrifice that. The cottage. Michael's hands shake on the wheel, just a tremor at first, fingers drumming the leather wheel cover, but soon so violently he pulls over. He bangs his palms on the dashboard. "No way," he shouts aloud. "No fucking way." In his chest his heart is double-beating. It takes his breath away. Blood pounds hotly in his temples.

This is no state to get into to see Angela. He rests his forehead on the wheel. All right. He'll see to it, they won't lose the cottage. They'll talk to the broker and the banker and among them work something out—he won't bother to figure what just now, he'll concentrate on driving, on making it to one set of streetlights, then the next. He pulls back into traffic and drives slowly. Get there late, he says to himself, but get there.

He maneuvers through lanes and waits in lines of flickering brake lights as cars crawl over the bridges. After a while his breathing returns to normal and his hands stop trembling, though his craving for a cigarette is so strong he's tempted to pull over at a convenience store and buy a pack.

Angela's place is a walk-up near the university. Generations of students who've forgotten their keys have jimmied the front doors, scraping a crescent into the cement landing. Inside, it's bright and cheerful. He knocks and then uses the key Angela has given him.

"Michael?" she calls out from the far end of the apartment. "I'm in the bedroom." He removes his muddy shoes. Angela's sitting in bed, propped up on two pillows, her knees bent under the quilt in a childish position. The bed is a futon, low to the floor. The other furniture includes a pine dresser, a full-length mirror, and a wicker chair, painted white. Angela has raised the pink blind on the one window, and Michael sees in its weak light how sick she really is. From the doorway she looks ravaged, even though she's put on a crimson shirt to bring color to her face, and she wears red bangles in her ears, giving her a rakish air. He pulls the wicker chair up as he enters and presents her with the book.

"Oh, Dorothy Sayers. I do like Lord Peter." He intends to sit down, but she says, "Kiss me." Up close he smells the sour of illness, as well as mint on Angela's breath and a hint of bath salts.

Her eyes are bright blue, but sunken, the flesh of her cheeks jaundiced. She smiles and says as he lifts his face from hers, "That wasn't so bad, was it?" When he doesn't answer she repeats, "I do like Dorothy Sayers."

"She works hard at nostalgia. At hanging on to the class system, the power of the Empire and all that." He sits on the wicker chair.

"I was thinking of romance," Angela says as she turns the book over in her hands. "I can use a little of that around here." She glances around the room so as not to meet Michael's eyes.

"We all can." Without commitment, without entanglements.

"But Harriet Vane. She's too—" Her eyes focus down, searching for the right word. "Too brittle. Emotionally brittle." She has grown pensive suddenly, a mood which frightens Michael into smiling.

"I've always thought her charming."

"Charming? The way she makes Lord Peter hang about?"

"Witty. And innocent, too, in a way that's gone now forever— what with Gracie Slick and Madonna." Michael stares at the book in Angela's hand, conscious of the precious tone that's come into his voice. He says in a clipped way, "And she's a woman making her way in a world of men."

"She's hard as nails. Her lips disappear entirely when she's angry. Which she always is with men."

"Maybe that's what was needed in 1920-whatever."

"Yes. But she should be more giving."

Like you? Michael wonders. So brave in the face of it all, so strong. He thinks of Uncle Charlie. What do you make of a world where the dying are strong and the strong dying? He moves his chair closer and, when she puts the book away on a shelf, takes her hand and turns it over in his. "Not everybody takes on life's misery headfirst." Her school ring glints blood red. "And Harriet won't be forced to change."

"Change? Is that it? I think that's a lot of rot—now." She repeats *change* in a bitter tone and stares at him with those blue eyes, refusing to be tragic, and forces him to look away. Over her head hangs a bright Miro print Angela bought in New York. He studies its sunny carnival figures and thinks that if she wanted, Angela could tell him what dying is like. She knows so much he doesn't. On her shelves there are books on dying, and she went to those classes to learn about the stages of death. She told him once about a dream where she was flying into white light and about waking one morning thinking she was already dead. She smiles thinly and asks him, "What about your own little mystery?"

For a moment he doesn't understand, and then he says, "I haven't seen the gunman again. In fact, I'm not sure that he *was* a gunman." Michael pauses, reconstructing in his mind's eye the figure on the beach from the fragments he can recall— camouflage jacket, boots, dark glasses. Their discussion at the pizza joint has led him to new conclusions. "The thing is, the first time, on the beach, he stood beside a tree with what I thought was a gun. But it could have been a walking stick or a fallen branch. The mind plays tricks. By the time he appeared again I'd convinced myself that's what it was and was looking for it. You know?"

"Uh-huh. You were guilty."

"Exactly. Then the second time he definitely did *not* have a gun, but for a moment I could have sworn one was cradled in his arms. But they were only folded across his chest. Threatening, yes, he was threatening, appearing like that in the black 4X4 and wearing those dark glasses and boots. The thing is, I expected to see a gun and so that's what I saw—or almost." He feels foolish admitting this, but better, too, as if saying it confirms he was only over-reacting. Maybe there was nothing to it at all.

"Well, then, what was he? Who?"

"I don't know," he says, sharply. And then, "I was going to hire a private detective to snoop around a bit."

"Don't do that."

"No?"

"Not if he hasn't appeared again." She rakes her hair back, strands of silver lifting through. "What about the letters?"

"One card. Weeks ago."

"What did it say?"

"It didn't *say* anything. A drawing of two people. Us."

"Us?"

"One with a beard, the other with dark hair."

"A hand drawing?"

"Yes. Like a child makes and shows to mommy and daddy."

"Clever," she says. She sits up, rubbing her lower back with one hand and thrusting her chest forward. She's suffering back pain now and takes the same medication for it as Michael does. When she resettles she asks, "Why did you say that about mommy and daddy?"

"I don't know. Just popped into my head. Does it matter?"

"Probably not. It's just that I've been lying here thinking about this business—threats, stuff in the mail. Who would do that kind of thing? That's what I've been asking myself. Kids? A student with a grudge? A demented neighbor?" Angela shakes her head. "I got some books from the library and talked to a guy in the crime division. It has to be someone close at hand. Emotionally, I mean. You don't send dogshit in the mail to strangers. It's too—too—"

"Intimate?"

"That's it. What I was thinking is—you're going to hate me for suggesting this—what about your daughter?"

"Jane? All her rage is up front. If she's angry, the kid just lets you have it." He says this, but something ticks over in his mind, like a gear clicking into place. Why? He pictures Jane on the mall parking lot, hands thrust deep in her pockets, rage flashing over her face.

"Well." Angela settles back. She closes her eyes. She adds, "It was a crazy idea. Forget it." She looks tired, thirsty.

"Do you want something?"

"Only for you to sit here." When she pats the quilt, he shifts off the wicker chair and onto the edge of the futon. "Do you know what else I've been thinking as I watch the sun go down on the days?" This close he hears the lisp and remembers how much he's loved her. "You still have desire, you know. That's what they say at the classes. You never lose desire." He nods. "Would you take off your shirt?" Though surprised, he slips out of the arms and tosses it over the back of the chair. On his skin Angela's fingers are warm, and the thin hair on his chest rises to her touch. "You have no idea what's it like lying here wasting away. The sun comes in through the window, phones ring in the apartment below, the water ticks in the radiators. Don't get me wrong. I'm not lonely. My parents are here every night. Friends drop by—too many." She sighs. "I'm pretty mixed up, aren't I?"

"It's all right."

"What I mean is, would you touch me?" Her eyes are pleading. "Do the buttons slow." His fingers touch her nipples and she watches while they bring them to hard little points. "This is what I'll miss," she says. "The mystery of why nipples do that."

He holds her then, shoulders thrust forward, his big back humped over her delicate body. Surprisingly, her grip is intense and carnal. He feels her breath ripple the hairs on the back of his neck. They've both kept their eyes open. "Oh, Angela," he says, "I feel like such a—" *Ghoul*, he thinks, but his lips can't form the word. "Cad," he says, thinking of Lord Peter and Harriet Vane.

"No. You've been very good to me. And I want to." Her words, simple and melodic, are like a song he's heard before but can't place. "Think of it as the last thing you can give me." She tugs at his zipper. He expected it would be gentle and slow, a moment from a film where lovers embrace in moonlight, but she urges speed on them, reaching down between his legs, parting her own for him to enter. The noises she makes, the urgency upset him, but fill him with desire, too. He feels panic when she cries out, and lust, and the need of flesh driving them forward. Angela groans in his ears, their bodies—shaped now to one end—make slapping flesh sounds as they go on and on, an engine blowing itself out. And then he feels the pain again, one, two spasms below the ribs. Or is it the middle of his chest? It takes his breath away. Everything turns sickly green, the walls of the bedroom, the skin of Angela's shoulder, the pillow in his face. He tries to lift upward and say something, to put his hand over his heart and reach back into the light of day, but his weight drives him forward into the green of the pillow turning black at the edges. The pillowcase is the last thing he sees.

* * *

Darkness. Michael's mind reaches out like a machine exploring the ocean floor, methodical and in slow motion. He smells fresh linens, antiseptic, the institutional flow of cool air, hears the sublittoral drone of electrical machinery and heating systems. White all around—sheets, walls, floors—and in the distance the marine glow of fluorescent lights. He hates hospitals. There's a pronged plastic thing shoved up his nose so far it irritates his gullet, and tubes running down the center of his chest, taped there on a disk with a red center. His skin itches. Somewhere behind him a machine ticks. Michael moves his head slowly. The red numbers on a digital clock near his face read 4:52. His hand is stiff. When he flexes it, he feels a plastic band dig into the underside of his wrist and this quick stab of pain tells him he's alive.

But am I brain dead? he asks himself. Have my gray cells been wiped out? He poses questions and forces himself to answer— the date of Kennedy's assassination, the opening lines of *Moby Dick*, and the distance from the house in Woodydell to the cottage at Willow Point. These are easy, and he closes his eyes to think of more challenging questions. The square of the hypoteneuse is equal to the sum of the squares of the sides. 14 January, 1917, his mother's birthday. If the heart attack has affected his brain, it's no worse than a bad drunk. He opens his eyes and repeats to himself Yankees, Blue Jays, Tigers, Indians, Red Sox, Brewers. Genesis, Exodus, Leviticus, Numbers, Deuteronomy. Pistil, stamen, stigma, style. The roof of his mouth is dry like after a long night's drinking and he feels tired. Things slip in and out of his mind, the names of ball players merging with proofs he learned in calculus. He closes his eyes.

* * *

At his side Mary is saying, ". . . lucky just minor or you'd still be in intensive care." She's been talking to him for some time because she arches her eyebrows when he looks at her, puzzled and amused, and then she sniffs as if she expects him to answer. This is a different room than before, and it is filled with the smell of flowers. Sunshine at the window. Mary is holding his hand, stroking his fingers. "The funny thing is," she adds, "that you'd be here the same time as Jane with the baby." She stops stroking for a minute, gray eyes lost in thought, before continuing. "You'll have to go down there when they let you on your feet." And when he blinks, "Second floor, maternity." She says something about the doctors mixing up Jane's date of conception and asks him what it feels like being a grandparent. His mind drifts. Galveston, Northstar Resources, Solomon Michael—everything jumbled together as if he's waking from a dream he can't remember but knows he has to or something awful will happen. He doesn't even know if Jane's baby is a girl or a boy, he doesn't know how he got to the hospital, how much Mary knows about Angela. Angela. Mary. Jane.

When Mary's gone a nurse comes and stands at the foot of the bed looking down at him. A dark girl, very pretty. From the pocket of her smock she takes an index card with words printed on it in black grease pen and holds it in front of his face. ANGELA

OKAY. He looks from the card to her unblinking eyes and nods. Brave girl, alone in her bedroom wondering about him. He thinks of the letter he will write her as soon as he's able, sentimental words which will hint that he has answers now, not questions.

He sleeps. Dreams. He is in a car on a freeway. The driver is a slim and handsome young black named Attus. The pride of his race, Michael thinks. In the backseat sit Mary and Jane. Suddenly the car jumps the freeway, crashing into a field below, half vegetable patch, half rubble heap. Michael knows as he scrambles from the car that Angela is dead. He stumbles about the field looking for her. He finds Attus in long grass lying on his back. Attus says, "You would have liked some of those chickpeas," and Michael thinks, yes, I like chickpeas. Then Attus lies back and closes his eyes. Dead. Michael lifts him to his chest. "Attus," he moans. The pride of his race. He stands, chest filled with grief. Mary, he thinks, my life will be empty without Mary, and he staggers to a metal shed and leans against it, thinking the years ahead without Mary will be emptyemptyempty. He is overcome by loss. He wants to cry out but his chest is constricted with grief. Michael wakes up. He lies with his eyes closed thinking about the way his dream shifted from Angela to Attus to Mary and finally settled on himself. Attus?

When he wakes again it's dark and he needs to pee. Someone has taken the pronged thing out of his nose, which feels swollen now. Raw. He would like some vaseline to put on his lips, too. He rolls onto his side and frees his arm from the intravenous tube. The sounds of nurses' shoes squeak by in the halls and voices echo in the distance, laughter, interns and nurses on the night shift flirting. Michael shifts his bulk to the edge of the bed, feet dangling to the floor. He puts his hand over his heart. Through the white hospital shirt he feels the steady throb and counts up to a hundred and then down again before standing. Easy. The tiles are cold. His legs tremble, a little out of control as they stiffen to take his weight. He holds his hands out to the side like a kid learning to skate. Easy. He's dizzy after all that time on his back and unsure of his footing in the dark, and he sees in the reflected light from the ceiling that the tiles have a high polish. In the cramped cubicle he clutches the horizontal rail on the wall and waits for the sound of his own tinkling. He is doing it, he's back on his feet. He catches water in his cupped palms and splashes his face. Have the nurses been washing him? The routine indignities of hospitals. Then one day you go in and never come out. When he lifts his head from the sink, he looks for stars in his peripheral vision and, not seeing any, takes larger steps on the way back to the bed.

His socks are in a drawer of the functional white dresser with the clock radio, the same argyles he put on to rescue Jane—it seems like weeks ago and less than an hour ago at the same time. *Life*, he whispers softly to himself. *Life*. He smoothes his hair and runs his fingers over his beard, tangled like the thatch on Ruggles' chest.

Michael stands at the window. Below, a parking lot is deserted except for the row of cars up close to the buildings in the staff spaces. Headlights flicker on the street through a light snowfall. He feels the same dread he felt looking out the window of his apartment on Pembina a decade ago. Vertigo of loneliness.

When his breathing is steady he slips along the hall like a criminal, looking into half-open doors. In the rooms thin bodies under white sheets stare at the white ceilings. A few have TV on, hands crossed behind their heads as if they're napping on the living-room couch, getting ready for a good night's rest and not the long sleep of the forever silent. Michael wants to shout a warning. He takes the stairs to the second floor.

Jane is also alone in a room, though there's another bed, too, unoccupied, between hers and the single window. She's lying back on the pillows with the baby on her breast. When she sees him her mouth drops open in a surprised way and she whispers, a little awed, "Pa." Her voice is husky, he remembers Patricia's got that way, too, something to do with postnatal weakness. He puts two fingers to his lips conspiratorially and steals into the room, taking the visitor's chair at Jane's bedside, an armchair with deep cushions into which he sinks thankfully. Motherhood has been tough on the kid. Her fair complexion looks gray, her fleshy cheeks consumed by fatigue. No vigor in her green irises, no energy, though she tilts her chin at him in the defiant way which looks out of her school portraits and smiles bravely. "Alison," she whispers, "Alison Jean." The baby is sleeping, curled into a tight ball facing toward him, little eyes pinched in, nose puckering with each breath. Michael reaches his hand to Jane's arm. His baby, his baby's baby. He feels the tension in her body. They look across the gulf between them in silence—her rage, his impatience, her demands, his resistance—their brief history forged in the heat of exasperation and fury. And love. In the glow of the hall lights their faces are ghostly, pale and shadowy. Jane stirs, shifting the baby higher on her breast, and smiles at Michael again, a smile he returns through eyes dancing with tears. He starts to say something, then changes his mind. After a while she leans forward and passes the baby across. In his arms he feels its weightlessness, the rubbery stir of new limbs under cloth. The cranium is molded and thatched with black hair. He touches it tentatively with his fingertips. The baby's lips are fleshy, like his mother's, like his own, and she has the same forked vein on the bridge of her nose that Jane does. Yes, he thinks. He strokes the baby gently, shifts her onto his chest, and tilts back in the chair. She whimpers and twitches her tiny hands and Michael senses warm breath on his fingers, the insistent beat of a heart through the thin nightshirt. "There, there," he coos to himself, "there, there."